THE OAKEN THRONE

BOOK FIVE IN THE TREE OF AGES SERIES

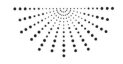

SARA C ROETHLE

T0204547

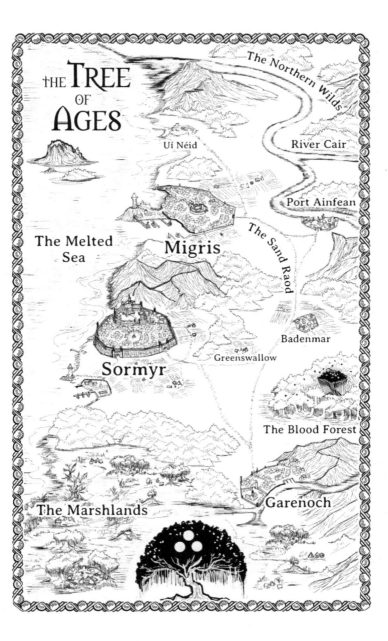

THE **TREE** OF **AGES**

The Northern Wilds

Uí Néid

River Cair

Port Ainfean

The Melted Sea

Migris

The Sand Raod

Badenmar

Greenswallow

Sormyr

The Blood Forest

The Marshlands

Garenoch

CHAPTER ONE

"*O*ighear will attack again soon," Keiren muttered to Ealasaid, "and this time, she'll be ready for you."

Maarav watched as Ealasaid, seated beside Keiren, peered down at the map spread out before them. Candles bedecked the table, accompanying the sunlight streaming through the window to light the lines of roads and rivers across the maps.

"And I'll be ready for *her* as well," she replied distantly.

Standing behind Ealasaid, Maaraav had an urge to touch the long blonde curl that had escaped her braid, the color crisp against her modest pale blue dress. Keiren's black gown, in contrast, hugged her thin torso and pooled over her toes provocatively. Her red hair, usually flowing wildly about her face, was also tied back in a long braid.

Maarav leaned forward to glance over Ealasaid's shoulder at the map. She was planning another expedition to find more mages, though where she'd house them was anyone's guess. Even though the collective magic of the mages had built a wall around the outskirts of the burgh, and had expanded and rebuilt many of the buildings within, Garenoch was near overflowing. There just wasn't enough space for further swelling of their ranks. Although, Maarav could not blame the new mages for flooding in.

Ealasaid had not only struck a grave blow to An Fiach, but to the Faie. There wasn't a mage in the land who didn't want to join her now, save those too cowardly to fight for their own lives.

Maarav gently laid his hand on Ealasaid's shoulder. She was a good leader, but he knew how much every death weighed on her heart. He feared every night that he'd wake up in the morning to find her grief had finally consumed her, and there would be no pulling her back.

"What about here?" Ealasaid questioned, pointing to a spot on the map. "Surely our scouts have not searched this region."

"That is the Marshlands," Keiren replied, shaking her head. "A truly desolate region, and far too close to Finnur."

He felt Ealasaid's shoulder stiffen at the mention of her friend's name. At least, they *used* to be friends. Maarav wished he could somehow get word to his brother, if only to let him know there was one human still on his side in Garenoch . . . for now. If Keiren convinced Ealasaid to confront Finn, he and Iseult would become enemies.

The thought of the potential loss stung him more than he expected. Ealasaid's soft-heartedness was rubbing off on him.

With a heavy sigh, Ealasaid stood, then turned to face Maarav. "What do you think? Where should we send our scouts next?"

He resisted the urge to tug her into his arms. He knew just how Keiren would look at him if he did, with that sly, predatory smile and those knowing blue eyes. If the sorceress hadn't used her powers to protect Ealasaid on more than one occasion, he would have killed her in her sleep long ago.

"I believe there are few areas left to scout," he replied, dutifully keeping his hands to himself. "All have heard of the magic users gathering here. If they want to come, they will."

Ealasaid smiled up at him.

Truly, he still couldn't quite figure out what he'd done to earn such a smile. He longed to tug her curly blonde hair out of her braid and run his fingers through the soft tresses.

He felt eyes on him, then noticed Keiren, giving him that *infuriating* look, like she knew exactly what he'd been thinking.

He stared back at her. He'd be cursed before he let her come between him and Ealasaid like she'd done with Finn. He'd kill her long before that day ever came.

Ealasaid's smile faltered, as if she too could read his thoughts.

He glanced out the window at the midday sun. "It's time to meet with Slàine," he reminded her.

Ealasaid's gray eyes widened. "Oh, I almost forgot." She turned to Keiren. "Until tomorrow?"

Keiren nodded with a smirk on her rouged lips. "Enjoy your lesson, though truly, why a powerful mage should need a sword is beyond me." She flicked her gaze to Maarav, *mocking*.

"If she finds herself evenly matched against Oighear," he replied tersely, "a sword might be a wise thing to have."

At least, that had been his reasoning when he'd asked Slàine to teach Ealasaid to fight. While he *did* want her to learn to defend herself without magic, he also just wanted her to spend less time with Keiren. He would have taught her himself, but knew Slàine, a woman of around Ealasaid's size, would have better tactics to share with her than he.

Ealasaid rolled her eyes at them both, then made her way toward the door.

Maarav followed, feeling Keiren's eyes on his every step, though he refused to give her the satisfaction of a glare.

Finn stared out at the pouring rain from the parapet. The awning above her dripped a secondary sheet of water, falling slightly faster than the rain.

She leaned her cloaked back against the damp stone wall, fighting a shiver. It wasn't often that she was left alone with her thoughts, yet now that she had a moment of peace, her mind was too scattered to focus. Or, perhaps she just didn't *want* to focus. She didn't want to focus on her friends depending on her, nor on the Faie that had flocked to the fortress, deeming her a preferable leader to Oighear the White. Most of all, she didn't want to focus on the Cavari, and what they might truly want from her. For now, they'd bowed to her will, but she held no illusions about their loyalty, or lack thereof.

As if summoned by her thoughts, her mother stepped out onto the parapet from the open door of Finn's chamber. She'd chosen the room because it was on the second story, and bridged the inner entrance to the high wall outside. It made her feel safe at the time. Now, it just made her feel trapped.

"They won't wait much longer," Móirne muttered, gazing out at the rain. Her face was so much like Finn's that if her dark hair were very light brown, and her blue eyes hazel, it would be like looking into a mirror.

"They will wait as long as I tell them to wait," Finn grumbled.

Her mother gave her a knowing look. It was odd, that look, considering Móirne had not truly known her daughter in over a century. "The Cavari fear the Snow Queen," she continued. "They will not stand idly by while she increases her forces. The time to strike is now."

Finn pursed her lips. "I care not for Oighear the White. Let her do as she pleases."

Móirne snorted. "What would please her most, is to place your head on a pike. The Cavari are her greatest enemy."

Finn was quite sure they were *hers* too, though they camped outside the fortress like loyal dogs.

She sighed. "I will not attack Oighear until I know what she plans." Instead, she wanted to focus on Keiren, and why she'd turned Ealasaid against her, though she would not admit it to her mother. While she wanted to trust her mother, there was a good chance anything she said would make it back to the Cavari.

"If you do not attack Oighear," Móirne began again patiently, "then the Cavari will attack *you*."

She shrugged. "Let them try. If I am truly fated to be their queen, then they cannot stand against me."

Móirne shook her head. "Nations revolt against their queens all of the time."

"*Human* queens," she countered, turning to fully face her. *Human queens*, her thoughts echoed. If only she could have been born human.

Móirne sighed. "I'll try to hold them off a while longer, though they listen to me less and less. I think they know I've been protecting you all along, even from them."

Finn wrapped her forest green cloak more tightly around herself as a gust of wind pelted them with raindrops. "Is it such a crime to protect your *queen*?"

Her mother gave her that knowing smile again. "When that queen is you, *yes*."

Finn smiled softly in spite of herself. She lifted her hand to the golden locket around her neck, a family heirloom that should have been passed along to her daughter. They'd been almost happy, once.

Both women turned their gazes back to the rain. The sky was growing increasingly dark, though it was only midday. It seemed the worst of the storm was still to come.

"Blasted, rock-brained, putrid little imps," Anna growled, tossing a few pieces of clothing and other random items onto the hard mat that served as her bed. This was the *third* time she'd caught the Bucca pawing through her things. The horrid creatures never went into *anyone* else's rooms, only hers.

"The Bucca again?" a male voice asked from the doorway.

She turned to see Eywen watching her, a soft smile on his lips. His silken black hair was pulled back from his angular face, showcasing his slightly pointed ears. Dark brown leather breeches and a loose white tunic covered his tall, lean, yet muscular form.

"Why do they only bother *me*?" she groaned, tossing the last of her things onto her mat to be brushed off and sorted.

Eywen crossed his arms and leaned casually against the doorway. "They like you. You should take it as a compliment."

She scowled. "They won't like me quite so well once I run my dagger through one of them."

Eywen moved to her side as she peered down at her meager belongings. Though they'd sent the remaining Aos Sí to gather any supplies the Bucca were too stupid to fetch, she still had very little to her name. In times of war, supplies were short for everyone, except perhaps the lords and ladies of the Gray City.

"I thought you might like to go for a walk," he said, surprising her.

She turned to survey his face, hoping for a hint of his intent. "Why?" she asked finally.

He shrugged. "What else are you doing?" He smirked. "Besides planning the demise of the Bucca, that is."

She sighed. "Alright, I suppose a walk could not hurt. It's

not like I have anything else to do in this gods-forsaken land."

Together, they departed Anna's chamber, venturing through the large stone entry room and out into the courtyard beyond.

The ground squished beneath Anna's knee-high boots, and mist coated her black vest, tunic, and cloak, evidence of the heavy rain that had rolled in that morning. It had decreased to a light drizzle, but she could see more dark clouds on the horizon.

"Perhaps we'll all drown in a flood long before the Snow Queen kills us," she quipped.

Eywen glanced over at her, mirth twinkling in his deep blue eyes. "I by far prefer rain to snow. In fact, I would gladly drown in the rain if it meant I never had to see snow again."

Anna smirked. While she hated the rain, she knew Eywen's aversion to snow was far greater. Centuries serving the Snow Queen would do that to a man.

They reached the gates to the courtyard, which had been temporarily replaced by half-rotted wood, though the Trow still stood guard on either side. They might currently look like peacefully rooted trees, but Anna had seen them in battle. They could crush a man in seconds.

Eywen pushed one side of the swinging wooden gate open just enough for them to slip through. It had to weigh twice as much as Anna, but he made it look easy.

Once they were through, he pulled the gate closed behind them, and Anna had to stifle a shiver. They were vulnerable outside the gates, but she had to remember she had an ancient Faie warrior at her side, and she was far from defenseless herself. She resisted the urge to stroke the long daggers that never left her hips in recent times.

Eywen walked forward, seeming none too worried about what dangers might lurk in the surrounding trees, or the marshlands beyond.

Anna stepped lightly at his side. She would *not* look in the direction of the Cavari. She'd fought them once before and had no intention of ever facing them again. She still could not believe Finn had allowed them to remain so close to the fortress.

"I wanted to speak with you about your gifts," Eywen said suddenly.

She turned to him so abruptly that she stumbled. She took a moment to compose herself, then affixed him with her most threatening glare. "I thought you said you just wanted to go for a *walk*."

"I know you do not like to speak of them," he sighed, "but this is important."

She debated turning around and running back toward the fortress.

Seeming to sense her inner conflict, Eywen gently took her arm and led her forward.

She sighed. "Fine, what is *so* important that you must force such discomfort upon me?"

"Not yet," he muttered, leading her into the more densely populated treeline. "I would not want anyone to overhear."

Her heart thudded against her throat. Though she rarely spoke of her *gifts*, everyone in their party knew about them. What could he need to say that no one else could hear?

Eywen continued on, leading her beside him until the

fortress was well out of sight. Anna's feeling of vulnerability increased the farther they went, but there was no way she'd admit that she was scared.

Finally, he stopped. He released her arm and turned to face her.

She let out a shaky breath, peering up into his strange, yet kind eyes.

"I'd like to speak with you about the wraith," he said, surprising her.

She blinked up at him. "Branwen? What about her?" She'd been just as stunned as their other companions when Branwen reached the fortress. They'd all thought her long since dead . . . but Branwen was harmless, wasn't she?

He nodded. "Yes, Branwen. What do you see when you look at her?"

Anna frowned. She'd never paid Branwen much mind. "A scared, simpering little girl."

Eywen laughed. "I mean, what do you *sense* from her?"

She sighed. With others, she could avoid any talk of her *magic*, but Eywen always asked her so directly. It was uncomfortable, yet oddly refreshing.

"I sense very little," she admitted. "She seems almost dead."

He nodded, his gaze going distant. "She technically *is* dead, or at least, she is no longer animated by the things that animate you and I. It is the energy of the in-between that keeps her as alive as she can be." He gave her a hard look, as if expecting her to make her own deductions.

Anna sighed, watching her breath fog the air. The woods were eerily silent, evidence that the Cavari were near. The other Faie feared the Cavari, and would not venture toward their camp. Fortunately, Anna would sense the Cavari if they came near enough to eavesdrop. "I give up," she said finally. "Why am I supposed to be worried about Branwen?"

His face fell, as if he were disappointed she hadn't figured out what he was hinting. She fought to not be disappointed too.

"She is a direct link to the in-between," he explained, "to a realm composed entirely of magic energy. With Finn's power, and Branwen's connection, they really could break the barriers to that realm. There's no saying what sort of chaos such an action might release."

She raised a dark brow at him. "I'm not sure if you realize this, but the land already *is* in chaos. The Cavari are here. The Snow Queen could attack us any day. Ealasaid is gathering mages. Why not add releasing in-between energy into the mix? Maybe if the worlds would combine, I wouldn't end up stuck in another realm in my dreams." She bit her tongue before she could rant further.

He smirked, though worry still darkened his eyes. "You truly are fearless, aren't you?"

She snorted. "Hardly, I just know better than to worry about possibilities that are out of my control. I already see into the Gray Place half the time when I'm awake regardless."

He smiled. "You speak more easily of such things than you did when we first met."

She fought to hide a sudden blush, pushing her slowly dampening hair out of her face. He seemed to bring out the idiot in her. "If it offends you, then I shall stop," she snapped.

He watched her for a moment, the ghost of a smile still

on his face. "You know that is not what I meant. I'm pleased that you've grown to trust me. I never thought I'd live to see the day when a human would speak easily around one of my kind."

Her lips parted for her response, but nothing came. What in the Horned One's name was she supposed to say to *that*? She was saved as the rain suddenly began hammering down.

Eywen looked up, impervious to the droplets collecting on his face. He turned his gaze back down to her, a smile still on his lips. "We should return to the fortress."

Anna nodded, then turned on her heel to lead the way. It wasn't fair of him to fluster her so. She needed to find someone to spar with to calm her down. Unfortunately Kai had been avoiding her, and Iseult would probably murder her. Perhaps Bedelia would do.

Eywen walked comfortably beside her. She briefly considered asking *him* to spar, then dismissed the idea. If she knew what was good for her, she would run far, *far* away from the ancient warrior. She trusted he would not harm her physically, but there were worse ways to hurt. She had promised herself that the first time she'd been betrayed, oh so long ago, would be the last. There would be no opportunity for it to happen again.

After hanging her damp cloak on a hook near the fire in the main chamber, Finn sought out Kai. She had bread and cheese stuffed into a satchel, along with a waterskin. She was still the only one who knew about the first bite he'd sustained from the Dearg Due, the one that had gone uncleansed, though others suspected something was amiss. It was difficult to continue keeping the secret when Kai had taken to sleeping during the day, while avoiding his highly perceptive best friend, Anna.

Glancing both ways to ensure she was alone, she climbed the stairs to the second level of the fortress, then took another set up to the third. While some of the remaining Aos Sí warriors, including Eywen, did not mind inhabiting chambers on the chilly third floor, Kai was the only human.

At least, Finn hoped he was still human.

Her steps echoed across the stone floor as she hurried to the end of one long hall, then turned and rushed down another, all the way to the southern back corner of the fortress.

She wrapped her arms around herself, wishing she'd donned a dry cloak over her thin blouse and wool breeches to ward away the cold.

Pausing outside of Kai's room, she took a deep breath, then lifted her hand to knock on the heavy wood and iron door.

"Come in," a voice muttered before her knuckles could touch the wood.

She shivered, this time not from the cold. Kai would not invite just anyone in. He knew it was her standing outside his door, and he knew she was alone. There was no way a human should have known those things.

She pushed the door open with a loud creak, then stepped inside, shutting it behind her.

The fire in the hearth had nearly died, leaving only

glowing embers to emit warmth into the room. Kai was nothing but a pile of dark blankets on his straw mat. If it weren't for the room's small window, she wouldn't have had enough light to see.

"You don't need to keep visiting me like this," he mumbled from beneath the pile. "I'm fine."

She stepped forward, then sat on the foot of his mat, the only place to sit in the barren room besides the stone floor. "You're a terrible liar."

The blankets shifted, then Kai sat up, revealing his face. He was deathly pale, with blue veins showing on one side of his face where the soft light from the window hit.

She removed the bread and cheese from her satchel and handed them to him.

Instead of eating, his food filled hands fell limply to his lap.

"You must eat," she pressed. "You're growing weaker by the day."

He shook his head. "I'm not though. I should be dead by now, but I haven't grown truly weak at all. Just . . . ill."

She bit her lip. Despite Kai's protests, she'd secretly asked Eywen more about the bite of the Dearg Due. She knew Eywen would not tell a soul of their discussion. He wouldn't dare since he'd named her his queen.

She'd learned that when human men were bitten, they became thralls. Their bodies decayed, and their minds became solely focused on serving their Dearg Due mistresses. Yet, Kai had not run off to find the creatures who'd accosted him. His mind was still his own.

The only reason she could conjure was that her blood ran through his veins. It had somehow protected him, yet not entirely. No one knew what would happen if one of the Dair was bitten, let alone if one were subsequently fed the blood of the Dearg Due for healing. She would not be surprised if Kai was the first. Most lesser Faie would not dare face one of Finn's kind. Not even in their diminished forms.

"Stop looking at me like that," Kai grumbled. "There's nothing you can do to help me."

She glared at him. "You have no idea of what I'm capable."

He smiled, a mere ghost of the smiles he used to give her. "And *you* have no idea what's happening to me. The only thing left to do is wait."

She sucked her teeth. It wasn't the *only* thing left to do. She worried that Kai would eventually turn into something just like the Dearg Due, and at that point he'd be lost forever. The fear of losing him had made her consider some rather dangerous ideas.

"What are you thinking?" he asked suspiciously. "I can always tell when you're plotting something."

"Nothing," she lied. Perhaps she could do it while he was asleep. She knew he'd never let her help him otherwise. He'd never let her sacrifice more of her magic to save him, making herself a little closer to human.

Anna would let her though. Finn would need to break her promise to Kai, but Anna would help her save him if she asked.

She knew it was selfish to risk herself when so many were depending on her. She was the Oak Queen, and countless Faie were now depending on her magic, including Eywen and the other Aos Sí . . . not to mention

Iseult, Bedelia, Àed, and the other humans she'd come to love.

Kai raised a brow at her, barely visible in the shadows obscuring half his face. "Now I *definitely* know you're plotting something. Out with it."

She shook her head. "Eat your meal, then rest. I'll be back this evening."

Kai reached for her hand before she could rise. Despite the cold in the room, his skin was like fire against hers. "If it is my fate to die," he said evenly, "you must let me go. You have more important things to worry about."

She returned his stare. "I will worry as I choose." She gave his hand a squeeze. "Now if you're not going to eat, then rest, and I will see you soon."

Kai nodded somberly, and Finn stood to depart. Not saying another word, she hurried toward the door, fighting the tears that stung her eyes.

Perhaps it was not her choice to make, but she would not let him die.

Kai stared at the door as it shut behind Finn. He should have made *her* eat the bread instead. She looked so frail and thin. She was pushing herself too hard, and soon she would break.

He could only hope he'd remain alive long enough to protect her when she did.

Setting aside the bread and cheese on the cold stone floor, he snuggled back down beneath his blankets. He was always so tired during the day, and the sun stung his eyes, yet at night, he felt renewed.

He was lucky he'd become faster, able to move throughout the fortress with silent footsteps, lest some of the Aos Sí on guard begin to suspect he was changing.

He knew the time would come when he'd have to end himself. He would not become a monster like the Dearg Due. In fact, he should have ended things already, but how could he? How could he abandon Finn and Anna in such a dangerous time?

Deep down he knew neither one needed him. They could both take care of themselves, and if they could not, Eywen and Iseult would watch over them . . . but he still could not release the very human part of him that wanted to protect them both. The same part of him that wished Finn was just a human girl, capable of living a normal life out of harm's way.

He closed his eyes, hoping sleep would come quickly. Just a few more hours to delay the decision he'd inevitably need to make.

———

Oighear lay on her back in the snow. The crisp white flakes cradled her, the only loving embrace she'd known in centuries. To any who might look upon her, they'd hardly see her with her pure white hair, skin, and gown blending into the icy white surroundings.

She reached a hand toward the sky, gently catching perfect snowflakes as they fell. She brought them near her face, marveling at the tiny facets. Most would see the flakes melt on their skin, but on her hand, they remained perfect.

She would miss them.

Slowly, her hand fell back to the snow-covered ground. It was only a matter of time before the Cavari would come for her again. They would seal her magic away once more, forcing her into eternal slumber. She'd failed to retrieve her mother's shroud, and had failed to best the Queen of Wands. She'd failed her people entirely. Once she was gone, her Aos Sí warriors and the other Faie in her command would fade away. They all knew it. That was why so many had defected to swell Finnur's ranks. They were less likely to fade away if they followed the one with the Faie Queen's shroud. Her *mother's* shroud.

She sat up. Her thoughts had lingered for many days on the human girl who'd nearly bested her. A tiny little thing with curly blonde hair and bland gray eyes. She was young, and far too strong for her age. If Finnur didn't come for her, surely the human girl would. One queen would live, two would die. Yet, what did that mean for the human queen and Finnur? She would not be the only one to die. Another would come with her.

She blinked at the snowflakes collecting in her eyelashes. If the human girl could be swayed to her side . . . she shook her head. *No.* She'd killed the human's mages, and her entire family. There would be no way to reason with her personally, but there was always the fiery-haired sorceress. She was no queen, but she did whisper in the human girl's ear.

She stood, brushing the snow from her gown. Perhaps Òengus would still be of use to her. He'd already saved her twice. She began walking, then stopped, an uncomfortable feeling twisting her gut. The second time he'd saved her . . .

She shook her head, pushing away the memory of waking up in his arms as he carried her through the melting snow to safety. No one had dared touch her in a very long time.

No one but the snow.

Branwen sat atop the eve of the fortress roof. The rain soaked her burgundy cloak and russet hair, but she barely felt it. She barely felt *anything*.

She knew she was as good as dead. She only still walked and talked because the Ceàrdaman had filled her with the energy of the in-between, the same place she'd been trapped while her brother had been murdered.

Her only choice now was to try and live for him. He'd sacrificed his life for hers, and she would not let him die in vain . . . yet, she was not sure that her current state of living was what he would have wanted. Would he have wished for her to aid the Ceàrdaman in destroying the barrier to the in-between?

She shook her head violently, sending rain droplets scattering around her face. She felt mad half the time. If she could not convince Finn to break the barrier, what then? Would the Travelers send her back to the grave? Would she really mind?

Sighing, she gazed out at the dark clouds. Perhaps her life should have ended when she first entered the Blood

Forest. The memory seemed so distant, and all her time since had seemed like a dream . . . or a nightmare.

Her current existence was perhaps the most nightmarish of all, and there was nothing she could do about it. For now, all she could do was watch and wait, and hope that she made the right choice when the time finally came.

CHAPTER TWO

*A*nna entered the courtyard. Finn's unicorn and the few horses they'd acquired needed feeding, and it was her turn to tend them. As she walked past the rough wood panels added to the old stone of the original stables, she sensed someone following her. She inadvertently rubbed the sides of her black breeches nervously, hesitating to complete her task.

Scowling at her sudden fear, she forced it away. If someone was watching her, the logical thing would be to lure them out. Walking past the stabled horses, she veered toward the newly constructed storage building which housed the feed for the horses, as well as saddles, bridles, and other supplies.

She casually unlatched the hook holding the thin wooden door shut, then walked inside, leaving the door hanging open behind her.

Instead of moving toward the feed, she plastered her back against the wall just inside the door and waited.

It was a while before she heard the footsteps, then a shadow loomed in the open doorway. Anna could see her magic shining before she entered, but now was even more perplexed since Finn had been avoiding her recently. She decided to wait and see what she did.

After a moment, Finn walked inside.

Anna darted behind her and slammed the door shut, trapping them both in near darkness within the cramped building.

Finn yipped in surprise, then whirled on Anna. Seeing they were alone, she relaxed.

Anna looked her up and down. Truly, she looked nothing like a queen with her long, unkempt hair and plain tunic and breeches. "Are you here to finally tell me what secret you and Kai have been keeping?"

She thought Finn's eyes widened, but it was difficult to tell with only slivers of light coming in through the wooden slats of the walls.

"Secret?" Finn asked.

Anna rolled her eyes, tired of whatever game they were playing. She knew something was going on with Kai, and suspected it had to do with the Dair blood running through his veins, given Finn's involvement.

Leaning against the closed doors, Anna crossed her arms, then waited.

Finn let out a long breath, her shoulders sagging. "I need your help."

Anna snorted. "Of course you do."

Ignoring her sarcastic remark, Finn continued. "Kai is in trouble, but he will not let me help him. I need your help to —" she hesitated, glancing over her shoulder as if someone else might be in the tiny building with them. "I need your help to hold him down," she whispered conspiratorially.

Now it was Anna's turn to be taken aback. "Hold him down? What in the Horned One's name are you talking about?"

Finn bit her lip, taking a step closer. "I swore to him that I would tell no one of his affliction, but I fear he hasn't much time left. I want to—" she glanced around again, then turned back to Anna and whispered, "I want to help him like I was able to that night we were in the in-between."

Anna's eyes grew even wider. The night they'd been in the in-between was the night Kai almost died from a poisoned wound. Finn had given him a measure of her immortal blood to save him.

"It's that bad?" she questioned. She knew something was going on with Kai, but she hadn't expected something life threatening. She truly thought he would have told her if that was the case.

Finn nodded, her expression somber. "I believe so. I don't even know if my blood will help him, but I think it's his best chance."

Anna recalled the night in the in-between once more. Kai had been unconscious at the time. She knew she'd have to do a lot more than hold him down if Finn tried to give him her blood while he was awake. In fact, she'd likely have to hold a knife to his throat.

He wouldn't thank her for helping with Finn's plan, but it wouldn't matter if he was dead. Alive, he could forgive her in time. Dead, he wouldn't be forgiving anybody.

Anna took a steadying breath. "Just tell me what to do."

Iseult stood on the parapet next to Eywen. They'd both seen Anna going to feed the horses, and watched as Finn crept along after her. Then both women disappeared into the feed room and had not returned. It would be dark soon, so hopefully they would hurry up and return to the fortress where they'd be relatively safe.

"What do you suppose they're doing in there?" Eywen questioned.

"Scheming," Iseult answered. Whenever Finn was around Kai or Anna, there was always scheming. From Finn, he found it endearing. From the other two . . . less so.

He'd also seen Eywen and Anna leaving the fortress walls together earlier that morning, but did not mention it. It was normal for alliances to be made in dire times, however unusual the pairings might seem.

"A decision must be made soon," Eywen muttered, drawing Iseult back to the present. "We cannot allow Oighear to continue gathering strength."

He nodded. As much as he didn't want to risk Finn, they could not just wait around for their enemies to attack. There was the prophecy to think about. Only one queen could live.

Iseult intended that queen to be Finn, despite any alliances he might have had in the past . . . despite his brother, his only living kin, choosing the opposing side.

"I'll speak with her," he assured, though Finn had been utterly unreasonable as of late. He knew she was hesitant to make her move, to risk more lives, but there was no other choice.

She could not live in peace, as much as she desired it.

Eywen nodded, still watching the feed room where Finn and Anna were hiding. "If you cannot convince her, I'd like to ask permission to search for more of my warriors. Others will want to defect from Oighear's ranks now that there is another option. We could strengthen our defenses while weakening hers."

"I'll pass along your request," Iseult said evenly, even though he knew Finn would say yes. She would not make anyone stay at the fortress if they wished to leave. Except, perhaps, the Cavari.

Finally, Finn and Anna emerged from the feed room, then hurried across the courtyard together. Naoki, Finn's now quite-large white dragon, hurtled across the courtyard upon spotting them, though he had not seen the creature prior to that moment. It was almost as if she'd appeared out of thin air.

Shaking away his speculations on the dragon, he watched as Finn and Anna, huddled close together and speaking in hushed tones, wove through the crumbled statues in the courtyard to reach the fortress doors.

Definitely scheming, he thought.

"I'll speak with her now," Iseult said aloud.

Eywen nodded, his gaze distant, deep in his own thoughts.

Iseult left him on the parapet and went inside. If he hurried down the interior stairs, he should catch Finn in the entry room before she could scurry off.

Though he was near her often, others were usually about. The thought of speaking with her alone made his heart race, just a little. He used to think it was her magic, or perhaps the touch of fate that brought them together, but now he knew it was just her. At some point, he'd stopped caring about what she was in favor of *who* she was. It made him question who *he* was, or at least who he was becoming.

Finn entered the main hall with Anna at her side. A fire blazed in the large hearth, and numerous candles decorated the sparse surfaces within the room, illuminating it as the windows slowly darkened.

They would not go to Kai, not yet. They would need to be quite sure of their plan first.

She lifted her gaze as Iseult descended the adjacent stairs. Her heart thumped a little admiring his cool approach, his sleek body in black, and his ebony hair bound partially by a leather clasp. At his hip was a sword, and she knew there were likely daggers hidden in each of his boots and beneath the long sleeves of his shirt.

"We'll speak later," Anna whispered as Iseult reached the landing and turned toward them.

Anna hurried off before Finn could reply.

To camouflage her worries, she forced a smile at Iseult, the most wildly confusing man she'd ever met. "If you're here to demand I confront Oighear, you can save your breath."

He reached her, then hesitated before closing the last step of distance between them. "I came to speak with you about Eywen, actually." Finally he stepped forward, then offered her his arm.

Feeling silly about being confrontational, she hooked

her arm in his. He led her across the main hall into a short corridor, then out to the exterior gardens.

Once outside, Finn exhaled a sigh of relief. While she did not feel the same connection to the earth that she once did, she still felt better outside. The fortress had begun to feel like a cage, with the Cavari out front, barren marshlands behind, and the ever looming threat of war everywhere else.

They walked together in the dim light of dusk, toward a small stone bench, still damp from the rain. Wordlessly, they both sat.

She smoothed her hands down her breeches nervously. She longed to tell him about Kai, about the decision she'd made to save him, but knew she could not. He would try to stop her, and he wouldn't be wrong to do so. In weakening herself, she was risking them all.

"You said you wanted to speak about Eywen?" she prompted, attempting to distract herself from her guilt.

He nodded. "If we have no plans to advance on Oighear, he wishes to depart. He would like to gather more of his people to strengthen our defenses. He fears Oighear will grow too strong while we wait."

She wasn't surprised by his words. She knew everyone was growing impatient with her. Everyone, except perhaps Àed, who seemed content to rest in the fortress now that he'd escaped Keiren, and Kai, too sick to even consider arguing the delay.

"I suppose that's for the best," she replied.

Iseult's gray-green eyes watched her intently. "So you still refuse to act?"

She took a long, tired breath, then looked down at her lap. She knew he'd bring it up eventually. Yet, what was she supposed to do? March far to the east to attack Oighear in her own element? March on Garenoch and *kill* Ealasaid? She didn't care about the prophecy. She would not harm anyone who was not actively attempting to harm her first.

Iseult's hand reached forward to cradle her chin, turning her toward him. As soon as she looked up, his hand dropped, and he was closed off once more.

Utterly infuriating man, she thought again. If he was going to be so closed off, he never should have kissed her in the first place.

"I have angered you," he observed.

She fought to hide her emotions, then decided against it. She had a right to be angry, and not just at Iseult. She was angry at the entire cursed world, and at fate itself for making her a part of its morbid prophecy.

Emboldened by her anger, she spoke without thinking. "If you must know, yes, I'm angry, but that is not at the forefront of my mind. I cannot think about wars, prophecies, or even *you* when I know Kai is in peril. I have been tip-toeing around for days, worried that you'll try to stop me from saving him, or worse, you'll kill him yourself instead."

Iseult's expression did not change as he said, "He was bitten by one of those creatures, wasn't he? Not the last time, but before, when he went missing?"

Her jaw dropped. "You knew?"

He shrugged. "I suspected."

"And you didn't try to stop me from seeing him?" she pressed.

"What you do with him is your choice," he said evenly. "You have a much stronger . . . *bond* with him than I."

She blinked at him, attempting to maintain her emboldening anger, though it seemed to be slipping away. "Well then," she replied, "I suppose that means you will not argue when I tell you that tomorrow at dawn, I'd like to combine my blood with his once more. It is all I can think of to save him."

His jaw stiffened, but he still did not argue.

She waited.

Finally, he gave her a stiff nod. "To weaken yourself is your choice. I will continue to protect you with my life regardless."

Utterly. Infuriating.

She opened her mouth to reply, but he held up a hand.

"Someone is listening," he explained.

Footsteps sounded from within the fortress, not far from where they were sitting.

They both rose and rushed to the door to catch the eavesdropper, but no one was there.

Iseult peered down the short hall for a moment, then shook his head and turned to Finn. "If you intend to carry through with this plan, at least try to rest first."

His eyes scanned her face. She knew she looked horrible from lack of sleep, but there wasn't much she could do about it.

She nodded. "I will do as you say. Anna and I plan to act at dawn."

Iseult gently touched her shoulder for a moment, then strode away.

She watched his back as he retreated down the hall, her thoughts lingering on whoever had been listening to them. Hopefully it was just one of the Bucca.

Her feet dragging with every step, she made her way

toward her chamber. She knew sleep would not come easy, but if Iseult could be so agreeable to her notions, she could stand to be agreeable to some of his.

Kai pressed his back against the wall, panting. That blasted Iseult had ears like a fox. How had he heard him waiting inside the doorway?

He forced his breathing to slow, then hurried back toward his room, mulling over what he'd heard. He could not allow Finn to sacrifice more of her blood to him, not when it wasn't likely to help.

He reached his room and began gathering his few belongings. He should have left long ago, back when he first realized the bite, and perhaps the blood he was fed, were *changing* him. Yet, he'd selfishly looked forward to his daily visits from Finn. He'd hoped he would improve enough to be able to protect both her and Anna in these dangerous times.

Now, he'd be doing quite the opposite if he stayed. He'd weaken Finn, and she'd be vulnerable to her many enemies. He could not allow it.

If only Iseult would have argued with her . . . he shook his head. He truly couldn't believe that he had not argued, but this was no time to dwell on it. He needed to escape the fortress before she came for him. He knew without a doubt that if he was forced to face her, he would be unable to say no.

With his belongings slung over his back, and a few weapons strapped about his person, he exited his room. He listened to make sure no one was coming, then fled, knowing he could not look back. If he looked back, he would not have the strength to leave them all behind.

Ealasaid limped toward the dining hall, the moon shining overhead to light her way. Slàine had forced her to practice for *hours*, and she'd been none too gentle about it. Her entire body was covered in bruises, and her new training clothes, a set of black breeches and matching tunic, were torn and muddy.

To make matters worse, as soon as the lesson had ended, Sage, who was now her second in command, had come to find her to discuss infighting in the burgh. The young, dark-haired mage had been inexperienced when they'd first met, but now his fire magic could nearly rival Ealasaid's lightning. He was a hard worker, and loyal, diligently training the new mages showing up each day. It turned out having so many mages in one town could be dangerous, as infighting escalated far beyond what would occur with normal men and women. She'd spent the remainder of her evening apologizing to the innkeep for his damaged property, when what she really wanted was a hot meal and a long bath.

Maarav appeared at her side as she walked, the pleasant smells from the nearby dining hall engulfing them. She used to jump whenever he approached her so stealthily, especially at night, but she was used to it now. In fact, she'd come to depend on the way he always showed up just when she needed him most.

"Carry me," she whined. "I cannot walk anymore."

He smirked, making no move to lift her off the exterior cobblestone path leading to the brightly illuminated dining hall. They walked between decorative hedges, adorned near their wiry trunks with waxy winter flowers, their colors washed out in the moonlight. "I see Slàine has not grown softer in her training methods."

She shook her head, her frizzy curls now mostly pulled loose from her braid. "If anything, she's grown harder. I cannot believe that she made all of her assassins train so rigorously."

Maarav smiled wistfully, his black hair trailing behind him in the soft breeze, intermingling with the darkness of night. "On my sixteenth birthday she made me climb to the top of the cliffs guarding our home in the North. When I reached the top, she aimed an arrow at me and forced me to walk along the entire effacement before I could come back down."

She stopped walking to turn and balk at him. She'd seen his homeland once, not long after they'd escaped Conall and his Reivers. The massive black cliffs hiding the city within were far too steep to climb, and their tops were jagged and sharp as daggers. "You're kidding," she pressed when he did not elaborate further.

He shook his head. "You can do impossible things when a woman is aiming an arrow at you."

"I'll have to remember that," she quipped, then forced herself to start walking. Her sore feet dragged with every step.

"So . . . " Maarav trailed off.

She knew what he was going to ask next. Though she'd agreed to marry him, she hadn't thought everything through. How could they possibly have a wedding when they were at war? It seemed somehow wrong. Not to mention that her family was dead, and she wasn't close enough to any of the mages to call them true friends. If they had a wedding now, their only witness would be Slàine. Perhaps Ouve and Tavish would have attended, but they were both dead.

"We are at war," she replied, not wanting to voice her other pathetic concerns. She was ruling over thousands of powerful magic users. She shouldn't be concerned about having friends.

"My point precisely," he countered. "We don't know what could happen tomorrow, and I'd like to be married to you today."

They reached the light of the dining hall. If she could just put him off until they were inside, they'd have no privacy in which to speak . . .

He gently took hold of her arm, halting her advance. "Is there another reason you're avoiding this subject?" he questioned.

She met his gray-green eyes.

"Ealasaid!" someone called, and her shoulders slumped in relief.

They both turned to see lantern light illuminating Ilsandra, one of the mages who'd been present since the battle against the Aos Sí. She was tall, only a few inches shorter than Maarav, with long hair so blonde it looked white.

She reached them, then hesitated, her dark eyes hinting that she'd picked up on the tension between Maarav and Ealasaid. Her freckled skin slowly turned red.

"It's fine," Ealasaid assured. "What do you need?"

"*Travelers*, my lady," she explained. "They wait outside the gates."

"The Ceàrdaman?" she questioned. "Have they said what they want?"

Ilsandra bit her thin bottom lip, then replied. "To speak with you, my lady. They asked for you by name."

Ealasaid turned her attention to Maarav.

He shrugged. "They're being polite if they're waiting outside the gate. Simple walls do not keep creatures like the Ceàrdaman out."

Well that was something, at least. She turned back to Ilsandra with a sigh. "I suppose I better go and speak with them."

Ilsandra nodded, then turned to lead the way. Maarav followed at Ealasaid's side without question.

Ealasaid's stomach growled. She'd been *so* close to a nice supper. "What do you know of the Travelers?" she whispered to Maarav as Ilsandra walked ahead of them.

"About as much as any," he replied. "They claim to be all-knowing, and are somehow related to the Faie. No one knows where they came from, or why, they suddenly just appeared at a random point in history."

Ealasaid sucked her teeth as they rounded the central building of the estate toward the gates leading out into Garenoch. What could the Travelers want with *her*?

Even at the late hour, many mages were still running around, along with the assassins who stood guard. Those who came near enough to recognize her in the dark watched on curiously as they reached the gates, motioning for the guards above to let them out into the burgh.

Ilsandra stood close to them while the massive gates

swung outward, prompting Ealasaid to keep her questions to herself, not out of distrust, but out of a need to appear like she knew what she was doing. Which, it was becoming increasingly clear to her, she did not.

With the gates now open, she turned to Ilsandra. "There's no need to accompany us any further. We'll be fine on our own." She flicked her gaze to the assassins who'd approached, ready to escort them into the burgh.

The black-cowled men and women turned their gazes to Maarav, who nodded.

Ealasaid sucked her teeth again, then turned to walk through the open gates. Even though she was supposed to be in charge, the assassins all deferred to Slàine, or to Maarav when Slàine was not around. Perhaps someday Ealasaid would earn their trust. She only hoped such a day would come *before* Slàine decided Ealasaid was worth more to her dead.

Together, she and Maarav walked out into the burgh. The gates slowly swung shut behind them, trapping them on the outside, though Ealasaid did not mind. She felt far safer in the burgh than she did around Slàine, or any of Lady Síoda's men. Though the lady of the burgh and her husband, Lord Gwrtheryn, had peacefully retreated to their own private area of the estate, Ealasaid could not quite push away the fear of a knife striking her in the dark. Gwrtheryn might be a coward, but Síoda was a woman to be watched.

Once they were out of sight of the guards perched atop the high walls, Maarav wrapped Ealasaid's hand in his. She took comfort in his warm palm against hers. At one time, she feared a knife in the back from him too, but that time was long since past. While few others would be wise to trust him, she did, and that was all that mattered to her.

They received a few glances here and there from those still out that evening, either closing their shutters for the night, or walking toward the inn for a meal, but no one bothered them. It was refreshing to feel for a moment like any other normal person.

Of course, that feeling would end as soon as they reached the outer gates where the Travelers waited.

Nearing the newly constructed gates, she stopped to look up at Maarav's shadowed features. "Is there anything else I need to know?"

He shrugged. "Just be careful what you say, Eala, and do not ask them for information that they do not offer freely. And do not take any gifts. If you do, they will expect something in return, something you will most certainly be reluctant to give."

With a nod, she took a deep breath, then approached the guards standing at the base of the gate, ready to gesture up to those posted above. Two of the guards were Lady Síoda's men, evident by their simple uniforms of dark blue coats and matching breeches. With them were two mages Ealasaid vaguely recognized, a man and a woman, though she could not recall either's name.

"They wait just outside the gates, my lady," the male mage explained. "We were not sure if we should admit them."

She didn't bother telling them that if the Travelers wanted to come in, they would simply come in, and there was little anyone could do about it.

"Open one side of the gates," she instructed, "but remain on guard. I will speak with them."

The mages and guards nodded. One guard gestured up to those mounted atop the wall. A moment later, one of the heavy gates began to swing inward, prompting those before it to step out of the way.

Ealasaid waited patiently as the gate opened, revealing five of the Ceàrdaman standing outside. They wore long white robes, obscuring their thin forms to the point where Ealasaid could not tell if they were male or female. Their perfectly bald heads and features that were neither overly masculine nor feminine added to their air of *sameness*.

Ealasaid stepped forward with Maarav at her side, and the guards and mages behind them, fanned out defensively.

One of the Travelers stepped forward. Ealasaid guessed she was female. In her hands she held a black velvet box, long and thin. To Ealasaid's surprise, the Traveler dropped to a knee, her people mirroring the movement behind her.

She bowed her bald head and extended the velvet box. "We of Clan Solas Na Réaltaí come bearing gifts for the Queen of Wands."

Ealasaid bit her lip to keep from gasping. Queen of Wands was what Oighear had called her too. She recognized the words of their clan name as something that roughly translated to starlight. Not far off from the name given to her gathering of mages, An Solas, simply, *the light*.

Her mind raced for something to say, but all she could come up with was, "Why?"

The Traveler lifted her gaze, but did not rise. "To swear fealty, of course."

Ealasaid glanced at Maarav, who shrugged.

"And what would you want in return for this *fealty*?" she asked, remembering Maarav's warning.

"We offer this allegiance freely," she explained. "We do not require a boon in return."

She glanced at Maarav again.

He pursed his lips, observing the Travelers. "They may twist their words, but they do not lie. If they say something directly, you need not question it."

Her shoulders relaxing, she received the velvet box. It was heavier than it looked, far heavier. She wondered by its shape if perhaps a short sword was hidden inside.

She peered at the Traveler as she rose, wondering if she was now expected to open the box.

Though Ealasaid asked no direct question, the Traveler nodded.

With a shaky breath, she balanced the heavy box in one hand and removed the lid with the other.

Inside was a silver scepter. The rod was decorated with tiny swirls and pinpricks of jewels that looked like stars. At one end was a perfectly clear, raw jewel, clearly unshaped by human hands. It was about half the size of her fist. With the way it twinkled in the moonlight, she could hardly imagine what it might look like in the sun.

"It is a relic of our people," the Traveler explained, "hidden away for centuries, waiting for a time when someone who walks the line between reality and the in-between would rule."

Ealasaid's mouth went dry. It was an ancient relic of the Ceàrdaman, and they were giving it to . . . her?

"Um, thank you," she muttered, unsure of what else to stay.

Seemingly satisfied, the Travelers began to back away.

Ealasaid opened her mouth to ask them more about what the gift of the wand meant, but they were no longer there. They had faded from existence as if they'd never been. Yet, the box with the wand was still very real in her hands.

Maarav moved to peer over her shoulder at the wand. "I don't like this. Not one bit."

She turned her head and blinked up at him, unsure of what to say.

The female mage cleared her throat. "We should retreat back within the gates where it is safe, my lady."

Ealasaid nodded, quickly putting the lid back on the box. She'd examine the wand further when she was safe within her bedroom.

While she had no idea what it meant, or what powers it might possess, if any, she was quite sure the tides of fate had just shifted.

She could only hope the change was in her favor.

CHAPTER THREE

*F*inn knew distantly that she was in a dream, but she couldn't quite seem to pull out of it. Moonlight lit her way. The mists of the Gray Place obscured her feet, parting, then reforming around the hem of her thick robe. The robe itself was a deep forest green, but was not the ratty robe originally gifted to her by Àed. This one was was well-made, with soft fur lining the hood. A heavy broach shaped like a golden leaf gathered the fabric near her left shoulder, below her collarbone. Her long, dirty blonde hair blew freely in the warm air.

She knew the area in which she treaded. She recognized the odd, scraggly trees, and knew a large lake was not far off. She wondered if she was meant to go to that lake. Perhaps it was the only way she would wake. Something butted against her bare hand, startling her.

She turned down to see Naoki, pushing against her palm for attention. The dragon's once sparse feathers had finished growing in, coating her head, body, and wings in glistening white. Tiny glittering feathers had even sprouted down over the base of her sharp beak. She blinked spherical, lilac eyes up at Finn, as if questioning her presence in the Gray Place.

Finn stroked Naoki's feathered head, rather comforted to have the company, then continued walking. The dragon's appearance in the Gray Place was no surprise. She'd appeared there before, and Finn knew she could find her way back to the real world whenever she chose.

With a shaky breath, Finn pressed onward, wondering if she had been summoned here, or if she had arrived on her own.

The shimmering lake came into view. Walking to its shore with Naoki by her side, she admired the calm, dark surface reflecting the moonlight. Her eyes darted about. No one waited for her, at least not that she could see.

Naoki trotted along the lake's edge a short way to examine a small boat lodged in the sand. Finn remembered the boat from a previous dream. She could still recall the feel of Oighear's icy fingers around her throat as she swayed on the boat, trapped in the middle of the lake. Nothing on earth could compel her to set foot in the vessel now.

She stared at the boat for several seconds, then turned, sensing a presence at her back. She scanned her surroundings, but there was no one there. She could have *sworn* she felt eyes on her.

Without warning, Naoki darted past her, back in the direction she'd come. Seconds later, she was out of sight.

Shaking her head in confusion, she wrapped her arms around herself as a cold gust of air hit her, so cold she began shivering. She began to grow nervous. The Gray Place was usually even in temperature, except for her one dream of Oighear. She blinked, and found herself surrounded by familiar trees, not the odd scraggly ones that were here before. Her eyes widened in surprise. What was happening?

The moon shone softly overhead, but the mist it once illuminated was gone, except for Finn's breath fogging the air in front of her face.

A final look around revealed the distant fortress. She was back in reality. She looked down at her muddy, bare feet, then stroked her palms down her white underpinnings, covered only by her ratty green cloak. Had she been sleep-walking?

"My apologies for interrupting your dream," a voice said from behind her.

She whipped around, then narrowed her eyes. "What are you doing here, Niklas?"

The Traveler stood alone, his pale gray robe cloaking all but his bald head, and the tips of his unnaturally long fingers.

"I've come to check on you," he purred, "and to make sure my wraith is behaving. I can't seem to find her."

Hmm, so Branwen had told her the truth. It was Niklas who turned her into little more than a ghost.

"She's fine," she replied sharply, fighting her chattering teeth. "If that's all, I'd like to return to my bed."

Niklas titled his head. "No, that is not all. I would like to offer you a gift."

Finn shook her head. She knew better than to take *anything* from the Ceàrdaman, especially Niklas. "I do not want your *gift*."

He smiled, revealing sharp teeth. "Oh trust me, my dear,

you will want this one, lest you give the human queen the upper hand."

Her eyes narrowed further. "What do you know of Ealasaid?"

Instead of answering, he lifted a small black velvet box from within the folds of his robe. It was roughly the size of his palm, not likely to hold a weapon, or anything else that might cause her harm.

He opened the box to reveal a ring. Curious in spite of herself, Finn stepped closer to observe it. The solid gold band had a thick base engraved with tiny leaves and acorns, embedding a deep green stone with a raw, irregular surface.

Niklas offered her the ring, still resting within its box.

She lifted her eyes to meet his gaze. She'd encountered the Travelers enough to no longer be startled by the reflective nature of his eyes.

Niklas smiled softly. "I offer you this gift on behalf of Clan An Duilleog, the Clan of the Leaf. That is the clan from which I hail."

She took a step back. "I do not desire your fealty."

His smile broadened. It was a predatory smile, the last thing some people saw right before meeting their ends. "You have it whether you like it or not. You have had it from the start." He held the box toward her.

"No," she said, taking another step back. "I do not want it."

He sighed. "Always such a difficult girl." He closed the box containing the ring, then turned and walked away, fading from sight.

Finn blinked, slowly lowering the hand that had darted to her thundering heart. She paused mid-motion, noticing a peculiar weight on her finger. She lifted her hand and peered down at the ring Niklas had offered her.

Disgusted with his trick, she tugged the ring off her finger, then dropped it in the dirt. She kicked soil and dead leaves over it with her bare foot, already throbbing from the cold.

With a final huff, she turned and walked back toward the fortress, wondering just what Niklas was plotting. She also distantly wondered about the eyes she'd felt on her in the Gray Place. She didn't think it was Niklas. Whatever it was, Naoki had chased it, and might be chasing it still, given she wasn't here.

She reached the gates to find one side slightly ajar, just enough for her to slip through. She glanced to the Trow on either side of the gate, resting peacefully in their rooted tree forms. She wondered if anyone besides the Trow had seen her depart, barefoot in the middle of the night. They'd probably think her quite mad, and after her strange night, she'd have trouble arguing with them.

When Finn finally awoke, the sun was already streaming harshly through her window. She'd missed dawn by a long shot. She was supposed to meet with Anna to enact their plan with Kai.

She sat up with a groan, peering down at Naoki curled happily by her feet. Her sleep must have been deep to not notice the dragon's return. She stroked her soft white feathers, then lifted her hands to rub at her eyes. She scowled, extending her hands in front of her. That cursed ring was on her finger again.

With a growl, she tore it off and slammed it onto the low table beside her straw mat. If it ended up on her finger again, she'd throw it out the window.

Naoki barely moved as she climbed out of the blankets and placed her bare feet on the chilly floor, noting the mud still speckling her skin.

She hurried to the basin of icy water near the hearth of burning embers. Shivering, she washed her feet, then dressed in forest green breeches, a loose tan tunic, and her ratty cloak. Finally, she tugged on her woolen socks and boots. It was time to find Anna. Hopefully she wouldn't be off with Eywen somewhere since Finn had missed their meeting.

She rushed down the hall, then descended the stairs, following her well-trod path to the entry room. It had become somewhat of a meeting place for their small group. If Anna hadn't finished her breakfast already, Finn would find her there.

She entered the large room to find not only Anna, but Iseult and Bedelia. Their expressions were grave.

"What's happened?" Finn asked, rushing toward them.

Anna waited for Finn to reach her, then explained, "I went to Kai's room this morning. I wanted to speak with him after all you told me. He wasn't there."

Finn glanced at Iseult and Bedelia, then back to Anna. "While it's odd for Kai not to be in his room given his current state, it isn't necessarily cause for alarm."

"I was on watch last night," Bedelia explained, her expression pained. "I saw him sneak through the gates. He seemed to think no one was watching." She pushed a lock of short brown hair behind her ear. "I would have been more suspicious, but I saw you go out a few moments after him. I apologize, I did not know of his condition, or I would have tried to stop you both."

Finn's heart fell. Niklas had lured her out the gates not long after Kai's departure. He might have even seen her meeting with the Traveler, but she had been too busy to notice him. Although, none of that answered the question of why he left. Had he finally succumbed to the bite of the Dearg Due? Was he even now seeking out his new mistress?

Iseult watched her carefully. When she did not speak, he explained, "I believe he was the one who heard our discussion last night. It may have prompted him to flee."

Finn closed her eyes, attempting to fight off the panic threatening to take over. She was such a fool. Kai had heard her plan, and left before she could sacrifice more of her strength for him. She had to *find* him.

Her eyes snapped open. "We must leave at once. If we start now, we may still be able to catch him." She turned to Bedelia, knowing her tracking skills were superior. "Will you help me?"

Bedelia nodded, her brown eyes wide. "Of course."

"As will I," Anna said immediately.

"You cannot," Iseult argued. "Have you forgotten the position we are in? We cannot waste time with this."

She raised a hand to halt his speech, then nearly screamed at the sight of the green-stoned ring on her finger. With a shriek of irritation, she pulled it off and flung it across the room. It went clattering across the stones, skidding to a halt before the fire.

47

Iseult, Anna, and Bedelia all looked at her like she'd grown a second head.

Sparing a final wary look for Finn, Bedelia moved across the room and retrieved the ring. Walking back to the group, she extended the ring to Finn.

Finn glared at it.

Anna huffed. "Is there any reason you're fretting over a ring right now instead of Kai?"

She sighed. Those gathered knew enough about her to not be surprised by her explanation. "Niklas was here last night, outside the fortress. I rejected the ring, but when I woke, it was on my finger. He said it meant his clan had sworn fealty to me."

Bedelia dropped the ring like it had stung her. It clattered to the stones.

Anna glanced at it, then up to Finn. "I suggest you throw it in a bog."

Iseult watched the exchange with thinly veiled rage, though whether it was directed at her, or the fact that Niklas had visited the fortress unbeknownst to him, she did not know.

With a sigh, she knelt and retrieved the ring, then stood, peering down at the odd green stone. "I have a feeling that even if I threw it into the sea, I'd still wake up with it on my finger the next morning." Not wanting to waste any more time on the ring, she stuck it in her pocket.

"Now back to finding Kai," Anna suggested.

"He left of his own volition," Iseult interrupted. "Let him make his own choices."

All three women glared at him, but it was Finn's glare that finally compelled him to raise his hands in surrender.

He sighed. "At the very least send a scouting party of Pixies to find him. There is no need to go yourselves. Pixies are more efficient."

Finn watched as Anna raised a dark brow at him. "And you think *Pixies* will be able to convince him to come back?"

"Then you go with them, but Finn must remain," he said. "There is much more at stake here than a single life."

Guilt twisted Finn's gut. She knew he was right, but . . . "I would never forgive myself if I did not try."

He flexed his hands, clearly on his last nerve. "Then send Anna and the Pixies. If they find him, the Pixies can fly back to retrieve you. Do not waste your time on what may be a fruitless search."

She pursed her lips. She supposed they could *all* live with that, but it still didn't feel right.

She turned back to Anna, who nodded. "I'll be fine on my own. I travel better that way."

Against her better judgement, Finn nodded her consent, and Anna stalked off to prepare.

Finn watched her go, but something still felt *wrong*. Some instinct told her that the incorrect decision had been made, and for that, someone she cared for would pay dearly.

Anna rushed around the fortress, gathering supplies in preparation for her journey. Too much time had already been lost. Thanks to Bedelia, she knew around what hour he'd left. If he'd traveled through the night, he could already be miles ahead of her. If only the fool had confided in her sooner.

If only she hadn't been too distracted by her own misery to ask.

Shaking her head, she shoved her few articles of clothing into a saddlebag. She'd be taking one of the few horses they had at the fortress. Hopefully the extra speed would be enough to catch Kai.

A knock sounded on the partially open door behind her.

"Come in!" she called, giving her room one last scan to make sure she didn't miss anything. She had no idea how long she'd be gone, so the more supplies she could bring, the better.

She turned to see Eywen pushing the door the rest of the way open.

Suddenly she felt oddly guilty. She hadn't told him she was leaving . . . not that she owed him any explanation. He had *no* reason to care.

"I've just spoken with Iseult," he said, scanning her mostly empty room. "He told me what happened with Kai."

Slinging the saddle pack over her shoulder, she turned to fully face him. "Yes, I'm a fool for not realizing the severity of his condition. The Pixies are going to help me find him so I can bring him back."

He nodded, not debating the fact that she was a fool. "I'll accompany you on your way out. I'll be journeying east to see if any of my people would like to join our cause."

Anna blinked at him. Here she had actually felt guilty for not telling him of her last minute plans, when *he'd* been planning on leaving for who knew how long.

Yet, she couldn't be angry. She had no *reason* to be angry. Her face reddened anyway.

"You'd think you would have mentioned that previously," she said curtly.

He tilted his head, cascading raven black hair over the shoulder of his tunic. "Are you angry?"

"Not at all," she said simply, then strode past him toward the door. She shouldn't be concerning herself with one of the Faie. Kai was more important.

He followed her out of her room. "Would you *not* like me to accompany you?" he questioned, following her down the hall.

She shrugged, not bothering to look at him. "You may do as you please."

"Then I *will* accompany you," he decided.

She ignored the nervous little flip of her stomach.

They reached the entry room to find Finn waiting by the fire. She turned at the sound of their footsteps, then hurried toward Anna, wrapping her in a hug before she could protest.

Grumbling in irritation, Anna pushed Finn away to arm's length to see tears glistening in her eyes. The woman cried *far* too much.

"Promise me," Finn began, "Promise me that if you need my help, you'll send the Pixies. Loinnir will carry me swiftly to wherever you may be."

Anna nodded, suddenly choked up, but she'd be cursed if she'd allow herself to cry.

Especially in front of Eywen.

"I'll find him and bring him back," she assured.

Finn turned to Eywen, offering him a warm smile. "May your journey be safe. I hope you'll return to us soon."

He nodded sharply. "I have sworn my allegiance to you, my queen. I shall return."

Anna rolled her eyes at him, gave Finn a final wave, then headed for the large double doors, already opened, revealing the damp green courtyard.

After a few more muttered words to Finn, Eywen caught up to her side.

Anna was not surprised to see Iseult standing near the gate, he'd want to be there to ensure Finn didn't ride off while he wasn't looking. What did surprise her, however, was that he stood ready with two mounts. It seemed Eywen had planned on accompanying her whether she liked it or not.

Reaching Iseult, Anna took one set of reins, belonging to a black and white dappled mare. Eywen took the other set of reins from Iseult with a nod, and climbed on a horse so deep brown it was almost black, except when the sun hit it, then there were tones of red.

Anna noticed Eywen's supplies already strapped to his mount. Suddenly she realized that perhaps he hadn't shifted his plans for her. Perhaps he'd planned on leaving that very day regardless, and he hadn't bothered to tell her.

Her mood darkening further, she slung her supplies over her horse's saddle, securing them in place with leather cords. She mounted without another word, then rode toward the gates, not bothering to look back to see if Eywen followed.

Of course, his horse reached her side as one of the Trow came to life to push the heavy gate open for them. They rode through, then the gate shut behind them.

Anna forced herself not to squirm at the sound of the

gate thudding into place, though she jumped when a swarm of Pixies flew overhead. One of the tiny shapes swooped down toward them, then hovered in front of Anna's face.

The little woman straightened her gauzy red dress, impervious to the cold, then put her hands on her hips with her wings beating as fast as a hummingbird's. "Follow whichever path you please," the Pixie said. "We'll scout in all directions, and loop back from time to time to report in."

Anna nodded. "Thank you."

With a nod in reply, the Pixie flew away. Anna urged her horse forward, refusing to acknowledge Eywen's presence at her side. She knew she was acting like a petty teenager, but she could not seem to help herself.

He rode beside her with a pleasant expression on his face, not seeming to notice either way.

The silence stretched on as they rode, broken only by the occasional visits from the Pixies. Though she saw no signs of Kai's passing, the direction they took was the most direct path toward the Sand Road.

The further they got from the fortress, the more Anna relaxed. She hadn't realized just how much the presence of the Cavari had weighed on her. For the first time in a long while, she didn't feel like a knife was going to pierce her back at any moment.

She glanced at Eywen. "How far do you intend to ride with me?"

He turned his head toward her, watching her curiously. "How far would you *like* me to ride with you?"

"I didn't ask you to ride with me at all," she growled, turning forward. "You may leave me any time you please. I dare say you'd do so regardless."

She felt his heavy gaze as he continued watching her, letting his horse amble along at its own pace. "Would you care to explain what that means?"

She scowled, flicking her eyes to him, then back to the path. "It means you were going to leave today without telling me anyway, so I don't know why you'd ask what *I* would like you to do." She glanced at him again to see him smiling. "Do I amuse you?" she hissed.

He shook his head. "I had only spoken with Finn about leaving less than an hour ago, just after I learned of your departure. I had been planning on discussing it with her, but not leaving for a while yet. When I heard you would depart, *without* telling me, I might add, I rushed my plans forward, throwing together whatever supplies I could find with such short notice."

Her jaw dropped. She stared at him a moment, trying to tell if he was just putting her on. "I—" she began, not sure what to say. She turned her gaze down to her hands on her reins. "I owed you no explanation," she said sourly. "I can come and go as I please."

"As can I," he said simply.

There was no malice in his tone, and she turned to see him smiling to himself, not angry in the slightest. She quickly averted her gaze once more.

Kai. Kai was the focus. Eywen would leave her soon, then it would be up to her to save her best friend . . . though she could at least admit, for now, that she no longer minded the company.

Kai rested on the ground within the shelter of the small cave. The sunlight stung his eyes more and more each day, and he feared it would only continue to get worse. He was turning into one of the creatures he so detested, even though it shouldn't be possible. The Dearg Due were female, an ancient race that only used humans or other Faie for breeding purposes. Their children were always female. He wondered if he could find one to ask her what was happening, then quickly dismissed the idea. They'd already tried to kill him once.

He shifted his head, resting on his pack. Before he'd begun to change so drastically, he'd learned all he could of the Dearg Due from Eywen and the other Aos Sí. They were dark creatures, pure evil, if such a thing existed. He did not relish the thought of becoming one of them, as impossible as it was supposed to be.

If he had allowed it, could Finn have saved him? Would he have been cured?

He turned on his side. It didn't matter. He would never let her do it. If she weakened herself, and died because of it . . .

It was a fate worse than death for him. He could not risk it. He would run as far away as he could, then he'd keep running some more. Once he was far enough away that Finn couldn't find him, he'd live out his final days alone. He'd lock himself away where he wouldn't be able to hurt anyone.

He might not be the most strong of will, but he at least had the strength for that.

Keiren lounged on the cushy chair in her chambers. She'd been spending more and more time at the estate in Garenoch, far more than she'd originally intended.

Ealasaid was too smart and ambitious, and leaving her for long, especially with Maarav around, didn't seem wise. While most in the estate had come to trust her, Maarav clearly did not. It was an issue.

And so, she remained in Garenoch, ready to steer Ealasaid in the correct direction whenever the opportunity presented itself. Of course, the *correct* direction had changed many times, especially with the Travelers' visit the previous night. The Solas Na Réaltaí Clan, or Starlight Clan's gift to Ealasaid was a complete surprise to Keiren. While she possessed the *sight*, the Ceàrdaman often managed to thwart her abilities.

After learning of their visit and what they'd brought, Keiren had spent the entire morning in her room waiting for Ealasaid to show it to her. Yet, she never came. Perhaps she had not earned as much of the girl's trust as she'd originally thought. She'd have to remedy that if she ever hoped to manipulate Finn into destroying the barrier to the in-between.

A knock sounded at her door. She smiled, then flipped her long red hair over her shoulder as she stood. The girl had come to show her the wand at last.

Her face fell as she opened the door, revealing a young boy. His trembling hands held a rolled up piece of parchment.

She observed him for a moment, noting his black hair, freckled face, and the inordinate amount of fear in his eyes. She'd seen the boy running around town before, and he seemed a normal child, brave because he was yet to be knocked down by life.

"What are you doing here, boy?" she snapped. "*Speak.*" How had he gotten past the guards at the gate, and the second set of guards outside the building in which she dwelled?

With one trembling hand, he extended the rolled up parchment.

Keiren took the paper, and the boy turned on his heel and ran.

Irritated, she slammed her door shut and returned to her soft chair, unfurling the parchment as she walked.

She slumped into her seat, then began to read the note.

As she read, her eyes widened, then a smile slowly curved across her lips. She'd thought Òengus was dead, likely killed in the battle with the Aos Sí.

Not only was he not dead, he was still in the employ of Oighear the White, and he wanted to arrange a meeting.

She could only guess at what such a meeting would entail, but there was one thing she knew for sure.

Things were finally about to get interesting.

CHAPTER FOUR

"*A*re you sure you don't want an escort?" Ealasaid asked, peering up at the red-haired sorceress from the bench where she sat eating her breakfast.

Keiren had found her outside the dining hall, with a plate of food balanced on her lap, enjoying a rare moment of peace.

Keiren smirked. "I can take care of myself." She slithered her palms down the sides of her heavy black traveling cloak. "I merely wanted to inform you of my journey. I have some personal business to tend, nothing that concerns you."

Ealasaid pursed her lips, glancing down at her plate of half-eaten eggs and sausage. While Keiren wasn't exactly a friend, she still worried about her safety, and not just because she was a powerful ally.

"I'll return within a week's time," Keiren explained, "so don't let Maarav talk you into anything foolish while I'm alway, like *marrying* him."

Ealasaid blinked up at her. "How did you—" she began to

ask, then cut herself off. Of *course* Keiren knew. She knew everything. She probably even knew about the jewel-encrusted wand in the velvet box, hidden beneath her mattress.

Keiren smiled at her. "Just promise me you won't make any rash decisions, one friend to another."

Ealasaid forced a smile and nodded, wondering if Keiren had read her thoughts about them not being friends. They'd fought together in battle, and were allies, but Ealasaid had no illusions as to *why* Keiren cared about her. Friendship had nothing to do with it.

"I won't," she assured, forcing her thoughts away in case Keiren really could read her mind.

Seemingly satisfied, Keiren turned and slinked away, her heavy black cloak billowing behind her.

Ealasaid let out a long breath. She wasn't sure whether to be worried, relieved, or suspicious. Worried that Keiren might be harmed, relieved that she'd be able to relax, if only slightly, with her gone, or suspicious about where she was going.

As she sat staring at her cooling eggs and sausage, suspicion won out. She almost debated having someone follow the sorceress, but whomever she chose would inevitably be found out.

"What was that about?" a voice asked from her left, near the corner of the building.

She turned to see Slàine, dressed in her fitted black clothes with her gray hair pulled back in a tight bun. She was in remarkable form for a woman her age, and could best Ealasaid in a battle with her hands shackled behind her back.

Seeing no reason to lie, she replied, "She's going on a journey. She'll return in a week's time."

Slàine walked around Ealasaid's bench and sat down beside her, their elbows nearly touching.

She fought the urge to scoot away.

"You should have sent someone to follow her," Slàine said casually. "She cannot be trusted."

"Are you volunteering?" she asked, then bit her tongue.

Slàine laughed. "Hardly. Someone has to stay here and make sure you don't impale yourself on your sword."

Ealasaid frowned, not sure if Slàine was joking.

Slàine's smile faded. "You don't like me, do you?"

She blinked at her, stunned at her bluntness. Where was Maarav with his abrupt appearances when she really needed him? She turned her gaze to the surrounding greenery, unsure of what to say.

Finally, she admitted, "It's not that I dislike you, I just find you rather terrifying is all."

She turned to see Slàine's eyebrows raise so high they nearly touched her hairline, then she laughed. "Oh, you may be a queen, but you are so very young. Let us take a walk."

Ealasaid gestured to her breakfast plate, hoping to use it as an excuse.

"Leave it," Slàine ordered. "One of the servants will clean it up."

With a heavy sigh, Ealasaid set her plate aside and stood, then followed at Slàine's side as she headed toward the back end of the estate.

"It's come to my attention," Slàine began, "that you and Maarav intend to marry."

Ealasaid fought her groan. Did *everyone* know? "Is that a

problem?"

Slàine shrugged. "No, except that those of mine and Maarav's order take an oath not to marry outside of said order. It can complicate contracts, and muddy one's priorities."

Ealasaid stopped walking. They'd reached the edge of the gardens, and were completely alone as far as she could see. "Maarav never mentioned that."

Slàine shrugged again. "He took the oath when he was but a child. He likely doesn't remember."

She narrowed her gaze. "What exactly are you attempting to say?"

"I said what I'm trying to say," Slàine replied. "Maarav cannot marry anyone outside of our order."

Ealasaid couldn't seem to get enough air into her lungs. Her palms began to sweat. How could he have forgotten such an oath?

"There must be a way," she breathed.

Slàine smiled, and Ealasaid knew she would not like whatever was coming next. "Well, *you* could take the same oath and join our order. If you were one of us, there would be no issue."

She watched Slàine's expression, searching for any hint that she was serious. When Slàine did not openly laugh in her face, Ealasaid shook her head. "I'm not an assassin, and I will not become one. I would never harm someone who did not attack me first."

Slàine snorted. "You likely wouldn't harm someone even then. I do not mean for you to become a killer. Maarav would never speak to me again if I tried. I simply mean for you to swear an oath of loyalty. Promise not to betray us, and we will remain equally loyal. It is strictly forbidden to take contracts on any members of the order. It would be a guarantee that none of our associates will ever take a contract on your life."

Ealasaid wetted her dry lips. A promise that none of the assassins would ever attempt to harm her, even Slàine? It seemed too good to be true. "Why would you offer this?" she breathed. "What if you disagree with my tactics in the future?"

Slàine's expression was suddenly serious. "I would not be swearing to serve you indefinitely. I would only be making an oath to treat you as I would anyone else in the order, and in exchange, you'll never send a hoard of mages after me. Truly, this deal is of much greater benefit to me than it is to you."

Now it made sense. Slàine finally viewed her as a worthwhile adversary, and so, wanted to ensure the safety of her order in the future. Ealasaid was fine with that. She would never harm the people Maarav had grown up with regardless. She'd sacrifice nothing and gain great peace of mind.

Having thought it over, she held out her hand. "I would like to speak with Maarav first, but I believe we have a deal."

Slàine took her hand, holding it tight. "Speak with him soon. I'd like you to swear your oath tomorrow night."

"Tomorrow?" Ealasaid questioned, her hand still trapped in Slàine's. "Why so soon?"

"Why not?" Slàine asked coyly.

Before Ealasaid could respond, Slàine gave her hand a shake, released it, then turned and strode away.

Ealasaid blinked after her, wondering if she'd just been tricked. Did Slàine know something she did not? It was the only explanation she could think of for needing to take the oath so soon.

She glanced around the expansive gardens, wondering where she might find Maarav. Perhaps he could make sense of it all.

That was, after she finished yelling at him for not remembering the oath he'd sworn.

Maarav watched from the cover of an alleyway near the front gates while Keiren departed. He'd seen her speaking with Ealasaid, and had noted the sorceress' traveling cloak. If he did not think she'd spot him sooner or later, he would have followed her out the gates to see where she was going. As it was, he was left with many speculations.

He raked a hand through his hair. They knew little of Keiren's life outside of Garenoch, except that she was suspiciously concerned with Finn. She'd even sent Bedelia to befriend and trick her.

More and more he wished he could speak with his brother, or even Finn. They were the missing pieces of an ever-complicating puzzle, and now he didn't even know what *they* planned. While he hated the idea of leaving Ealasaid, it might behoove him to make the journey to find them.

As the gates closed behind Keiren, he turned away from the wall he'd been leaning against, then began his walk back toward the estate. He'd learn from Ealasaid Keiren's excuse for leaving, and if she'd be gone long enough, he'd broach the subject of finding his brother.

He walked openly down the bustling main street now that Keiren could not see him. The market was active, far busier than it had likely ever been with all the newcomers to both shop and sell their wares. The burgeoning war had not grown bad enough to harm food supplies, but he knew it was only a matter of time. While the townsfolk out buying bread, withered vegetables, and eggs were aware of the possible dangers, they had no way of knowing just how bad things would become . . . except the few apprised of the prophecy.

He continued onward, occasionally returning a wave from those he recognized. It was an odd feeling, being on friendly terms with common folk. While many had known him at his inn in Migris, most would not attempt to befriend him. The only reason they did so now was because of Ealasaid. Anyone who met her loved her, except Lady Síoda, and perhaps Slàine. He might not have been loved, but he was at least liked simply by association with her.

He reached the wall surrounding the estate, his mood darkening. He wouldn't mind moving to a new place where no one knew him, and he could slink about unnoticed, but the same thing would only happen again. He would have to accept that this was the way his life would forever be once he married the woman he loved.

Love, he thought, gesturing up to the guards atop the gate. Such an odd thing, and something he never thought to experience, especially without a soul, or whatever it was that Finn had taken from his people over a century prior. Of course, it might all be for naught, since it seemed as though Ealasaid no longer wanted to marry him. He was a fool for even asking.

The heavy gate to the courtyard opened. He strolled in through the gate, seeing Ealasaid not far off, red-faced and huffing.

Upon spotting him, she put her hands on her hips. "I've been looking for you everywhere. How dare you forget you swore an oath that prohibits our marriage?"

He walked toward her, moving far enough out of the way for the gates to close behind him. Her curls were puffed out around her head as if she'd been anxiously pawing at them, and her face glistened with sweat.

"What in the gods are you talking about?" he asked as he reached her.

She glared up at him. "I'm talking about Slàine, ambushing me and telling me we can't get married unless I join your order."

He burst out laughing. He couldn't help it.

Her gray eyes shot daggers at him. "Don't you dare laugh at me! This is serious!"

He glanced around to see if anyone was watching them, then held a finger to his lips, though he couldn't help the final chuckle that emerged. Before Ealasaid could continue yelling, he put an arm around her shoulders and led her further away from the gates, veering left to circle around the main building.

"Now," he began calmly as they walked, "please explain to me what in the gods you're talking about."

She turned her head to scowl at him, but continued walking. "I'm talking about the oath you swore when you became an assassin," she hissed. "You swore to never marry outside of your order to avoid any contractual conflicts."

He snorted. "That? I swore my oath when I was but a

boy. I don't even remember half of what it entailed."

She sighed and stopped walking. As she turned to him, his arm fell away from her. "It entails you forfeiting your life if you break your oath, which you would be doing in marrying me."

Finally, he felt compelled to return her scowl. "But you don't even *want* to get married, so what does it matter?"

Her eyes opened so wide he thought they might pop out of her head. "Why would you think that!" she gasped.

He rolled his eyes. "You change the subject every time I bring it up."

She blinked up at him, stunned, then her tears began to fall.

"Now why are you crying!" he hissed, slipping his arm around her shoulders once again to lead her somewhere more private.

She allowed him to guide her only a few more steps, then stopped and pulled away to look up at him. At least they were near the far side of the estate now, where few guards were posted to watch them.

"Do you really want to know why I avoid the subject?" she sobbed, her tears flowing freely.

He fought to keep his expression hard, though her tears clawed at his insides. "Yes, I do."

She glared, though the effect was lessened by cheeks glistening with moisture. "I avoid the subject because marriage is supposed to be a joyous occasion where you are surrounded by family and friends. If you haven't noticed, I don't have any friends, and my entire family was slaughtered on Oighear's command."

His expression softened. He truly was daft at times. Here

he'd thought it had been something *he'd* done. That she'd realized she was about to marry an ex-assassin and had thought better of it. He was such a fool.

Heedless of any who might be watching, he pulled her into his arms, gently cradling her face against his chest. Her tears soaked his shirt.

"Just tell me what you want me to do," he muttered, at a complete loss for any other words.

She pulled away enough to look up at him. "Tomorrow night I will swear whatever oath Slàine wants me to swear, then we will get married."

He frowned, now thoroughly confused. "I thought you said you didn't want to get married because it wouldn't be a happy occasion."

She shook her head. "I thought that until it seemed Slàine was going to prevent our marriage from ever happening. When she said that—" she shook her head, casting her gray eyes downward. "When I thought I would not be able to marry you, I realized I don't want to wait another moment. I want to do it *now*."

Still a bit confused, he removed one arm from her waist to place his fingers under her chin. He pushed up gently until she met his gaze. "I would have married you yesterday, or any day before that, but you needn't swear an oath to Slàine. She will not actually kill me."

Ealasaid laughed, though it sounded a bit like a sob. "No, I'll swear her oath. I like the promise that she won't kill me in my sleep."

He grinned. He quite liked that promise too. His hand still on her chin, he leaned down and kissed her.

Suddenly, it didn't matter if townsfolk recognized him

enough to wave, or if he had to behave himself around infuriating sorceresses. He'd accept his new life happily, in exchange for spending it with the fiery, sometimes confusing woman in his arms.

Finn stood on the parapet, her eyes trained in the direction of the Cavari, though she could not actually see them past the wall. She barely noticed the damp, icy air stinging her cheeks.

She knew she needed to speak with them soon. To come up with a plan before they turned on her. She'd bested them once, but the effects of that battle would only last for so long. She turned her gaze down to the courtyard where Loinnir grazed, free of her stable. Finn could have sworn the unicorn had spoken directly into her mind on multiple occasions, but in recent times, the beast had been calm and quiet. *Waiting*, just like everyone else.

Finn longed for word from the Pixies searching for Kai, but she knew it was likely too soon. They'd only just left the previous day, and the morning sun had only just begun to shine above the treetops.

She heard shuffling footsteps at the door behind her, then turned to see Àed approaching, his expression sour, like usual. Still, he looked far better than when he'd first come to the fortress. His long silver hair had been combed free of knots, and his shapeless gray robe had been cleaned.

She met his sky blue eyes with a smile. "You're up early."

He hobbled toward the edge of the parapet and leaned his arms against the low wall beside her. "I could say the same for yerself." He looked her up and down. "Or perhaps ye didn't sleep at all."

She grimaced. She hadn't slept well for ages. She actually preferred the nights she ended up in the Gray Place in her dreams, otherwise her dreams were filled with the horrors of her past. Her daughter's death. Her curse upon Iseult's people. Sometimes her dreams were about the more recent past, about forsaking the peace she so desired in favor of fighting to protect those she now cared about.

Àed watched her, a knowing expression creasing his already lined face. "Nightmares lose their power when ye come to terms with the things that are haunting ye."

She shivered at his words. "Far easier said than done."

He chuckled, then turned his gaze out toward the courtyard. "Yer right about that, lass, which is why I must speak with ye. I think it's time that I leave."

She turned to face him, shocked. "But we only just got you back."

He nodded, his eyes still distantly settled on the greenery beyond. "I know, lass, but ye no longer need me, and there are things in me own life I must settle."

"Things?" she questioned.

He nodded. "Ye have yer ghosts, I have mine. Seeing me daughter once again made me realize as much."

She watched him, the wheels in her mind turning. "You want to find her again. You want to try to save her, even after all she has done?"

He snorted. "Yer far more perceptive than ye used to be, lass."

She couldn't help her smile, though her heart ached at the thought of him facing Keiren. She'd not seen the sorceress since she and Ealasaid had found her in the Gray Place, so there was no saying what Keiren was plotting currently. She ran her fingers across the collar of her thick, cream colored tunic forlornly. She supposed it wasn't entirely her business.

"She's likely still in Garenoch with Ealasaid," she explained with a sigh, "so you should not have terribly far to journey."

He raised a bushy white brow at her. "No arguments on me leavin'?"

She smirked. "You have your ghosts, I have mine. I cannot prevent you from doing what you need to do. I only wish Iseult could understand such a concept."

He shook his head. "Ye should listen to the lad. He's a good balance to yer . . . impulsive side." He glanced over his shoulder. "Speaking of, I'll be off. I'll come to see ye before I go."

Finn followed Àed's gaze to see Iseult, now waiting behind them. She hadn't heard him approach. Then again, she rarely did.

Without another word, Àed ambled off, past Iseult into the open door leading through her chamber and into the fortress beyond.

With Àed gone, Iseult quietly took his place beside her on the parapet.

She eyed him askance, wishing she could read him as easily as she did Àed.

"Waiting for the Pixies?" he asked.

She turned her eyes back toward the courtyard and nodded. "Among other things. Àed plans to leave us."

Iseult nodded. "He spoke with me as well. Bedelia

intends to go with him."

Finn clenched her jaw. Was *everyone* going to leave her? Did Bedelia truly want to see Keiren too, even after she'd controlled and mentally abused her? Did everyone think she no longer needed them, now that she had the Cavari and droves of Faie under her command? She *did* need them. She needed all of them.

"I suppose next you'll say that you're leaving too," she said caustically, still angry that Àed had not mentioned Bedelia.

"You know that is not the case," he said evenly, "as much as you might sometimes wish it."

She felt her hard expression softening. Did he truly believe that? "Iseult—" she began, then cut herself off, unsure of what to say.

"Look," he said, gesturing toward the sky beyond the wall.

Her gaze turned outward, noticing the little specks of color heading in their direction. In a matter of seconds, three Pixies branched off from their group, zipping downward to hover before her and Iseult.

"Did you find him?" she gasped, barely able to breathe.

A male Pixie with green hair shook his head. "Still scouting, but we found something else, far north."

Her mind raced. The only thing to the north was Sormyr, the Gray City, and that was a three to four day long ride away. "What did you find?" she asked, shoving away her disappointment at it not being Kai.

"An army," the Pixie explained, his two female comrades hovering silently behind him. "Largest army I've ever seen. All men too. They must have gathered in the city."

"An Fiach?" Iseult questioned.

The Pixie bobbed in the air as he nodded. "We think so, though fortunately, they do not head this way. They have veered east on the Sand Road."

Finn turned wide eyes to Iseult. "Do you think they're going to Garenoch?"

He nodded. "That seems a reasonable assumption."

Her stomach twisted into knots. Ealasaid may have spurned her friendship, but she still did not wish her harm. "We have to warn them," she breathed. But how? They'd met in the Gray Place once before, but she had no idea how to summon Ealasaid there.

"Bedelia and Àed," Iseult suggested. "If we spare them two more horses, they will be able to travel more quickly than an army. They could arrive in time to warn them . . . if they even need it."

Finn blinked at him, confused.

"She is gathering mages, Finn. She likely does not need our help."

She knew he was right, but she could not simply allow Ealasaid to be attacked without warning. With a warning many days in advance, many lives might be spared . . . at least those lives Ealasaid cared about most.

She turned back to the Pixies. "Thank you for your information. Please keep an eye on the army if you can, but search for Kai as well."

The green haired Pixie nodded, then the trio sped back toward the rest of their group, waiting in the distant trees.

Iseult watched her cautiously. "Please, do not say what I think you're going to say."

"We cannot risk these men attacking at the same time as

Oighear," she argued. "Your brother is in Garenoch too."

Iseult shook his head. "I will not argue with you. The choice is yours."

She turned her gaze outward. She wanted to find Kai, to wait for Anna to return with him, and to wait for Eywen to return with more Aos Sí . . . but she was finally realizing she had waited long enough. This war would happen whether she liked it or not, and her friends would be caught in the middle. The time had come to act.

———

Night had come and gone, and Anna had seen no sign of Kai. The Pixies reported in from time to time, bringing word of an army of men on the Sand Road. With that news, any plans Anna had of using the road for ease of travel were dashed.

With that in mind, she and Eywen had awoken the next morning to continue riding through the forest, mostly in companionable silence, waiting for any more news that might once again sway their course.

Eywen rode silently beside her, yet to leave her side, though he was supposed to be branching off to search for more of his kind in the Northeast. Perhaps he feared the human army, but she had not brought herself to ask.

She tensed as her ears caught the sound of voices not far off. Apparently Eywen had heard it too, for he drew his horse to an abrupt halt. He lifted his hand to signal her to do the same, but she was way ahead of him. An Fiach should not be this far from the road, but there was no telling who else would feel the need to travel in such a remote region.

They both waited, listening, but the voices did not draw nearer. Whoever it was, wasn't moving.

As agile as a cat, Eywen dismounted, his boots landing silently on the forest floor. He then began leading his horse further away from the voices, gesturing for Anna to follow.

She quickly dismounted. Perhaps she made slightly more noise than Eywen had, but the voices never stopped their indecipherable conversation. She quickly led her horse away, hoping the animal would not snuffle and alert their possible enemies of their presence.

Once they were far enough away, they both tethered their horses to a tree.

"You wait here," Eywen whispered. "I will determine if they are friend or foe, and dispatch them if need be."

She put her hands on her hips near her daggers and glared up at him. "I'm just as capable of determining such things. More so, in fact, since they're likely human, and thus will be more apt to respond positively to *me*."

"Or they are Aos Sí," he countered with a smile, pushing a strand of black hair behind his pointed ear, "and will skewer you as soon as you approach."

"We'll see about that," she grumbled, then turned away from him, focusing on the direction the voices had come from. If they had innate magic, she would sense it.

She focused for several seconds, but felt nothing. She turned back to Eywen. "They are human. I win."

Before he could argue, she snuck off, leaving him to watch over the horses.

She stepped lightly over the rotting leaves and fallen branches littering the ground, weaving her way between trees while listening for the voices. Soon enough, she caught a hint of sound again, changing her path to approach. It sounded like there were only two people, a man and a woman, unless there were more present who did not speak. They weren't terribly aware of their surroundings if they hadn't yet sensed they weren't alone.

She continued forward, then caught sight of them. The man sat on the ground, his legs crossed, while the woman desperately attempted to build a fire. Both wore threadbare clothes in muted hues, their clothing far too sparse for the cold nights. Just judging by appearances, they seemed like simple country folk, not threats in the slightest . . . but what were they doing way out here?

She crouched behind a shrub to watch them, hoping to catch a hint of their conversation.

"We're never going to find another village this far out," the man muttered. "Even if we do, the folk that live in the marshes *can't* be friendly. Who would choose to live in such a wretched place?"

"Us," the woman said with a huff, "and anyone else who doesn't want to be caught up in the coming war. We couldn't very well stay in a burgh brimming with magic users, now could we? Not with a child on the way." She stood and rubbed her barely rounded belly lovingly, giving up on the fire.

Anna shook her head. These people may have made it a long way on their own, but as things looked, they likely wouldn't survive another week. She spotted their small packs of provisions leaning against a nearby tree. They were probably already almost out of food.

She sighed, then stepped into the clearing. The least she could do was scare them back to whatever burgh they came from. From the mention of mages, she guessed Garenoch.

The woman screamed when she saw her, then backed away, her eyes on Anna's twin daggers.

The man hopped up from his seat a moment later, dutifully stepping in front of his wife.

Now that she was closer, Anna noted that they were younger than she'd first thought, likely not past their twentieth years. Both had the sandy blonde hair and freckled skin most common to the southern regions.

"What do you want?" the man hissed. "We don't have anything for you to steal."

She smirked. "That's the last thing you should say to a thief."

The man reached for a small skinning knife hanging from his belt. *Utterly pathetic,* Anna thought. She could cut them both down before they could blink.

Suddenly the pair's eyes widened, but they were no longer looking at Anna, they were looking behind her. The man's hand was frozen at his belt, his fingers on the knife, but not drawing it.

Anna sighed and glanced over her shoulder to find Eywen standing a few paces behind her. "I told you I'd handle it," she grumbled.

"Why are you harassing these poor people?" he questioned good-naturedly, moving to her side.

She scowled. "I'm not! I was simply going to tell them to go back to their burgh if they want to stand any chance of survival."

She turned back around to face the couple, both practically trembling in their boots. She supposed Eywen had accomplished her goal. The man and woman were definitely scared pissless now.

"We're not going to hurt you," she sighed. "We heard your voices and wanted to make sure you posed no threat. It is quite clear the only threat you pose is to yourselves."

"W-what do you want?" the man stammered.

Anna sighed, then turned to Eywen. "Let us go. I believe they have been scared out of their stupidity."

"Wait," the woman said, stepping around her husband. She glanced warily at Eywen, then turned her focus back to Anna. "We cannot go back to Garenoch. Lady Ealasaid has taken control of the burgh, and is inviting mages in left and right. We didn't want to be there when the creatures came back."

Anna raised her brow. "Creatures?"

The woman flicked her eyes to Eywen again. "Like him," she muttered. "They attacked us once. They'll do it again. My brother died that day."

Anna frowned, taking offense to the woman's classification of the Aos Sí . . . though she supposed at one time, she'd thought the same.

"Then go to another burgh," she replied. "There are Faie in the marshes. You'll die long before you find an inhabitable village, if there are even any left."

"The larger burghs are no longer safe," the woman argued. "They've either been overrun by the Faie, or raided by An Fiach. We'd never make it all the way to Sormyr, or any of the burghs up North. We have *nowhere* else to go."

"I do not believe you will convince them," Eywen interjected, looking at Anna.

The woman gasped, though she'd already heard him

speak. The man looked ready to wet himself.

Anna sighed. She never should have stopped. Truly, she just wanted to ensure they would not be ambushed. Now she was just wasting her time.

She walked forward, ignoring the trembling couple, then began stacking the sticks and dried grass where the woman had been trying to build a fire.

Eywen walked up behind her, then handed her a flint and steel. "They can keep it," he muttered. "I have another."

Anna turned her eyes up to him, surprised he'd be so kind to people calling him a *creature*, then turned her attention back to building a fire.

"Why are you helping us?" the woman questioned, daring to venture forward a step.

Anna struck the flint, creating sparks that soon caught the dried grass on fire. She gently blew on the smoking grass, coaxing out a flame. "If you're too stupid to listen to me, I can at least give you a chance to survive the night. The fire will keep the lesser Faie away. Don't let it die. When you're ready to travel again, head northwest. Don't go any further south or your fates will be sealed."

As if finally making a decision, the woman hurried forward and crouched to warm her hands by the burgeoning flames. At the woman's wary look, Eywen stepped back, giving them space.

Anna watched as the man, remarkably gaining courage, slowly approached the fire, moving to the side of his wife farthest from Eywen. *Coward.*

"I hope your chivalrous husband at least knows how to hunt," Anna said to the woman.

She shook her head. "We've nothing to hunt with, but I

know which roots and plants are safe to eat. Insects too."

Anna widened her eyes in surprise. The husband definitely wouldn't survive, but the woman might. She stood, stepping back from the fire, then leaned forward to offer the woman the flint and steel.

She took it gratefully.

"We'll leave you then," Anna announced. "We've wasted too much time already."

"Wait," the woman said before Anna could turn away. "We still have some food to share. Please, I apologize for my rudeness."

To Anna's complete surprise, Eywen walked forward and sat, warming his hands by the fire. The husband skittered away, but the woman warily stayed put.

"What are you doing?" Anna hissed. "We don't have time to waste. We must find Kai."

Eywen peered up at her, mischief twinkling in his sapphire blue eyes. "We haven't seen a single sign of his passing. For all we know, traveling onward might take us in the wrong direction. We should wait for the Pixies to report in."

"Pixies?" the woman gasped, looking between Anna and Eywen with her jaw agape.

Anna glared at him, but found she could not argue. Plus, the warmth of a fire sounded nice on her cold, achy bones. She crossed her arms. "We should at least bring the horses near."

He pointed further behind her, toward a dense copse of trees where Anna could see the dappled rump of her mount. He had silently moved them while she'd been dealing with the frightened couple.

"Infuriating Faie," she muttered, then sat beside Eywen.

"I'm Ranna," the woman introduced, the fear in her brown eyes now replaced with glittering curiosity. She pointed to her coward husband, "This is Therin."

"Warm greetings," Eywen said politely.

Anna's scowl deepened.

"Please," Ranna began, "tell us where you came from. I never thought to see a human woman traveling with one of the . . . " she trailed off, glancing at Eywen.

"My name is Eywen," he introduced, "and I am Aos Sí. My cheerful companion is Anna."

Ranna glanced at Therin. "Fetch them some of our bread and cheese," she ordered. "We must thank them for their kindness."

Clearly still debating running away, Therin shuffled toward their supplies.

"No need," Anna interjected. "We have supplies of our own." She gave Eywen a cool look. "And we'll be *leaving* soon."

"Yes," he replied, "but first I'd like to hear any news you might bring. You mentioned a Lady Ealasaid?"

Anna's eyes widened, realizing perhaps Eywen wasn't just trying to infuriate her. If they could glean any new information, they could send some of the Pixies back to relay the news to Finn.

Ranna nodded. "Yes, Lady Ealasaid. She's a magic user, if you can believe it. Late one night she claimed Lord Gwrtheryn's estate with a hoard of black-clad fighters. Now they've taken over the entire burgh, inviting in any magic user willing to fight for their cause. They've even constructed extra defenses around the burgh."

"Then why did you leave?" Anna questioned. "You'd think a well-fortified burgh would be preferable to Faie infested woods."

Ranna shook her head. "No one is safe around so many magic users. Their powers cannot be trusted. Not to mention they draw the attention of An Fiach and the . . . " she glanced at Eywen again.

"Aos Sí," he finished for her.

She nodded, then turned her attention back to Anna. "So you see, we had to leave, if not out of fear of the Aos Sí, then because of the mages."

Anna felt her back stiffen at the woman's attitude. She herself would likely be deemed a *mage* if they knew she could travel to the in-between in her dreams, and sometimes even in waking.

"Do you know what Lady Ealasaid plans?" Eywen questioned.

The woman shrugged. "Your guess is as good as mine. All I know is she's gathering an army, and wherever armies are gathered, destruction follows."

Eywen gave Anna a meaningful look, and she subtly nodded. If the prophecy were to come true, Ealasaid would become Finn's enemy. One would need to die, and it seemed Ealasaid was actually taking her preparations seriously. They needed to warn Finn.

While Eywen continued speaking with Ranna, Anna cast her gaze overhead, hoping to spot the Pixies. With an army of men to the north, and an army of mages to the east, it seemed things were escalating.

All that was left to learn of was what sort of army Oighear had amassed . . . and when they would all collide.

Keiren cleaned her fingernails with a dagger while she waited at the disgusting little inn in Badenmar. If Óengus didn't show soon, she'd find him herself.

She leaned back in her wooden chair, balancing precariously while the fat little innkeep watched her with a wary expression on his sweaty face. She knew she stood out in the tiny burgh with her fine clothes and skin not marred with dirt or sheep manure, but she couldn't bring herself to care. A woman of her apparent age traveling alone would stand out no matter how she looked.

She heaved a sigh of relief as Óengus strode through the open door of the near-empty common room. His pale blue eyes, so pale they almost seemed white, spotted her immediately.

Observing him from his worn plain travel clothes to his slightly overgrown silver hair and beard, she frowned. He looked about ten years older than when she'd last seen him.

He approached her table and sat across from her, lifting a hand to halt the innkeep's advance.

Keiren watched as the fat little man glanced between them both warily before retreating back behind the bar.

She turned her attention to Óengus. "Whatever you have to say better be *good*. I left a fine room in a well-guarded estate for this."

He raised a silver brow at her. "Growing quite comfortable around the Queen of Wands, I see. I would have thought her to be your enemy, given her previous travel companions."

Keiren waved him off. "The girl is a naive little fool, easy to mold to my needs. A far better choice for an ally than the Snow Queen, I'd wager."

"Actually, that is why I'm here," he explained.

A small smile crossed her lips. Of *course* he wanted to come back to her.

"Do not smile so soon," he taunted. "I am here not to leave Oighear's service, but to offer you a deal on her behalf."

She tilted her head, cascading red hair over her black cloak. "And what could the Snow Queen possibly want from me? You would assume I'd be her enemy after I helped Ealasaid's mages defeat her Aos Sí."

Óengus shrugged. "Oighear is rather pragmatic for an ancient Faie. She views Finnur as the primary threat. She would like to work together to eliminate that threat, so that she and Ealasaid might face each other for the final battle."

Keiren smirked. "And why would I ever agree to that? Finnur is more likely to attack Oighear than Ealasaid. If I truly cared which of the prophesied queens survived, I would let Finnur eliminate Oighear all on her own, while Ealasaid bolstered her ranks unhindered."

Óengus smiled, though it was more just a baring of teeth. "Do you truly believe either could crush the tree girl on their own? Against each other, the battle would be fair, but against Finnur? Oighear fears her. She does not fear Ealasaid. The only chance either Oighear or Ealasaid stand against her is to work together."

Keiren resisted the urge to laugh in his face. Did he truly believe she cared? Her *only* concern was breaking down the barrier to the in-between. Unless Oighear could offer her that, there was nothing she wanted from the Snow Queen.

Still, the situation was rather curious. "We both know Ealasaid will never willingly work with someone who killed most everyone she cared about. Barring that, what does Oighear wish me to do?"

"Simply lead Ealasaid in the right direction," he explained. "When the time comes, Oighear will be there."

She stroked her chin in thought. She had no intention of granting Oighear's wishes, but it might prove useful to let her think she would, at least for a time.

She straightened in her chair. "I'll need time to think about this, of course."

Óengus nodded, then reached into the pocket of his cloak, withdrawing a large crystal. He offered it to her. "When your decision is made, hold this against your bare skin. You'll be able to sense when it is ready for you to speak."

She took the crystal gingerly, quickly dropping it into the satchel resting on the floor beside her chair. She'd be careful not to speak around the thing, touching or no.

His crystal delivered, Óengus stood.

She gazed up at him. "One last question, if you do not mind."

His eyes cool, he nodded for her to continue.

She smiled. "What do you stand to gain in serving Oighear? Do you truly believe she can return your shadow?"

His expression remained utterly emotionless as he replied, "I no longer know what to believe, but I stand a better chance serving a queen wishing to save her race, than a lonely sorceress who'd not only betray the woman she once loved, but her own father."

She smirked, though inside her heart felt as if it had been suddenly encased in ice. "Who are you to speak of loyalty?"

He shrugged. "No one at all, but that does not mean I cannot value it in others."

With that, he turned and walked away, striding back out the open door of the inn.

She scowled at that open doorway long after he was gone. She and Óengus were more alike than she'd ever enjoy admitting, but it wouldn't stop her from stringing his body up for the crows once she was done with him.

Rising from her seat, she gathered her things in preparation to depart. Yes, she'd have her revenge on Óengus, but not before she proved to him that she could have granted his wish, if only he'd been *loyal* to her.

Naoki crept along through the mists of the in-between. She'd been spending much of her time there, searching for an unknown force that beckoned her. The one she thought of as her mother was fading. Dark things lurked in the spaces between realms, things Naoki could never catch. If she did, she would quickly end them.

She stretched out her white wings, wishing she could fly across this strange place. Surely she'd find what she was looking for more quickly that way. Yet, her wings no longer seemed able to hold her. They hadn't held her since she was a baby, sailing haphazardly across the sea toward a light she could not resist. The light that had beckoned her was her mother, whose magic tasted of *home*.

CHAPTER FIVE

*B*edelia deftly secured her saddlebags onto her horse's back. She felt bad taking one of the few mounts they had, but it was the only way to reach Garenoch in a timely manner. Àed prepared his horse at her side. For added height, he stood on a large chunk of stone, previously one of the many Druidic statues adorning the fortress courtyard.

Bedelia checked that her bedroll was properly shielded from the rain they'd surely encounter, then stuffed her icy fingers into her breeches pockets, letting her soil brown cloak fall forward over her shoulders. Turning to stare back at the stone fortress, she shifted her weight to her good leg. She still hadn't told Finn that the poison from the Faie wolf bite had returned, just as she hadn't told her about her encounter with Keiren.

She wasn't really sure why she hadn't. The information that Keiren hoped to destroy the barrier to the in-between might prove valuable to Finn, especially since Branwen, the wraith, hoped to achieve the same end. Yet, Keiren had shared that secret with her, and her alone. Keiren might not be capable of loyalty, but she herself was, however displaced.

Sensing movement behind her, she looked over her shoulder. Finn emerged into the courtyard with Iseult trailing her. She seemed ethereal in the morning mist, with her long hair billowing behind her. Her thin form appeared weak, as if she might break in half at any moment, even though she was one of the most powerful beings in the land. She'd proven as much by not only enlisting the Faie as her servants, but by forcing the Cavari to fall to their knees before her.

Reaching her, Finn pulled her into an embrace. Bedelia returned the hug, guilt snaking through her. Part of her hoped the Faie bite would take her life soon, just so she wouldn't have to feel the guilt of deceit any longer . . . and she wouldn't have to confront Keiren either.

Finn released her, then peered into her eyes. "Promise me you'll be careful, and tell Ealasaid the same. I know she's faced An Fiach before, but this army of men is seemingly endless, or so say the Pixies. Their threat should not be taken lightly."

Bedelia nodded. "We'll do our best to reach Garenoch before them."

With a final smile, Finn turned next to Àed, wrapping him in a hug. "If I do not see you again," she muttered, "I will assume Keiren has you locked in a dungeon some-where, and I'll drop everything to find you."

Àed chuckled as he pulled away from her embrace.

"Don't be doin' that, lass. Me old life isnae worth much anymore."

"It's worth something to me," she stated firmly. "Your daughter has put us all through a great deal of trouble, and I will not stand idly by if her antics continue."

"Aye, lass," Àed said, patting her arm. "I know ye will not."

As Àed turned away to mount his horse, Bedelia lifted her gaze to Iseult.

He nodded in acknowledgement, not needing to speak to convey the silent promise between them. As warriors dedicated to a cause, they would both do what needed doing, and Iseult would protect Finn while she was away.

With a heavy heart, Bedelia mounted her horse, wishing it was Rada. She wondered if her long-time companion still lived somewhere within the Snow Queen's realm, or if she'd fallen in battle with one of the Aos Sí atop her back.

She waved to Finn and Iseult as she and Àed turned their mounts toward the open gates. It would take several days to reach Garenoch, even with pushing the horses to swiftly reach the burgh.

She wasn't sure if she hoped Keiren would still be there, or not. In her heart she knew she had unfinished business with the sorceress, but matters of the heart had always frightened her far more than any battle or threat of death ever could.

Iseult watched as Bedelia and Àed departed, then turned away as two of the Trow sealed the gates behind them. Finn left his side to approach the stables, weaving her way around fallen chunks of statue.

He followed, reaching her side as she stopped in front of Loinnir's stall and stroked her palm up and down the unicorn's white forehead, ruffling the portion of silky white mane resting between her ears. Finn wore the shroud tied around her waist instead of stored away in her private chambers.

"I'll take Loinnir when I meet with the Cavari," she explained distantly. "She will nullify their magic if necessary."

He stared at her, but she did not turn to meet his gaze. "You intend to address them soon?" With the shroud out of hiding, he should have known. She'd want the extra power.

She nodded. "This evening. My mother is right, I cannot put it off forever. Now that our friends have all left us save the few remaining Aos Sí, there is nothing else for me to do here, and I cannot stand idly by while Ealasaid is attacked."

He hesitantly placed a hand on her shoulder, unsure if his touch was welcome.

Finally, she looked up at him.

"You do not have to do anything you do not want to do," he said softly. "While I encourage you to grow your army, it would be far better for you to face Oighear in a defendable area. You can make her come to you."

Finn shook her head. "You would let Ealasaid face An Fiach on her own? What about your brother? Oighear could very well use the opportunity to launch her own attack. Her realm is not far from Garenoch."

He took a steadying breath. He did not like the idea of Garenoch's vulnerability, but he liked even less Finn marching into battle before she was prepared. As things stood, her help might not even be welcomed, though he did not have the heart to say so out loud.

"I will come with you to meet with the Cavari," he said instead.

She frowned. "I do not believe that is a wise plan. They will not speak freely in front of you."

"You are their queen," he countered. "They will speak if you tell them to."

A small smile spread across her lips. "I keep telling myself that, but somehow it does not feel like the truth. I suppose I just know them too well, and all that they are capable of. Even weakened, their magic is great."

"Then allow me to accompany you," he pressed, "regardless of how freely they will speak."

She turned her attention back to Loinnir. "I suppose we can go together," she breathed finally. "I truly don't like the idea of separating now, even for a little while." She turned her dark hazel eyes up to him, and he felt for a moment as if he could become utterly lost in their depths. "I feel as if you might disappear too, just like everyone else."

"I fear the same," he replied softly, unable to help his words. "Every time I close my eyes, I worry you will no longer be there when I open them."

Her mouth formed a small *oh* of surprise.

He was such a fool. He could not cross that line, not again. She needed a protector, not a lover. "I'll meet with the remaining Aos Sí," he said quickly. "I will tell them what we plan so that they might be prepared in the event we require their aid."

With that, he turned and stalked away, ignoring the

thundering of his heart in his ears, and the weight of Finn's eyes on his back.

Later that evening, Finn stroked her fingers through Loinnir's mane, feeling the warmth emanating from the unicorn's skin. She rode her bareback, since she didn't intend to go far, at least not yet.

"Are you sure about this?" Iseult asked again, though they'd gone over it countless times since that morning.

It was too late regardless. They'd already passed through the fortress gates, and soon would reach the small camp where fires never burned, and voices never sounded. Her people truly were little more than phantoms, though they appeared as flesh and blood.

A few of the cloaked forms came into view. Though she knew there were more of them elsewhere, whenever she dared look toward their camp there were always just three or four still forms staring in her direction. *Waiting.* She did not see her mother amongst them, though it was difficult to tell with their hoods.

As she reached them, with Iseult's horse keeping pace at her side, one stepped forward from the group. Broad shoulders beneath the billowing fabric of his black cloak hinted at his gender.

She debated climbing down off Loinnir's back, but thought better of it. The unicorn seemed immune to the Cavari's magic. She could stop any conflict before it started.

"The time has come," Finn announced, looking first to

the figure in front of her, then flicking her gaze to the three who stood behind. "I need an army."

The cloaked figure nearest her bowed his head. "If we are to go to war, we need a proper queen. Accept our oath. Return our full power."

Her stomach clenched. This was *wrong*, but how else was she to defeat Oighear *and* An Fiach? The Cavari were the most powerful tool at her disposal.

Iseult was silent beside her. They'd had their arguments over this, but in the end, she was queen. It was her decision.

"I will accept your oath," she breathed despite her better judgement. "I will be your queen in more than name. I will share my power with you, but I will not restore you fully."

The cloaked figure in front drew back his hood, revealing shoulder-length golden hair and piercing green eyes. He was just as she'd remembered, except for worm-white skin. Once upon a time, his skin had been perfectly tanned. Finn had been deemed lucky to receive him as her consort, the most powerful male member of her tribe.

"Sugn," she hissed. "I did not expect you."

His smile made her skin crawl. "Why ever not? Without you, I was the most powerful amongst our tribe. *Someone* had to lead the search for you."

She swallowed the lump in her throat, fighting against the contents of her stomach as they threatened to make an appearance. Sugn had been the father of her daughter, Niamh, but he was father in title only. He did not deserve the pride that came along with the word. He hadn't cared when his child had been cast aside for being weak, nor had he cared when she died.

"Will you refuse our oath?" Sugn questioned, one golden brow raised.

"No," she growled, sudden rage making her skin hot. "I like the idea of a world where worms like you must kiss my feet."

One of the still-hooded forms snorted at her comment.

Her own words shocked her, but she refused to take them back.

Sugn simply inclined his head, a sly smile on his wide lips. "I'll kiss you wherever you like, my queen."

Her face burned, eliciting a wave of power from within her. It seared through her chest then down to her fingertips. The earth beneath Sugn's feet rumbled, then a massive root shot upward. It swung down toward him like the arm of a giant. He hopped aside, a heartbeat before it would have clobbered him. The other cloaked forms calmly stepped back out of reach of the root.

"You will not speak to your queen in such a vulgar manner," she said haughtily as the massive root hovered above Sugn, dripping clumps of soil.

He swept an arm across his chest and bowed, though his face when he raised it held no fear.

"Finn," Iseult muttered, drawing her attention. His horse stamped its hooves, unnerved by the giant twitching root.

She took a deep breath, then nodded to him, suddenly more embarrassed than before. She'd never told him Sugn's name, but he'd likely drawn accurate conclusions about who he was, especially since violence usually was not her first reaction.

She relaxed her shoulders, and the root withdrew into the earth just as quickly as it had arisen, leaving violently turned soil in its wake. While Sugn did not seem cowed, the remaining three Cavari maintained a respectful distance.

Loinnir snorted, as if trying to remind her of her task.

Finn glared down at Sugn. "As the current leader of the Cavari, you will swear your oath to me at midnight. I will return at the appointed time."

He raised that infuriating golden brow at her again. "So we are not allowed within your fortress?"

"Do not question your queen," Iseult growled.

All humor left Sugn's expression as his green gaze turned to Iseult for the first time. "Do not speak to me *human*, and don't you dare think I do not know who you are, and what your people did to my daughter."

His daughter? Finn thought, rage and revulsion washing through her once more. She stifled a shiver, forcing herself to remain calm. She would not give him the satisfaction of eliciting another reaction from her.

She glared down at him, letting her hatred shine through her eyes. "She was never yours."

Sugn's smirk faltered, ever so slightly.

Having said all she needed to say, Finn tugged at Loinnir's reins, turning her away.

She heard Iseult's horse moving to follow behind her, but she could not look back at him. She could not let Sugn see her tears.

Kai wasn't sure just what had brought him to Garenoch. He only knew he'd traveled there unbelievably fast. As long as the sun was down, his legs never seemed to tire. Now he stared up at the newly constructed high walls, astonished at how the burgh seemed to have grown.

Though the moon shone bright above, a few travelers still came in and out of the burgh, likely returning to the nearby farmsteads after selling their goods at the market within, or conversely, retreating from the farms for the safety of the burgh.

He shook his head, marveling at the high stone wall. There was no way normal men could have constructed such a wall so quickly. Magic had been used. Given that, he wondered just what else the mages might be capable of.

Casting away his thoughts, he approached the gates, wondering if they'd let him in, or if he should just scale the wall unseen. He felt himself quite capable of the latter, though he would have felt better about his abilities if he weren't starving.

He'd snared two rabbits to add to his meager supply of hard bread, but the meals he'd made only seemed to make him hungrier. He needed a proper stew, and perhaps some honey bannocks and wine. Surely that would make him feel better.

Of course, he had no coin, but he'd been skilled at thievery even before the apparent effects of his bite had set in. Now, with all the changes he'd incurred, it would be nearly effortless.

He started toward the high gates, then stopped as they opened to let someone out. Kai moved back, observing from the darkness. He recognized the tall man exiting the burgh by himself. *Maarav.*

Kai watched as Maarav walked a few paces down the path, then veered left, hurrying past the few small, abandoned buildings outside the gate and into the woods beyond.

Without considering his actions, Kai followed. In a matter of seconds he reached the trees nearest to where Maarav had disappeared. He stopped to listen for a moment, then continued on into the darkness. He saw no sign of Maarav, but knew he could not have gotten far.

He continued weaving his way through the dark trees, stopping to listen every few steps. His eyes were far more keen in the darkness now than they used to be, but all he saw was dead grass and the pale trunks of trees, illuminated softly by moonlight.

He slowed, wondering what Maarav was doing out here in the first place.

"It's rude to spy," a voice said from behind him.

Kai whipped around. Maarav was standing a few paces behind him. He shouldn't have been able to sneak up on him, not with his improved speed and senses. How had he moved so quietly?

Kai turned to fully face him. "Can you blame me for being curious?"

Maarav stepped forward, closing the distance between them. His black hair hung forward to partially obscure his features in shadow. "If anyone gets to be curious right now, it is I. What are you doing here? Are Finn and Iseult with you?"

Kai shook his head, wondering how much he should tell him. "No," he said simply. "I came on my own. I was hoping to find a hot meal, then I'll be on my way."

Maarav looked him up and down. "There's something different about you."

Kai's heart sputtered. He just stared at Maarav, unsure of what to say. Could he actually sense the changes in him?

After a moment of thought, Maarav smiled. "Come now, I'll buy you a drink at the inn and you can tell me all that has transpired since we parted ways."

Kai watched him cautiously, then nodded. He'd said nothing of what he'd been doing sneaking around in the woods, but he was apparently willing to abandon his task now. Perhaps he could learn something useful from Maarav, and he wouldn't snub a free mug of wine, not after all he'd been through.

Still wary, he nodded, then followed as Maarav turned and led the way back into the burgh.

He hoped he would not regret his choice. Many humans would kill one of the Faie on sight. At one time, he might have been one of them. That position had altered slightly, considering he was quite sure he'd soon be more Faie than human himself.

Maarav gestured to the men manning the gates to readmit him. He'd unfortunately not made his meeting with his scout, but the chance encounter with Kai had proven too interesting to pass up. He'd meet with Rae, one of the assassins, later. He'd been gone for nearly a week gathering information to the west, information Maarav was desperate to learn, but it would have to wait.

He rolled his shoulders, loosening a twinge of guilt as he and Kai walked through the open gate. Truly, he'd not requested Rae meet him outside the burgh in an attempt to hide things from Ealasaid. He'd made the request that all meetings take place outside before Keiren had left. If news came of Finn and Iseult, he wanted to hear it long before the sorceress caught wind.

Now, with Kai's appearance, such news had dropped right into his lap at the perfect time. He would at least know what Finn planned, if not more of what was occurring out west. Keiren had said she'd be gone a week. It should be safe to talk.

They walked in silence down the rutted dirt road toward the inn. Though Maarav was glad for the opportunity to interrogate Kai, something felt off. He'd always had excellent senses, and they were currently sounding a warning in his mind. A warning about *Kai*. Not to mention how quickly and silently he had moved. Fortunately, Maarav had spent many years perfecting the art of being the watcher, and never the watched.

They reached the inn, bustling with the sound of those having late night wine and whiskey. A warm glow emanated from the open doors, supplied by dozens of candles and a massive fire blazing in the hearth.

Together, they stepped inside.

Maarav gestured to the innkeep, another person within the burgh who knew him on sight, and waved to him when they passed in the streets.

He grimaced at his thoughts, then took a seat at a small open table near the door.

Kai sat silently across from him, glancing up as one of the barmaids approached.

"Whiskey?" Maarav questioned.

Kai nodded, and the barmaid walked off to fetch their drinks.

Once they both had drinks in their hands, the two men proceeded to stare at each other. While Maarav had known Kai for quite some time now, as they had traveled together after returning to Migris, they'd had few conversations. All he really knew about him was that he'd been a thief before he met Finn, and now he was quite obviously in love with her. It would make him guard her secrets closely, but at least he *knew* her secrets. He might let something slip.

He raised a black eyebrow at Kai. "Are you truly going to make me ask what you were doing skulking about outside the burgh?"

Kai took a sip of his whiskey, seeming to resist the urge to down it one gulp. "I could ask you the same question."

Maarav steeled his gaze. He knew he'd likely need to give information to get information, but not just yet.

He sipped his drink, biding his time before asking, "Did Finn send you here? I find it odd that you would travel so far from both her and Anna."

His expression somber, Kai shook his head. "Much has happened since we first left Garenoch—" he hesitated, staring down at his whiskey. "It's difficult to explain, but Finn has a tendency to sacrifice herself for others, and I could not let her do so for me any longer. Not with so much at stake."

That sounded about right, Maarav thought. Finn and Ealasaid were astoundingly alike. It made the conflict in their friendship all the more tragic. There were few selfless people left in the world, at least, as far as he could see.

"And what of Anna?" he questioned.

Kai shrugged. "Anna has her own troubles to worry about."

Maarav watched him for several more seconds, weighing the odds that Kai might actually be a spy sent by Finn.

He found it highly unlikely.

"Well," he began, pausing to take another sip of his whiskey, "you may as well stay within the estate until you decide what to do. I'm sure Ealasaid would like to see you."

Kai raised his eyebrows in surprise. "Truly? She was the one that told Finn never to return here."

"Ah, but you are not Finn," Maarav countered. *But he was close enough*, he added in his mind. Someone close enough to Finn to perhaps bridge the gap between her and Ealasaid. It was the only way he could think of to get rid of Keiren without killing the sorceress in her sleep . . . not that he'd mind killing her in her sleep, but Ealasaid would never forgive him.

Kai's shoulders slumped, then he shook his head. "No, I cannot stay. I do not want to bring trouble to anyone—"

"Nonsense," Maarav interrupted, not about to let him slink off into the night. "You'll return with me to the estate and we'll find you a room. My girl is a bit low as of late, she'll be happy to see a friendly face."

Kai's jaw dropped as he fumbled the small cup in his hands. Setting the cup down and wiping the sloshed liquid on his breeches, he stared at Maarav. "*Your* girl? Truly?"

Maarav nodded, unable to help the proud smile on his face.

Kai shook his head and laughed. "My perceptions of

reality have been challenged on a daily basis these past months, but never as much as they have this evening."

Maarav chuckled, then downed the rest of his drink. While he still felt there was something different about Kai, he still seemed to be the same person, not possessed by some dark Faie force.

"Come," he instructed as he stood. "We'll find you a room, and," he sniffed the air, "a *bath*."

Kai smiled graciously, finally agreeing with a nod.

Maarav led the way out of the inn, wondering how he'd explain to Ealasaid what he'd been doing when he'd discovered Kai. He supposed he'd think of an excuse when the time came, then he'd think of another the next night when he'd finally be able to meet with Rae.

Regardless, he was glad Kai had come. Perhaps they could commiserate on their dealings with idealistic, frighteningly powerful women. They both knew them better than most.

Branwen watched from the protection of the dark, dense trees as Finn once again approached the Cavari. It was nearly midnight, yet the cloaked forms had stood there all evening, knowing she would come. Branwen had known it too. She'd watched when Finn and Iseult had visited them earlier that day. In fact, she'd been watching *everyone* since she'd arrived at the fortress, yet no one ever seemed to notice. She could walk right past someone, and they wouldn't even see her unless she spoke. Though her body felt real, it was as if she'd become little more than a ghost. It was fitting, perhaps, considering how much, or how *little*, everyone seemed to care about her.

Finn had told her they would further discuss destroying the barrier to the in-between, but the discussion was pushed off over and over as each new emergency arose. First, they had to gather supplies after the battle Branwen had missed. Then Kai was sick. Then Kai ran away. Now Anna, Eywen, Àed, and Bedelia all had gone. They all had *plans*. Plans that had little to do with her.

She chewed on her lip as the waiting cloaked forms bowed before Finn. Iseult waited some distance behind with Finn's unicorn. It was clear that neither man nor unicorn were allowed to take part in whatever ceremony was about to occur.

Branwen nearly screamed as something nudged her in the back. She turned to view Finn's white dragon, nearly the size of a small pony, though more sinewy and lithe.

The creature blinked its spherical lilac eyes at her, intelligence shining through the large orbs, reflecting moonlight.

Branwen lifted a finger to her lips, urging the creature to remain silent, but it reached its beak forward and nudged her again.

Beginning to panic that she'd be discovered, she glanced toward the Cavari. They stood huddled in a small circle around Finn, still not noticing her or Naoki.

Still nervous, she turned back to the dragon, then nearly screamed again as the beast darted its head down and clamped its beak around her wrist.

Her eyes slammed shut against the pain. She clenched her jaw to keep from crying out. Suddenly, her wrist was released. She opened her tear-filled eyes, and this time she did scream.

She screamed not in fear, but in rage and frustration. She was surrounded by mists she knew all too well. She was back in the in-between. The dragon, now standing before her in the misty marshland, had somehow taken her back to the prison that she'd only recently escaped.

"Take me back!" she desperately cried. She could not be stuck here, not again. The Travelers had given her back her body, tethering her to the land. She should not have been able to come here again. Niklas had said she *couldn't* come here.

The dragon blinked at her, as if expecting her to do something.

She shook her head in frustration, swatting at the tears that streamed down her face. "You don't understand," she muttered. "I was given life by the magic of this place, I'm not supposed to be able to come here. You may have very well killed me."

She sat down on the loamy earth with a huff, looking down at the angry red lines on her arm, created by Naoki's beak. The area was already beginning to bruise. She supposed she should not fear the harm done, as she was probably as good as dead.

Naoki took a step forward, then extended her long neck to nudge Branwen's shoulder with her beak.

Cradling her wrist, Branwen glared up at her. "Well, you can at least show me why you brought me here. Maybe you'll actually be able to take me back too."

The dragon bobbed her head, as if actually comprehending Branwen's words.

Her eyes wide, Branwen climbed back to her feet, curiosity outweighing fear.

With an excited stomp of her talons, the dragon turned around and darted off.

Branwen stared at her quickly retreating white rump for a moment, then took off at a run, awkwardly cradling her injured wrist.

While she was furious with the dragon, it was at least nice that *someone* was paying attention to her, even if it likely meant her death.

Ealasaid walked through the mists of the Gray Place, though her physical body was safe in her bed. She was beginning to grow more comfortable being there. She'd explored many of the seemingly endless stone halls, and had searched the dark marshlands. She wasn't even sure what she was looking for. Answers perhaps.

She was finally beginning to believe she was the third queen from the prophecy, especially after the Travelers had presented her with the ancient wand, but she still didn't understand *why*. Finn and Oighear were both centuries old. They had a long history that made them enemies, but why her? Her life had little to do with either of them, or with the politics of the Faie.

Her boots squished into sticky mud and she cringed, then turned as she sensed a presence at her back.

She gasped at the sight of a woman but a few paces away. Finn? No, this woman's hair was darker, and her eyes blue.

She might not be Finn, but she was most definitely one of the Cavari. Ealasaid could sense it.

"What do you want?" she demanded. She clenched her hands into fists, wondering if she could summon her lightning when she wasn't truly in this realm.

The woman tilted her head, trailing long brown hair over her black-cloaked shoulder. "Isn't it odd that the gods would face a mortal girl with not one, but two inhuman enemies?"

Ealasaid sealed her lips into a firm line, wondering if she'd absentmindedly muttered some of her thoughts out loud for this woman to hear.

"I would think the gods have little to do with it," she replied tersely.

The woman smirked. "I suppose not. Something stronger than the gods has led you down this path."

"What do you want?" Ealasaid asked again.

"I want to warn you to run far away," the woman stated. "You do not understand what you are up against. You may be Oighear's equal in power, but you will never defeat my daughter. She is more powerful than even she knows."

Ah, so this was the mother Ealasaid had heard mention of. "I don't want to defeat anyone who means me no harm," she snapped, "but I will protect those who need protecting."

"There is another," the woman said, stepping forward.

Ealasaid resisted the urge to step back. She'd faced the Snow Queen and survived. She would not be afraid *now*.

"The prophecy has begun," Ealasaid stated calmly. "Finn returned and made it so. From what I'm told, there is no other way."

"What do you think this place is?" Finn's mother questioned, lifting her arms to encompass the misty land around them.

Ealasaid was so caught off guard by her question that she blurted, "The in-between, of course, what does that have to do with anything?"

The woman stared at her, her blue eyes unwavering. "Everything, my dear, absolutely everything. A barrier separates this land, a land composed of pure magic, from ours. What do you think would happen if that barrier came crashing down? Why, it could change the fates themselves, prophecies included."

Ealasaid blinked at her. While what she said was intriguing, it wasn't like she could destroy such a barrier herself, so why tell her this at all?

"Think about it," the woman said simply. "Otherwise, your fate is all but sealed." She turned away.

Before Ealasaid could think of anything to say, Finn's mother disappeared into the mist, leaving her alone in a magical world, far different from her own.

CHAPTER SIX

*K*ai awoke in a strange bed with a gasp, then quickly shielded his eyes from the sun streaming in through the nearby window. Cursed nightmares. He sighed. Or perhaps they were portents of his future. He saw no other reason to be dreaming about the Dearg Due, the strange women who'd inflicted his current condition upon him.

With a groan, he crawled out of bed and walked toward the light, wincing at its brightness. He hadn't thought things through when he agreed to stay within the bustling estate. He no longer enjoyed being up during the day like everyone else.

Forcing his eyes open to mere slits, he peered outside, grateful he was on the second story so no one would see him cringing.

Outside was an expansive, beautiful garden, its hues darkening with winter's cold. Could it truly already be winter, not just the unseasonable cold they'd been experiencing for months? So much had happened he'd barely noticed the seasons changing.

He peered out at the garden, and the occasional figures hurrying down the main path on one errand or another. He couldn't help but think Finn would have liked it there.

A knock sounded on his door, turning him from the window. His shoulders relaxed once the light was at his back and no longer stinging his eyes.

Reluctantly, he strode across the room toward the door, wishing he'd thought to change his dirty traveling clothes before he'd collapsed onto the soft bed to rest.

He paused before opening the door, wondering if an enemy might be waiting outside.

The knock sounded again.

He opened the door, then stepped back, hiding his surprise. Ealasaid stood framed in the doorway, her normally fluffy blonde hair held back from her face in a tight braid. She wore an emerald velvet dress, plain and simple except for the expensive fabric. Behind her stood Maarav.

"I told you it was him," Maarav muttered.

Ealasaid looked Kai up and down, her gray eyes showing no mercy. "Why have you come here?" she demanded. "Did Finn send you?"

He blinked at her, surprised by her tone. "N-no," he stammered. "Truly, I had only planned on visiting the burgh for a quick meal before moving along. Maarav insisted I come to this estate." He flicked his gaze past Ealasaid to Maarav, hoping he'd validate his story.

Maarav rolled his eyes. "I did try to tell her that."

Footsteps sounded from the exterior hall, then a young,

dark haired man appeared in the doorway behind them. "Lady Ealasaid," he huffed. "You asked to be alerted the moment Lady Keiren returned. She is at the gates."

"Already?" Maarav groaned.

Kai stiffened, wondering if now would be a good time to hop out the window and flee, though he'd be hindered by the stinging sunlight.

Ealasaid nodded to the dark-haired mage. "Please tell the guards at the gate to instruct her to meet with me right away." As the man scampered off, she turned back to Kai. "You will come with us. Keiren has *the sight*. She will be able to divine your true intentions."

Kai gulped. If this sorceress truly could see more than what met the eye, he was cooked. He was in a human burgh filled with human mages, none of whom felt any love for the Faie.

He said a silent prayer to the gods as he followed Ealasaid and Maarav into the hall, hoping they would not turn on him. Although, despite his fear, he was quite intrigued by the idea of finally meeting the sorceress who'd wanted to steal Finn's immortality.

Ealasaid's thoughts whirled as she walked at Maarav's side down the hall, with Kai following behind them. Keiren had said a week, but it had been only a matter of days. The anxiety she now felt made her realize just how uneasy Keiren made her. Even if she seemed solidly on her side, she could not forget that Keiren had brought An Fiach to Garenoch when she'd first arrived. For all Ealasaid knew,

Keiren's *errand* might have been a meeting with the mage-hating humans.

They reached the end of the hall and walked out onto a wide staircase, descending to the ground floor lined with large stepping stones leading to the various outbuildings.

Ealasaid glanced at the other paths longingly, then took the one heading toward the main estate.

Maarav leaned near her shoulder. "Does this mean you will not be taking Slàine's oath this evening?" he whispered. She glanced back at Kai, who was shielding his eyes from the sun. Leave it to Maarav to get the man bladdered enough to be sick the next morning on his first night in the burgh.

"No," she whispered, turning her attention back to Maarav as they walked. "I'll still take it . . . we'll just perhaps push it a bit later, after Keiren has gone to sleep."

He sighed. "You know she'll know as soon as she sees you, there's no point in hiding it from her, but you are queen here. She cannot tell you what to do."

She snorted as they reached the massive double doors to the estate. "Try telling that to *her*."

Two guards opened the doors, and to Ealasaid's surprise, Kai scurried in ahead of them.

With Maarav next to her, Ealasaid entered, looking Kai up and down, noting his pallid visage and the way he hunched like he'd just been whipped. Something odd was going on with him, but she suspected her original guess was off. Perhaps he wasn't a spy, but a man in dire need of aid.

"Let's go," she said, her tone softer than before. "We'll meet with Keiren, then we'll find you a meal and a bath."

Kai blinked at her, surprised.

Suddenly embarrassed for acting so paranoid in the first place, she walked past him and toward the wide stone stairs.

Behind her, she heard Maarav mutter to Kai, "I told you it would work out."

She could not make out Kai's reply as both men started up the stairs behind her, their boots drowning out their words. Perhaps Kai and Keiren showing up so close together was a sign that she should not wed Maarav that night after she took Slàine's oath. Maybe she was being selfish to worry about such a thing when so many were depending on her for leadership.

Reaching the top of the stairs, she turned right toward what had once been used as a sort of throne room for Lord Gwrtheryn and Lady Síoda. It had since been repurposed as a place for her to greet new mages, and to hear reports from her scouts.

As they neared the room, Ealasaid eyed Slàine's two assassin guards who had replaced the usual estate sentinels. One man opened the heavy door for her to walk inside, followed by Kai and Maarav.

She scanned the large room with a sigh, relieved for some reason that she'd made it there before Keiren.

The maps they'd been perusing what felt like weeks ago were still splayed across the massive wooden table, illuminated only by the sunlight streaming in through the row of windows in the north-facing wall.

Without her needing to ask, Maarav instructed one of the guards to light the sconces on the wall opposite the windows, but not the many candles, unneeded in daylight hours.

She slumped into an empty seat, her emerald dress

billowing about the chair, then gestured for Kai to do the same. Curious about his strange state, she observed him watching the guard light the sconces with a small torch procured from the hall. Kai seemed to flinch as each new light flared to life.

"Are you ill?" she questioned. "At first I thought you were just suffering from too much whiskey, but you seem to be in pain. Perhaps you need to see a healer."

"I *told* you we only had one drink," Maarav sighed, taking a seat on the opposite side of the table.

Ealasaid pursed her lips, observing Kai.

"I'm not ill," he muttered, "and I must say, you are far different from the girl I remember."

Her expression softened. Had she changed that much? She did not have long to think about it as Keiren strode into the room, still wearing her heavy black traveling cloak.

At first she looked annoyed, then she spotted Kai, and tilted her head curiously, pushing a strand of fiery red hair behind her ear.

She took a step toward him.

"This is Kai," Ealasaid introduced, but Keiren raised a hand to cut her off.

"Why is there a Faie man sitting in our meeting room?" Keiren questioned, never removing her eyes from Kai.

Ealasaid frowned, turning to Maarav, who was staring at Keiren. "He's not Faie," Maarav explained.

Keiren shook her head, tossing her red hair about. "He might not have started out that way, but he is now."

Kai slowly slunk from his seat, taking care to remain as far away from Keiren as he could.

"I'm not Faie," he explained, backing away. "I was just . . .

bitten by one."

Ealasaid stood, staring at Kai as if just seeing him for the first time. His pallid skin, his red-rimmed eyes, the way he flinched from the sun . . . it was all because he'd been bitten by one of the Faie?

She glanced at Keiren, apprehensive to let Kai out of her sights. Maarav rose and stood slightly in front of her protectively.

Kai backed away, his hands raised as if to ward off a blow. "I've no evil plan," he blurted. "I didn't even want to come here, you must believe me."

"He's not lying," Keiren observed, her voice calm.

Ealasaid swallowed the lump in her throat. She believed Keiren if she thought Kai not a threat, but that didn't change the fact that he'd been . . . *infected* by one of the Faie.

"I'll gladly leave," he said when none of them spoke.

"No," Keiren said, her voice suddenly sly. She turned her bright blue eyes to Ealasaid. "I advise that we keep him. He is Faie, but not Faie. He could prove useful."

"He's not a puppy," Maarav interjected. "You can't just *keep* him."

Keiren rolled her eyes at him. "You might change your tune when you hear what I have to say."

"Which is?" Ealasaid interrupted.

"Return the Faie to his room," Keiren ordered, gesturing to Kai, "I must deliver this news in private. It concerns the Snow Queen."

Ealasaid observed Kai as he continued to back himself into a corner, watching the exchange like a trapped animal.

She took a deep breath, wishing the exchange could have gone more pleasantly. "Would you mind returning to your room for a time?" she asked Kai politely, ashamed for treating him so poorly when she'd once considered him a friend. "If there is a way to help you, I promise I will do my best."

He nodded, though he seemed suspicious.

"Have at least two mages escort him," Keiren instructed.

Ealasaid sighed derisively at Keiren, keeping her attention on Kai. "Do you mind?" she asked, not hating the idea. He'd been a cunning man when human, and she really didn't want him to try escaping.

"Do I have a choice?" he replied.

She frowned. She *truly* hated being queen. "No," she sighed. She turned to Maarav. "Please ask the guards at the door to find two upper ranking mages, preferably Sage and another of his choosing. They will escort Kai, then stand guard until told otherwise."

Maarav nodded, then headed toward the door, stopping near Kai. "My apologies," he muttered, "I never would have brought you here had I known."

Ealasaid's face burned with embarrassment. It was a sad day indeed when Maarav showed more compassion than her. Later, when she was alone, she would have to consider exactly what she'd become since being named queen, and why.

―――――

Once Kai had been escorted from the room, Ealasaid slumped down into her chair with a sigh of relief. It had taken *ages* of awkward silence before Sage had been found . .

. not that Keiren seemed to mind. She wouldn't know social graces if they bit her on the bottom.

"What is your news?" Maarav said tersely to Keiren, clearly irritated with how Kai had been treated.

Keiren sneered at him from her seat, then turned to Ealasaid. "The Snow Queen wishes to form an alliance with you against Finnur. She believes it the only way either of you will stand a chance at being the remaining queen in the prophecy."

Ealasaid's jaw dropped. "*That's* where you were? You actually met with Oighear?"

Keiren snorted. "Hardly. I met with a human emissary, one I trust to deliver accurate information."

"Who?" Maarav asked.

"That is none of your concern," Keiren snapped. Her gaze fell back to Ealasaid. "What do you think?"

Ealasaid fought against the hot rage zinging up her spine. That evil creature actually thought to make an alliance! *Hah.* "I think you know exactly what I think of *that*," she growled. "That monster killed over half my mages. She killed Tavish and Ouve. She killed *my parents.* I would not ally myself with her, even if she truly was my sole hope at survival. I say let Finn crush her if she so chooses."

Maarav stared at her for a moment as if she'd just shape-changed right in front of him, then a small smile graced his lips. He lifted a hand to hide his laugh at her behavior.

She glared at him, then turned back to Keiren. "The answer is no."

Keiren nodded. "As I thought, though Oighear *does* have a point."

"Which is what?" Ealasaid asked, feeling entirely over-whelmed.

Keiren rolled her eyes. "That neither of you stand a chance against Finnur on your own. At least, not without an excellent plan."

Ealasaid had lost count of how many times she'd told Keiren she had no interest in attacking Finn. She could say it a thousand times and the sorceress would not listen. So this time, she just tilted her head and waited for Keiren to divulge her plan.

"The barrier to the in-between," Keiren stated. "We must destroy it."

Ealasaid bit her lip, recalling the woman she'd met in the in-between who looked eerily similar to Finn. She'd said the same thing.

"Why?" Maarav asked. "Not that I understand *anything* about the in-between. For all I know you women have made it up in your minds. But, if it *does* exist, it seems a monu-mentally bad idea to destroy it."

Ealasaid tended to agree with him. She could not entirely fathom just what the in-between was, or what might happen if it were melded with reality.

"To change your fate," Keiren said simply. "The prophecy came into being on the terms of *this* reality. If you refuse to work against Finnur, work *with* her to create a *new* reality in which you might both survive. Create another possible ending to the prophecy."

"I thought you wanted to kill her," Maarav interjected.

She raised a red brow at him. "You forget, I've been tracking her since she first returned to this realm. If I wanted her dead, I would have killed her before she remembered who she was."

"But you could not see her for much of the time," Ealasaid argued, the wheels in her mind churning furiously. "That's why you sent Bedelia to her."

Keiren rolled her eyes. "Yes, and I could have had Bedelia stick a knife in her back, but I did not."

Ealasaid noticed Maarav watching Keiren intently, as if he'd just realized something. She desperately wanted to ask him what that something was, but it would have to wait just a moment longer.

"I'll think upon what you have said," she decided. "I'm sure you're tired from your journey. We can discuss this in greater detail once I've figured out the proper questions to ask."

Keiren nodded sharply. For an offhand suggestion, she seemed rather vested in this new plan.

"I'll take my leave then," she announced, rising from her seat. "Though, do not take too long. Oighear awaits an answer, and when we tell her no, she will surely try her best to destroy us to prevent you from allying with Finnur instead."

With that, she stalked out of the room, leaving Maarav and Ealasaid alone.

Ealasaid waited until the click of Keiren's boots had retreated all the way down the nearby stairs, then turned toward Maarav. "What did you realize while Keiren was speaking of her plan?"

His brows were furrowed, his eyes grim. "I realized that she's not lying. She never wanted to kill Finn, which means she wanted to use her for the same thing she's trying to use you for now. Destroying the barrier to the in-between has been her goal all along. The only question is, why?"

Ealasaid raised her brows as she considered what he'd said. "If that's the case, then why ally herself with *me*? What do I have to do with it?"

He leaned forward across the table, his gaze intent. "Think about it. How many people do you know that might stand a chance of convincing Finn to go along with this plan? How many people with the power to go to the in-between and meet with her themselves?"

She shook her head in disbelief. "But if Keiren wanted this all along, why did she advise me to keep Finn away?"

He rubbed his brow and shook his head. After a moment, he replied, "Because if Finn were around, allied with you, neither of you would need to worry about Oighear's forces to begin with. She has fostered distrust between you, so that you each will be desperate enough to want to change the prophecy."

Ealasaid's heart skipped a beat. He was right. He was absolutely right. This had been Keiren's plan all along, and she had played right into her hands.

"We need to speak with Finn," she said gravely.

Maarav nodded. "Let us hope she has not turned too far against us."

Keiren leaned her ear away from the door. Part of her was disappointed in Ealasaid for falling for such a simple illusion. While the sound of footsteps had signaled her retreat, if Ealasaid had actually tried, she could have *sensed* her eavesdropping on the other side of the door.

Stifling a growl, she hurried down the hall, her footsteps utterly silent. Curse that Maarav. She should have killed him long ago. *Of course* he would be the one to figure out her plan.

It was lucky no one passed her as she made her journey toward her chamber, else they would have felt the wrath she would have liked to aim at Ealasaid and Maarav. Fortunately, or perhaps *un*fortunately, she reached her door without being bothered. Withdrawing a slender key from her traveling cloak, she unlocked it and went inside. She would not remain around long enough for Ealasaid to confront her. That would only make matters worse.

Hastily, she began packing her belongings. Searching for things she wanted to bring, her eyes caught sight of the large crystal she'd tossed on her bed before seeking out Ealasaid. She blinked at it, pondering. If she so decided, she could use it to speak with Òengus, and through him, Oighear, to set events in motion. She could crush Ealasaid for so foolishly doubting her.

She turned back to her things, angrily wadding up silky dresses and tossing them into her pack with jewels and other baubles. She'd done *so* much for Ealasaid, and the girl chose to be wary of her *now*? After all they'd been through? Sure, she was using her, but she'd also protected her. She'd provided *invaluable* advice. She felt herself a fool to think it could be any other way. She'd never been good at making actual friends.

She was, however, good at running away, which she would do now before Ealasaid turned on her fully. Instead of biding her time, she would set this cursed war into motion, and would force Ealasaid and Finn into giving her what she wanted.

A throat cleared behind her, and she whipped around, but there was no one else in the room. Her door remained shut and locked.

The throat cleared again, and she darted her gaze to the floor length mirror dominating one corner of her modest chamber. Framed in the glossy surface was Niklas, draped in his usual robes with his bald head bare.

"Going somewhere?" he asked.

She scowled at him. "Yes, if you must know, though I have not given up on my quest—" she hesitated, "or should I say, *our* quest?" She'd found it wildly convenient at the time that she and Niklas' goals would align so perfectly, but he hadn't been much help since.

He nodded. "The clans have named their champions. Clan Solas Na Réaltaí has sworn fealty to the Queen of Wands, Clan An Duilleog to the Oak Queen, and Clan An Gheimhridh to the Snow Queen. The prophecy's fulfillment is near."

She raised a red brow at him. "And just how does the swearing of Ceàrdaman fealty fulfill the prophecy?"

He tilted his head, his strange eyes searching her face through the mirror's surface. "Truly, you do not yet understand?"

She glared at him, but shook her head.

He smiled wickedly. "Two queens must die, and one must live, but that is not the end. The fulfillment of the prophecy means this world will be irreparably changed. What sort of change do you think that might be?"

Her lips parted. Could it truly be so simple? "The breaking of the barrier to the in-between?"

He nodded. "Yes, but that fate only lies with the Oak Queen's victory. If the Snow Queen survives, the land will see endless winter."

"And what of the Queen of Wands?" she asked.

His smile broadened. "With the loss of their queens, all but the lesser Faie will fade away. The power of the mages will continue to grow, and an even greater war will take place. The humans will destroy each other out of age-old hatreds."

It was a lot to take in, but she supposed only one part was important, and she had to admit, it rankled. "So we need Finn to survive? She must kill Ealasaid?"

He nodded.

"Then what in the Horned One's name have I been wasting my time here for? *You* said this was where I needed to be."

Niklas chuckled. "*Someone* had to lure the Oak Queen to war. If you had not encouraged the Queen of Wands to grow her strength, An Fiach would not have marched. Oighear would have killed Ealasaid, then would have moved on to Finnur. Everything I have done has set another tiny cog in motion toward the outcome we both desire."

She slumped down onto her bed, overwhelmed. For once, she felt utterly out of her depth. How had this all gone beyond the realm of her *sight*?

"Do you understand now?" Niklas questioned.

She nodded. "All except for one aspect. Why swear fealty to the queens? Do some of the clans truly desire endless winter, or for the humans to destroy each other?"

He rolled his eyes. "Truly, child, you know very little. When our clans were cut off from the in-between, we lost most everything, except for three great relics, items made purely of in-between magic. A ring to control the living green things. A wand to control the sky. And a glittering crown to control the cold and darkness."

"The wand?" she mused, still bitter that Ealasaid had neglected to show it to her.

Niklas nodded.

"But why?" she pressed, still unsure of the significance of the items.

Niklas sighed. "Truly, I don't know why I put up with you. With these three items, our lovely queens will have true power over their elements. Finnur and Oighear have both survived their power being sealed away, Finnur by choice. The power of these objects will make our queens capable of *fully* destroying each other, ensuring the prophecy's fulfillment."

"But it's a prophecy," Keiren countered. "Won't it fulfill regardless? Was it truly necessary to make them *more* powerful?"

Niklas crinkled his brow in irritation. She suspected he might disappear from the mirror's surface, but he finally answered, "My dear, who do you think created the prophecy to begin with? Who do you think has tugged the strings of fate this entire time? When the Ceàrdaman were cut off from the in-between, we had only three relics of power to guide us back. The stars helped us choose our queens, and word of the prophecy was spread by *us*. We have made each of the queens powerful enough to carry out what comes naturally to them. Oighear the White will wrap the world in snow, because that is her nature. Her cold heart will infect everything around her. Ealasaid will start a war, because she is loyal, and duty bound to protect her kind. Finnur," he began patiently, eyeing her intently, "Finnur, will destroy the barrier to the in-between not only to free the souls she cursed, but to regain that which was stolen from her over a century ago."

Fully intrigued, she tilted her head. "Which was what?"

Niklas smiled. "Her daughter."

Her eyes widened. She'd known that Finn had lost a daughter, but to still try and reclaim her, after all this time? Thinking of her lost mother, Keiren shook her head ruefully. Perhaps she and Finner were far more similar than she could have ever imagined.

Kai sat stiffly on his bed. Against his better judgement, he'd remained within his room since being escorted there. Of course, the two mages standing guard might have had something to do with it. Both had stayed in the room with him, but spoke little. In fact, they seemed quite well trained for men who were likely no more than twenty. One was tall with dark hair, and the other shorter, plump with white-blond hair. They wore plain clothes, simple tunics and breeches, rather than uniforms of any sort. The taller one cast a bored look his way. Kai guessed he was Sage, the name Ealasaid had mentioned, given the apparent hierarchy.

Kai sucked his teeth, wondering what he'd have to do to prompt the mages to speak and possibly divulge useful information. Not that information was his primary concern. The sky had darkened with clouds outside, and he was beginning to feel less ill. He should really try to escape while the cloud cover remained.

A knock sounded on the door, which Sage opened, then Ealasaid and Maarav came barreling in, bringing with them a wash of excited energy.

Kai's spine stiffened in anticipation. At least Ealasaid was no longer looking at him like she might have him hanged.

"We need to speak with you," she explained breathily. She turned to Sage and the other mage and added, "*Privately.*"

Sage nodded, then both boys dutifully vacated the room, shutting the door behind them.

Ealasaid wrung her hands. "We have a proposition to offer you, a possible alliance, and hopefully we can find help for your . . . condition too."

"That is," Maarav added, "if you still care about Finn."

Kai's jaw fell open. "Of course I do. What in the Horned One's name are you talking about?"

Ealasaid sat on the bed beside him, suddenly relaxed in his presence, no longer wary. He wondered what had changed. She cleared her throat and met his gaze. "First, I would like to apologize for earlier. In my position—" she hesitated, "well, let's just say it is difficult to not suspect most everyone of secretly plotting against you."

He nodded. "I suppose I understand, but what does this have to do with Finn?"

Ealasaid bit her lip, as if afraid to speak.

Maarav sighed. "Let's just say Ealasaid's judgement regarding Finn has been clouded. We would like to make things right, to rally against Oighear and An Fiach."

Kai was quite sure they'd both gone mad if they thought he had any idea what they were going on about.

"We need to know," Ealasaid began anew, seeming to take his silence as agreement, "have I turned Finn too far against us? Is it too late?"

Kai shook his head. He'd expected to be cast out, or perhaps executed. He had not expected *this*. "When I left she was still the same old Finn, worrying about everyone else when she should have been worrying about herself. I'd say your chances of alliance are good, unless the Cavari have gotten to her. She has a sore spot when it comes to them."

"The Cavari?" Ealasaid breathed. "We'd heard she'd called a truce with them, but little else. Do you believe they have the power to influence her?"

He shrugged. "I'd like to say no, but back when she was part of their tribe she did go a bit . . . mad."

Ealasaid glanced at Maarav.

He nodded. "It's still worth a try. She may be willing to choose us over the Cavari."

Ealasaid nodded a little too quickly, as if trying to convince herself of Maarav's words. She turned her gray eyes back to Kai. "That brings me to our second question, and a third, actually. First, I'm hoping to attempt bringing you to the Gray Place with me. I'm not sure if it can be done, but Keiren brought me once, so I'd like to try. It's a small chance, but if we can find Finn we can offer her an alliance. Yet, the last I saw her I told her to stay away. I want you there to assure her of my sincerity."

He narrowed his eyes in thought. "But what if she is not there? I find it unlikely that we will meet with her."

"We at least have to try," Ealasaid sighed. "We have no other way of reaching her. It is our only chance. If we fail tonight, we will go again tomorrow. Every night until battle prevents us."

Kai's shoulders slumped. He supposed there was a small chance they could find her, or perhaps even Móirne, who'd used the in-between to contact them on more than one occasion.

"There's something else," Ealasaid continued, drawing him out of his thoughts. He raised a brow at her. "Something else beyond dragging me to the in-between?"

Ealasaid grinned. "Yes, Maarav and I will marry tonight, and I'd like you to stand witness."

"*Me?*" he balked. His thoughts were still hung up on the idea of going to the Gray Place, now she wanted him to stand witness to a marriage?

As his thoughts caught up to him, he turned his head to stare at Maarav. "*You,*" he began skeptically, "are getting married to *her.*" He gestured to Ealasaid.

Maarav scowled. "It's not *that* unbelievable. I *told* you we were together."

Kai laughed. Yes, Maarav had told him that, but he hadn't fully *believed* it, and now to suddenly be getting married? They really had gone mad. In fact, in that moment, it seemed the fates themselves had completely lost all semblance of reason.

Ealasaid pursed her lips as she glared at him. "It's not funny."

He shook his head. How had he ended up in such a backwards situation? "I apologize. I'd love to stand witness for your ceremony. In fact, if it will keep you from hanging me, I'd even marry the two of you myself."

"I wouldn't have hanged you," Ealasaid mumbled, finally seeming like the sweet, naive girl he'd known before.

"Shh," Maarav warned jokingly. "We have him where we want him. Don't let him know he's safe."

Kai shook his head, laughing again for the first time in what felt like ages. "I'm hardly safe if you want to drag me to the in-between. The last time I was there I nearly died."

"You were already dying," Maarav scoffed. "Just be grateful you get to be a part of negotiations. I have to stay here and guard your sleeping bodies."

Kai shook his head again. They truly were mad, but then again, he probably was too. At least they seemed happy. It had been a long time since he had viewed true happiness. He might never be able to find it himself, but at least he could be glad for the strange couple before him.

"I agree to all of your terms," he said with a grin.

Maarav clapped him on the shoulder. "Then we've found ourselves a witness, even if he's more Faie than man these days."

Kai's shoulders slumped back down. In all of the excitement, he'd nearly forgotten about that part. There might be some brief happy moments in the near future, but beyond that, he knew his days were numbered.

Branwen clenched and unclenched her fists as she walked, reminding herself that she was in her physical form. This wasn't like the last time she'd been trapped in the in-between, when her body was gravely wounded back in reality. Her body was whole and well, and she intended to keep it that way, though night had come and gone and she was still trapped.

Sometime ago, the loamy ground beneath her feet had become more solid and rocky. The strange scraggly trees had thinned, giving way to tall grass and wildflowers. While the mist of the in-between remained, it now seemed somehow lighter, less stifling, lifting strands of her russet hair with occasional gusts of cool air. The sun shone over-head, delicately kissing her freckled cheeks. She'd never reached this place during her previous entrapment, but perhaps this was just a place where only physical bodies could go, not those visiting in their dreams.

Her eyes scanned the gently swaying grasses for Naoki, who periodically bounded to her before disappearing, since the previous evening. She seemed to be searching for some-thing, but what could a dragon so desperately want to find? Her only hope was to help Naoki in her search, then perhaps she'd bring her back to reality. Niklas had told her that as a wraith, she could not come here. She'd proven him wrong, but now feared what might happen when she returned to her home realm. *If* she returned.

A bright, pulsing light drew her attention to the other end of the meadow. The light was cool, like a captive star, not the warmth of the sun flickering through the yellow grass. A tickle of fear crept through her, but she knew she had little choice but to reach the light. Anything was better than wandering through the endless expanses of the in-between for another day.

The grasses swished against her breeches as she hurried forward, her eyes trained on the flickering light. At first it increased in brilliance, then nearly halfway across the meadow, it winked out of sight.

Her heart fell, but she continued onward, hoping she could still find whatever it was. Eventually her feet slowed, reaching the area where the light had been. She stopped, peering around, then nearly jumped out of her skin as she spotted a small child sitting in the grass, the long yellow tendrils nearly obscuring her from sight.

The child, a little girl, hung her head, her small arms wrapped around bony knees. A white dress covered her delicate frame. A *funeral* dress. Her golden hair was adorned with tiny braids and white flowers, and her tiny feet were bare.

Branwen wondered if this girl was dead, and waiting to move on. Finn had claimed she'd seen Anders in a golden meadow after he died, right before he'd passed on to wher-ever the dead went in the end. Yet, the custom of white funeral gowns was old. It was rumored to have originated with the Druids, and so had been rejected not long after the Faie War.

Branwen crouched down, hoping she would not scare the little girl. "Greetings little one," she crooned, "what are you doing out here by yourself?"

The girl blinked hazel eyes at her. "Druantia has bade me to wait for any who might seek her counsel."

"Druantia?" Branwen questioned.

The girl nodded. "Queen of the Druids. She rests here

because her home is in turmoil. She belongs with the dead now."

Branwen tilted her head, wondering at this strange child and her alleged Druid Queen.

"Do you wish to see her?" the child asked.

"Perhaps," Branwen replied. "What is your name?"

The girl opened her mouth to speak, then turned wide eyes toward something suddenly crashing toward them through the grass.

Branwen quickly stood in time to see a flash of white, then Naoki skidded to a halt, nearly crashing into the girl. Seeming frantic, Naoki, lowered her beak and sniffed the girl so fiercely she nearly knocked the child onto her side.

"Naoki!" Branwen hissed, shooing the dragon away. "Leave her alone!"

Naoki craned her long neck to gaze up at Branwen. Her spherical lilac eyes were open wide, un-blinking, as if trying to tell her something.

"Is this who you've been looking for?" she asked.

Naoki seemed to nod.

Branwen turned her attention back to the child, though the child did not seem to fear the dragon.

Still, Naoki was an alarming sight. "Don't worry," Branwen consoled, crouching back in front of the girl. "She will not hurt you. In fact, I think she brought me here to find you."

The girl nodded. "I think she wants me to bring you to Druantia."

Knowing she might regret it, Branwen nodded. "Yes, that may be the case. Will you take us to this Druid Queen?"

The girl nodded, then climbed to her feet. Without

warning, she took off across the meadow, bounding with the grace of a deer toward a distant copse of fir trees.

Naoki instantly took off after her.

Cursing under her breath, Branwen hurried to follow, wondering just what they might find within the copse. The legends spoke of the Druids as a peaceful race, but their magic had been feared by humans. They'd been hunted down and eradicated. Branwen worried their Queen might not have warm feelings toward mortals.

The child reached the copse far ahead with Naoki at her heels. Huffing with exertion, Branwen ran faster, not wanting to get left behind despite the risks. If this was why Naoki had brought her here, she had to see it through.

Naoki and the child had disappeared into the trees by the time she reached the forest. She slowed, peering around for them, but all she saw were tree trunks wider than her chest, and the deep green foliage underneath.

Carefully picking her way along, she listened for Naoki and the child, but heard nothing. Growing increasingly worried, she continued on, deeper into the tree shadows.

She wiped the sweat from her brow as she walked, rapidly losing hope. They'd left her behind, and now she'd be lost in the woods alone. Her head fell as her heart was consumed with despair. Thinking the worst, her loud thoughts almost drowned out the sound of a woman's voice not too far ahead.

"What have you brought me?" the voice said.

Perking up, Branwen crept in the direction of the voice, distantly noting the sound of running water. As she neared, she could hear the low murmur of the little girl's voice too, though she spoke too softly to be understood.

Branwen's eyes caught sight of a small pond in the middle of the forest. The opening in the trees allowed the sun to shine through, glistening across the pond's surface. Beside the pond stood the little girl and Naoki, but no woman. Curious, Branwen crept forward until she reached the little girl's side.

"A wraith traveling with the dragon," the woman's voice commented. "How peculiar."

Branwen's head whipped around, searching for the source of the voice.

"Down here," the voice said with a chuckle.

Branwen looked down at the water. "Down where?" she questioned.

The little girl pointed down at the pond, her bare toes nearly touching the edge.

"Does the dragon know you?" the woman's voice asked. As she spoke, the sparkling surface of the water rippled.

Her heart thudding in her throat, Branwen knelt beside the pond's edge. "Are you . . . in the water?"

The voice chuckled. "Silly child, I *am* the water. It's a nicer form than a tree. More . . . *fluid*." The pond let out a bubbling laugh at her own joke.

Branwen turned wide eyes to the child. "Is this the Druid Queen you spoke of?"

The child nodded. "Her name is Druantia."

"Forgive me for luring you here," the pond, Druantia, interrupted. "I was curious."

Branwen furrowed her brow, then looked back down at the water.

"The light you saw," Druantia explained. "I provided it to

draw your attention. When I sensed a wraith in my realm, I feared the worst. Has the balance shifted even further?"

"Balance?" Branwen asked, still confused. "I'm here because Naoki brought me. I believed she was looking for this child. Now I'm not sure."

"The dragon?" Druantia asked. "Yes, I suppose that makes sense. Dragons are excellent trackers. In the old times, they served as familiars to the Druids, along with unicorns and other mythical beasts. Once they were bonded, they could track their masters to other realms and beyond."

"Well this one belongs to Finn," Branwen explained, "so I don't know why she brought *me* here instead."

"Ah yes," Druantia replied. "Finnur. That child is lost to me now. She has chosen the mortal path, rejecting our ways."

The child beside Branwen began to sniffle.

"What's the matter?" Branwen asked, but the child simply shook her head.

"Enough of sad talk," Druantia sighed. "I do not know why the dragon brought you to this realm, but she has gravely wronged you. Wraiths cannot come to the in-between."

"But I'm here," Branwen argued, "so really, they can."

Druantia sighed again. "My apologies, I was not clear. Wraiths cannot come here and survive. The energy that animates you belongs in this realm. Now that you are here, it will slowly seep from you until you die."

Branwen's stomach twisted into a painful knot. She suspected something like that might be the case, but suspecting and knowing were two very different things. "What if I go back?" she croaked. "Is it too late."

"You cannot go back," Druantia replied. "The barrier will keep your energy here. If your mortal body returns to the other realm, it will still die."

No, she thought, this cannot happen now. Not after her brother had sacrificed his life to save her. "What if the barrier were to be broken?"

"You would dare to suggest such a thing?" Druantia hissed. "Has not the balance been altered enough already?"

"Just answer the question," Branwen begged.

"Yes," Druantia grumbled, the water's surface seeming to churn with her displeasure, "if the barrier were to be broken, you would most likely retain that which animates you, but many more will die. Magic would run rampant in your realm. This place would meld with that."

Branwen shook her head, frustrated. "But magic is already running rampant there. A war is brewing because of it. The mages fight the non-magic humans, and the Faie war with both."

The water's surface seemed to shiver with a heavy sigh. "Yes, I have felt the disturbances. The Dair draw nature power into reality. They are not one with it, they *use* it. Everything they do draws magic from the earth and releases it into the lives of mortals."

That seemed about right. Though she hadn't experienced Finn's magic firsthand like the others, she'd been held captive by the Cavari for quite some time. "So maybe the barrier breaking would be a good thing?" she suggested, her thoughts lingering on the Dair. "Surely things cannot get any worse?"

The pond bubbled with a snort, seeming to grow more animate the more it spoke. "You are a fool. Adding *more* magic will only make things worse. It would restore the Ceàrdaman to their full power, and who knows what it would do to the Faie?"

Branwen fell silent. Was that why Niklas wanted to destroy the barrier? "The Ceàrdaman?" she questioned.

"They are from here, you know," Druantia explained. "The Ceàrdaman left this place to play with the mortals. They started the flow of foreign magics into that land. Eventually, the hole they had created repaired itself, and they became trapped."

Branwen curled her legs under herself, hunching her back in defeat. She knew she was Niklas' pawn, but she had at least trusted him to give what he had promised. He'd promised her she could return to a somewhat normal life after she helped Finn break the barrier, but how could her life be normal if breaking the barrier would do such horrible things to the mortals of her realm? How could she live a life with her family, if she risked all of their lives to meet her own ends?

She needed to accept the only possible answer. "I suppose I'll die here then. I will not try to break the barrier. My family will be safer never seeing me again."

"I'm sorry, child," Druantia soothed. "You may remain here with me if you wish. I've lived many lives, and have many stories to share with a former scholar. Perhaps together we can figure out what the dragon wishes as well."

Branwen sighed, not questioning how Druantia knew she was a scholar. At one time, her life had been all about stories. She'd left her home in search of more. Now she was being offered the opportunity of a lifetime, but she wouldn't be able to write anything down for generations to come. The stories would die with her.

"Yes," she sighed, settling in. "Please tell me your stories." She aimed a glare at Naoki. "Though I couldn't care less about what *she* wants."

Naoki ignored her in favor of sniffing the poor child again, but the child no longer seemed afraid. Perhaps Branwen would learn more about her too, and what sort of magic had trapped her in this awful place.

CHAPTER SEVEN

$\mathcal{F}$inn sat atop Loinnir's back, making her way through the forest. At her side rode Iseult, and behind her, the Cavari. Sugn had gone to gather more of the Dair. As the afternoon sun glimmered through the trees, she thought of Branwen, whom she'd not been able to find the night before, or the morning of their departure. In truth, she'd nearly forgotten about her with everything else going on. At least the remaining few Aos Sí, who'd stayed behind to watch over the fortress, could inform Branwen, if she deigned to show up, where Finn had gone. Or perhaps she never would. Perhaps Branwen wanted to be far from the chaos that swirled around her. She shook her head. She could not blame her. She'd like to be away from it herself, but there was no other choice. Naoki too, had gone missing, but she knew the dragon could track her anywhere. She'd proven so on many occasions.

Pushing aside her thoughts, she glanced at Iseult, observing his perceptive eyes and grim expression. She wanted desperately to ask his advice on strategy. She had never faced a true battle, and now she might be facing many. The first threat was An Fiach, but Oighear's Aos Sí might be lying in wait too. It would not do to charge in blindly.

She glanced at him again to find him watching her. "What is it?" she questioned, her voice barely audible over the creak of their saddles and the gentle hoofbeats of their mounts.

He eyed her intently, shadows passing over his face from the bows above. "Are you sure about this?"

She glanced over her shoulder, noting a few of the Cavari on horseback, well out of hearing range. That did not mean Faie weren't hidden about with ears eager to listen, but she trusted them far more than her own people.

"It is the only way," she explained. "If An Fiach will attack Garenoch . . . " she trailed off, shaking her head. "I cannot just let that happen, especially not with Kai and everyone else roaming about. There is too much danger, and I am the only one strong enough to protect them all."

He continued to watch her. "What of the prophecy?"

A shiver went down her spine. Something in her bones told her the prophecy was real, that it would need to be dealt with, but she could not bring herself to face it. At least, not yet.

"I'll deal with that when the time comes."

His eyes were all too knowing. With a quick glance behind, he tugged his horse's reins.

She stopped beside him, wondering at the sudden emotion in his gray-green eyes.

"Finn," he began patiently. "The prophecy states that

either you or Ealasaid will die, yet you will risk yourself to save her. Perhaps in doing so, you'll fulfill part of the prophecy with your death."

She knew he was right, but . . . "What else am I supposed to do? Let so many others die in my place? Ealasaid deserves life far more than I—" She sealed her mouth shut, surprised at her own words. She wanted to *live*, truly she did, but a deep, dark part of her soul argued that she'd already had her chance at several lifetimes.

His eyes scanned her face, but he did not speak.

She blinked back tears. She would not cry *now*. Her task was laid out before her. She needed to be brave.

"I care for Ealasaid," Iseult began, surprising her further, "and I care for my brother, but Finn," he shook his head, "I would let the entire world burn if it meant you would live. I would leave my ancestors' souls to rot in the in-between. I would cast aside my own soul, and everything else in this life I hold dear. I would lay down my life, if it meant you would continue to brighten this world, because that is precisely what you do. You think your are the darkness, a creature unworthy of life, but I think you are the most worthy person I've ever laid eyes upon. You are the only hope this cruel, spiteful land has. You are the only hope *I* have."

She only had a moment to blink at him in shock, then he was down from his saddle, wrapping his arms around her waist to lift her to the ground. He wrapped her in his embrace and kissed her, and this time it was a *real* kiss. No pulling away. No stalking off into the night.

She reveled in his warmth, in his *aliveness*. In that

moment, she didn't care what she deserved, she only cared about what she wanted. *Needed*.

With the love she felt in that moment, she felt the power to break *any* prophecy, because there were greater powers in existence than the fates.

Slowly, he pulled away from her.

Reluctantly, she let him go. "Why now?" she questioned. "Why wait until now?"

He stroked a strand of her long hair back from her face. "Because there is no telling what might happen tomorrow."

Gazing up into his eyes, she wanted to give up her title, and her duty. She wanted to run away with him and let everything else fall apart.

Yet, she could not. There were others depending on her. While there was a time for love, now was not that time.

The time had come for war.

Anna's horse ambled along beneath her, the rhythmic movement not budging the scowl on her face. They'd spent far too long conversing with Ranna and Therin, and had parted ways after giving the couple far too many supplies. Though, at least the pair might survive now. Being non-magical humans, An Fiach would likely leave them be on their way to Sormyr, where they might find work on a farm.

She lowered her gaze to the loamy ground ahead, seeing no sign of tracks, though she hadn't expected any. If the Pixies were unable to find Kai, what chance had she? She wasn't sure why she still pursued her quest, riding farther from the fortress, except that Eywen was still riding that way with her. He would soon veer off on another path to scout for Aos Sí warriors, but she was reluctant to turn back. Once she did, she feared she'd never see him again. The thought stung more than she'd like to admit.

"We should rest the horses," Eywen said, drawing her out of her thoughts. "Let them graze while we speak of your plans."

She frowned, suspecting he'd noticed her confidence waning, and would now ask her to turn back.

Without waiting for her reply, he stopped his horse and dismounted.

She followed his example, ready to give her sore backside a break from the saddle. As soon as her boots hit the ground, she stretched her arms over her head, grasping her reins loosely in one hand.

As she lowered her arms, Eywen handed her a crumbly bannock wrapped in parchment, no doubt stolen for them by the Bucca, then led his horse toward a tree where it might graze, loosely anchoring its reins on a sprawling branch.

"I'll build a fire," he stated as she tied her horse near his.

She wished she could see his expression, but saw only his broad back as he looked for dry wood . . . not that he was likely to find any. They'd endured intermittent rain throughout their journey, leaving Anna's clothes in a constant state of damp.

Taking bites of her bannock, she turned her back to him to check over her horse for any signs of physical stress, then wrinkled her nose at the smell of smoke.

As her brain caught up with her nose, she whirled on

him. He crouched before a small pile of wood already smoldering with the first hints of flame.

"How did you manage that?" she questioned curiously, approaching him as she plopped the last portion of bannock in her mouth, then stuck the crumbled parchment in her breeches pocket.

He leveled his deep blue eyes up at her, a small smile on his pale lips. "I may not have much magic of my own, but I am not without my tricks."

At the mention of magic she sighed, then plopped down beside him, lifting her palms to warm them by the burgeoning fire. "Tell me about these *tricks*."

Settling in on the ground more comfortably now that the fire was surviving on its own, he inclined his head toward her. "You truly want to know?"

She nodded, unable to quiet her curiosity.

"You know that the Aos Sí who have pledged themselves to Oighear survive off her power," he began, telling her something she did in fact know, but still didn't fully comprehend. "We Faie are beings of magic, and we need magic to sustain us," he added, seeming to sense her hesitation.

"The lesser Faie," he continued, "can survive off the magic of the earth, to a degree, but the Aos Sí are not connected to the earth in such a manner. We are immortal soldiers, always connected to a queen. When my queen was Oighear, I had the minor magic to survive the cold, in addition to my natural physical abilities."

She nodded for him to go on, thoroughly intrigued.

He smiled at her. "Now that I have named Finnur as my queen, my abilities have changed. While Oighear is the cold and darkness, Finnur is the warmth and light. She is the seed growing in the soil. Hence," he gestured to the fire.

She tilted her head, actually beginning to understand. "So you now have powers of life and warmth instead of cold," she said with a nod, "but there's one thing I still don't understand."

He nodded for her to go on.

"Where do mages get their power?" she asked, leaving her true question unspoken. What she really wanted to know was where did *she* get her magic?

"Excellent question," he complimented. "As far as I've been led to understand, most mages siphon their power from the energy of the elements. That's why most tend to express their magic as fire, ice, wind, and so on. Since Finnur's return, magic has flown more freely. The mages seem to have grown in strength, though minor magic was accessible to some while she was gone."

She nodded, a frown creasing her brow. That still explained nothing of why her magic had increased since her experience with the Travelers.

"Now your magic," Eywen began, "is more of a mystery. It is the magic of the in-between, and is not related to this land. I imagine somewhere far back in your bloodline is an ancestor not quite human, providing you with this link."

She raised a brow at him. "Are you proposing that one of my ancestors was Faie?"

He shrugged. "Perhaps, or perhaps something else. The Dair and the Ceàrdaman are magical races, but are not quite Faie."

She stared at the fire in thought, barely noticing that her clothes had finally begun to dry. She highly doubted she had any relation to the Dair, but the Travelers? They had sensed her magic long before she even knew it existed. Could they have known even more about her lineage than they'd let on?

"I apologize if that's not what you wanted to hear," he muttered.

She startled, realizing she'd been scowling. "No," she smiled, "it's alright. At least I have some vague idea now of why this has happened to me."

He returned her smile.

Suddenly she found herself gazing into his sapphire eyes, only then realizing how close they were seated to one another.

To her utter surprise, he leaned forward and kissed her. To her greater surprise, she did not pull away.

A mighty torrent of thoughts collided in her mind. Her tragic past, her many years spent alone, her fading fear of the Faie. They all halted when she realized she was kissing an immortal Faie warrior, and she was *enjoying* it.

She pulled away abruptly, shakily climbed to her feet, and ran.

Not looking back, she fled past their horses and into the trees, heedless of any dangers that might be lurking. Her thoughts were too loud to perceive if he followed. Had he really just kissed her? Her lips burned, and her stomach was all twisted in knots. Her skin felt like it was on fire. She hadn't felt like this in *years*. She hadn't *allowed* herself to feel like this in years. She staggered to a stop and fell to her knees on the slippery leaves, breathless.

Footsteps sounded behind her. She would have turned to face him, but didn't want him to see the tears now streaming down her face.

"Anna," Eywen began, his voice hesitant. "If I over-stepped, I apologize."

"It's nothing," she snapped, wiping at her eyes. *Please, go away*, she thought, but couldn't bring herself to say it. Part of her wanted him to stay.

"Anna," he began again, his voice soft. "Why are you crying?"

Curse him, did he have to be so perceptive? She turned to look up at him, wiping at the last of her tears. "I wasn't crying," she argued, though she knew there was really no denying it.

He took a step toward her, his gaze wary. Once, she would have found his unearthly blue eyes strange, but not anymore. Nothing about him seemed strange to her anymore, except for the way he made her feel.

"I haven't—" she cut herself off, turning her gaze back down to her lap. Was she really going to tell him this? She'd never even told Kai. She took a shaky breath. "I was betrayed, long ago," she explained, her voice barely above a whisper. "He was the only man that was ever truly dear to me, though I suppose he was more of a boy. We were both seventeen."

Why was she telling him this? Her face was flush with embarrassment. She should just end whatever was going on between them, here and now.

"He broke your heart," Eywen observed, stepping closer.

She nodded, fighting back her tears once again. "More than that. He *sacrificed* me, or, at least he tried to."

Eywen sat beside her in the damp dead leaves, his hand alighting on her shoulder.

She flicked her gaze to his long, pale fingers, fingers that had slain countless foes, yet comforted her so gently. Closing her eyes, she began the story she'd never planned on beginning again.

"I grew up in an orphanage in the Gray City," she admitted.

"Orphanage?" he questioned.

She began to feel insulted, then opened her eyes to see his confused expression. She sighed. "It's a place where unwanted children go. Those without parents to claim them."

He nodded his comprehension. "Please, go on."

She licked her dry lips. "When I was old enough to fend for myself, I turned to thievery. It was the only way to survive in the city when you grow up like I did. I was good at it too. I was able to survive when others were not." She closed her eyes, giving in to the images of her past.

"What of the other children in the orphanage?" he asked.

She shrugged like it didn't matter, but really, it *did*. "Some of the girls were lucky enough to marry, and some of the boys found crews to sail with, or farms to work on, but many others didn't make it that far. I had no desire to marry a farmer, but could find no other work. That's when I met Yaric."

With a shuddering breath, she hunched her back, wishing she could curl up into a little ball until the painful memories left her.

Eywen's hand dropped from her shoulder, granting her space to collect herself.

She inhaled sharply. She'd come this far, she might as well finish the tale. "Yaric did not grow up unwanted, as I had, but his family lived in servitude to the Gray City. Many end up with great debts just to survive, then work their entire lives in an attempt to pay them off. Not wanting to be saddled with his family's debts, Yaric abandoned them. I should have known that he would show me the same loyalty, but I was young and idealistic. I thought he loved me."

She glanced at Eywen, wondering if he was bored, then quickly looked away, uncomfortable with the rapt attention he was paying her.

"Though I had already started stealing on my own, Yaric taught me better ways to apply my skills. Instead of stealing bread for my next meal, I began stealing jewelry and other baubles. Yaric knew a merchant willing to buy such things without asking questions."

Absorbed in her recollection, she leaned against Eywen's shoulder.

"Eventually I learned that Yaric was working for a notorious thieving ring. I knew they were dangerous, but he assured me he'd keep me safe. I believed him." Memories flashed through her mind, one in particular. Yaric's face watching impassively as his employer beat her within an inch of her life. He'd carried her outside, leaving her for the Gray Guard to find, her pockets filled with stolen jewelry.

"Yaric's employer was under investigation from the Guard," she sighed. "Too much had been stolen, and someone had to hang. Yaric sacrificed me to that cause. I was beaten, and left to be punished for the crimes."

"How did you survive?" Eywen asked softly.

She looked up at the cloudy sky. It would be dark soon, not a good time to be sitting far away from their horses with no fire near them, but she'd started her story, now she might as well finish it.

"By luck alone," she admitted. "The guards found me at sunrise and arrested me. I told them what happened, and begged them to let me go. I would have hanged were it not for an older guard taking pity on me. He thought I looked like his daughter. He let me go the day before I was to die. I fled the city. Too many of the guards knew my face."

"What happened to Yaric?" he asked.

She shrugged. She'd always wished she'd gone back to kill him. Even if it meant she'd die too.

"I heard he hanged less than a year later," she sighed.

"Good," Eywen muttered.

She turned to him, surprised.

Eywen eyed her steadily. "If he were still alive, I would find him and separate his head from his body."

She laughed, bringing her tears forth as she rested her head on his shoulder. "I do not need you to defend me."

"I know," he said simply, "but I will do it anyway."

Somehow, that comforted her. She might be in a strange place, with her head leaning on the shoulder of one of the Faie, but she suddenly felt lighter and happier than she had in years.

"I'm sure these horses are theirs," Bedelia argued, sitting atop her own halted mount as she observed those tethered to a tree.

"What does it matter, lass?" Àed grumbled. "We're losin' daylight."

Bedelia frowned. While she wanted to reach Garenoch as soon as possible, she knew the two horses belonged to Anna and Eywen. They might not yet be aware of the human army marching toward the burgh, and she felt it her duty to tell them.

She turned toward the sound of voices, proving she'd been right about the horses. Anna and Eywen appeared from within the trees, walking companionably side by side. Anna's face seemed puffy, like she'd been crying, though she seemed in good cheer now.

Bedelia lifted a hand in greeting.

Anna stopped dead in her tracks upon spotting her, but Eywen seemed unfazed, as if he'd already known she and Àed were there. He lifted his hand to return her greeting.

"Ye must have been takin' yer time for us to catch ye," Àed taunted.

Anna glared at him as she reached her horse. "We were detained, if you must know, by a human couple bearing news of affairs in Garenoch."

Bedelia perked up at the mention of the burgh. "What news? Is everything alright?"

"Yes," Anna answered, "except that Ealasaid is amassing an army of mages. The couple we met were afraid to remain within the burgh, afraid enough to brave the wilds on their own. Is that where you're headed? I can't imagine any other reason for the two of you to be out here."

Bedelia bit her lip, wondering if answering yes would bring on more questions, but Àed made the decision for her. "Yes," he growled, "though that shouldnae be of concern to ye. I take it ye've seen no sign of Kai."

Anna's expression darkened. Instead of answering, she

tugged her reins from the tree and vaulted up into her horse's saddle.

Eywen climbed into his saddle without a word.

Observing Anna, Bedelia thought it best not to question them further.

"Well," Àed announced in the somewhat uncomfortable silence, "we best get movin'."

Bedelia nodded her agreement. While she was anxious to reach Garenoch to confront Keiren, she wouldn't mind extra company for a time, if only to grant her a reprieve from Àed's gruff behavior.

"Will the two of you be heading to Garenoch as well?" she questioned. "Perhaps that is where Kai has ended up." She secretly hoped it was. The more allies present when she faced Keiren, the better. Not to mention she wouldn't mind speaking with someone else suffering from an infective Faie bite. She suspected her wolf bite was different from the injuries he'd sustained, but there might be some thread in common that could save them both.

Anna shrugged off her question, a scowl on her face. Perhaps she wouldn't be an improvement to Àed after all.

"I must continue northeast," Eywen answered when Anna did not, "though Garenoch may be a good place for Anna to take respite."

Bedelia didn't miss the sharp look Anna darted his way. She wondered what it might be about, though Anna would likely never tell her.

To her dismay, they continued on in silence after that. She missed Finn and Iseult, two friends who actually seemed to value her presence, and who had both understood just why she had needed to leave.

She hoped she would survive her meeting with Keiren to see them again.

Iseult sat staring at the fire, with the quiet, dark woods at his back. He couldn't help occasional glances at Finn, though she seemed to be resting soundly, with her unicorn grazing only a few paces away. Without meaning to, he found his eyes scanning up and down Finn's bundled form. He'd meant every word he'd said to her. He would gladly let the world burn if it meant she would be safe. Unfortunately, the world was already burning, and they were riding straight toward danger. That was a thought for another day, though. He'd deal with what they found in Garenoch when the time came.

He was glad for now, at least, that they camped alone, though many of the Faie milled around in the surrounding forest. The Cavari who'd accompanied them spoke little, and seemed to have no need for sleep, unlike Finn, who seemed the most human amongst them. Human and frail. The more powerful she grew, the more her physical form seemed to be wilting away.

"She seems so sweet when she's sleeping," a voice said from behind him.

He tensed, not having sensed anyone approaching. It was rare that someone could actually sneak up on him. He turned his glare to observe Sugn, his golden hair seeming to glow with the flickering firelight.

Uninvited, Sugn stepped forward, then sat on the fallen log beside Iseult.

"What do you want?" Iseult asked, unable to hide the venom in his tone.

Sugn's gaze was on Finn as he answered, "I want assurances. Finnur marches us to war, but to what end? Are we to fight for insignificant little mages and other mortals now?" He turned to look Iseult up and down. "No offense meant, *mortal.*"

While Sugn had clearly meant to offend, Iseult had forsaken the notion of prideful vanity long ago. "She is your queen," he said evenly, keeping his voice low. "You would dare question her?"

Sugn sneered, turning his handsome face ugly. "She was born under the needed alignment of stars, that is all. If she were to truly die, another would replace her."

His blood boiled at Sugn's words. He debated killing the man right then and there. He forced his heartbeat to slow. "And you believe that *someone* might be you?"

Sugn smirked. "Now you're catching on." He flicked his gaze once again to Finn's sleeping form, then back to Iseult. "Although, I'd be happy to follow a queen who adhered to the wishes of her people. I'd imagine someone who cared deeply for her would lead her in that direction, if only to ensure her continued health."

Rage washed through him once again. He would protect Finn with his life, and he wanted to kill Sugn right there, but something stopped him. He was not a foolish man, and he knew when an adversary could not easily be slain. He would not be able to do it on his own.

"I'll think upon your words," he forced himself to say. He needed time. Time to reach the others. Time to *plan.* Finn would never abide the Cavari's wishes, so it would be her or them.

Sugn stood. "I see you're a wiser man than I'd originally thought. See that you do not think for too long." With that, he walked away, fading into the darkness.

Iseult peered down at Finn's sleeping form, curled up by the fire.

She groaned in her sleep, clearly slipping into another nightmare, though he was reluctant to wake her. It was rare that she slept long at all, and he needed time to process his conversation with Sugn, and to figure out how to approach her with the newly garnered information.

He found himself wishing for Kai, despite any jealousies he might harbor toward him and his relationship with Finn. Kai always knew what to say to her. Out of everyone, he was the one who'd truly become her friend.

Iseult would have liked the role, but he'd never been good at friendship. He'd been on his mission for too long. Instead of resolving it, things had only become more complicated, making him perhaps less agreeable than he'd ever been before.

His thoughts dark, he gazed down at Finn, clenching and unclenching her fists in the fabric of her bedroll. Though he'd met her what seemed like ages ago, he knew their journey had only just begun.

CHAPTER EIGHT

*E*alasaid's heart raced. Keiren had not emerged from her chamber since their meeting, so she'd not bothered telling her what would occur that night. After Maarav's revelations, she would not have wanted to tell her either way. She'd known Keiren likely had ulterior motives, but to realize she'd never cared about the mages from the start . . . she shook her head, glancing first at Kai on her left, then Maarav on her right as the trio made their way through the gardens to the place Slàine had chosen for her to swear her oath. She had decided to wed Maarav in the same location. It was, after all, where he'd proposed.

Kai followed their lead as they made their way through the decorative hedges toward their destination, the massive stone centerpiece bearing the names of those who'd fallen under Ealasaid's command. While seeing the names made her heart hurt, it also reminded her just what they were fighting for. It reminded her that there were still good, brave people in the world.

As they approached the stone centerpiece, she eyed Slàine and two female assassins waiting there. The trio were clad in their usual black, without their face-obscuring cowls.

Kai hesitated as he saw them, but Ealasaid nodded to him that it was alright.

Slàine stepped forward, placing herself in front of the memorial stone. "Tonight we welcome a new sister into our order, both through solemn vows and marriage."

Ealasaid looked to Maarav, smiling. He might be overly pragmatic, greedy, and a seasoned killer, but the only important thing to her in that moment was that he was hers . . . and that he no longer killed for coin.

"I assume this man stands witness?" Slàine questioned, nodding toward Kai.

Ealasaid turned to see he'd backed away toward the hedges, but was still close enough to be part of the gathering. She noted a slight reflection in his eyes, and once again wondered just what was happening to him. It would have to be discussed later though.

"Yes," Maarav answered when Ealasaid failed to speak.

His voice was steady and confident, and she wondered if he was somehow not as nervous as she was.

"Then let us begin," Slàine said, holding a hand out to one of the woman standing off to her right.

The woman stepped forward and handed Slàine a large leather-bound book, then retreated to stand by her assassin sister.

Slàine opened the book, then began reciting the words which Ealasaid suspected she had memorized, given she only had the light of the moon to see by.

"Tonight, Ealasaid Ó Corraidhín joins us in a solemn oath as old as the barrows of the Faie. She will pledge her life to her brothers and sisters in arms and blood, to carry our secrets to the grave. We are the executioners of fate, let no man stand in our way. The punishment for breaking our solemn oath is death. Do you swear your life to us?"

Slàine looked up from her book toward Ealasaid.

Maarav took her hand and gave it a squeeze. "You just have to say yes," he whispered.

She really didn't like the idea of swearing her life to Slàine, but she supposed she'd already sworn her life to others ten times over when she first took charge of An Solas.

She cleared her throat. "I do."

Slàine extended the book to the woman who'd originally offered it, then from the other woman took a silver dagger. The blade gleamed in the moonlight, the hilt glittering with pure black and red jewels.

Turning back toward Ealasaid, Slàine held out her free hand. "In blood, our oath will be sealed."

Maarav cringed, then glanced down at her. "My apologies, I forgot about that part."

Ealasaid sighed, then extended her hand palm up, guessing at what Slàine might want.

Slàine cupped her free hand under Ealasaid's, then drew her dagger across her palm.

Ealasaid's breath hissed out at the sharp sting, then blood welled in her cupped hand. She thought Slàine might cut her hand as well, but instead laid the flat edge of the dagger across the pool of Ealasaid's blood. She watched in awe as the dagger seemed to absorb the blood.

"It's magic," she breathed.

"Many relics still hold power," Slàine explained. "We are not superior fighters through skill alone. Our vows give us strength. This is the secret you must never speak." Her eyes darted to Kai, waiting quietly a few paces back from the group. She addressed him firmly, "As witness, you are bound by our laws. Betray the trust Ealasaid has granted you, and you shall know the full fury of our order."

Ealasaid watched as Kai raised his hands in surrender. "Trust me, I'll be blocking this out of my mind as soon as possible."

Slàine smirked, then turned back to Ealasaid.

Ealasaid gasped as she glanced the slice on her palm. The dagger had absorbed all traces of blood, leaving behind a clean cut. Slàine sheathed the dagger at her belt as if it were something entirely ordinary.

"Now on to the next ceremony," she announced. "It would honor me if you'd allow me to oversee this most sacred rite as well."

Maarav laughed. "Well I don't know who else is going to do it."

Ealasaid scowled at him, but it soon turned into a smile. Slàine might not be her first choice of a person to wed her to Maarav, but she was basically his mother, and she liked the idea that family would be involved.

Slàine looked again to Kai. "We'll need your participation for this part." Then she turned to the two women. "You may go."

The women both nodded, then slunk off silently as Kai moved to Maarav's side.

Slàine mirrored him, standing next to Ealasaid. She

lowered her hands to her waist, unfastening a braided leather cord.

Ealasaid turned to Maarav and held out her hand, the cut stinging as the cool night air hit it.

Facing her, he took her left hand in his right, gripping it firmly.

Without a word, Slàine began winding the leather cord around their wrists, binding them together. When she'd wrapped it several times, she stepped back, offering Kai the loose ends. He silently tied them in a loose knot, beginning a ritual as old as time itself.

Ealasaid met Maarav's gaze, twinkling in the moonlight. She was well aware that he was the only person alive that truly watched out for her, and had her best interests at heart, and she did the same for him.

Really, she could not have asked for anything more.

Óengus eyed Oighear sitting at the head of a large wood table, her face buried in her pure white palms. A twinkling crown, encrusted with tiny white crystals, and a raw blue stone at the crest, bedecked her shimmering tresses. While she often wore jewels, he'd never seen her wear this one before.

"I've not heard further word from the sorceress," he explained, still observing her from afar. "An alliance might not be possible."

Oighear lifted her head from her hands. "So be it," she sighed. "We go to war, for better or for worse."

She seemed in such a morose mood, he was hesitant to

speak. Yet, he could not allow her to die in battle without first fulfilling his wish.

"And what of my shadow?" he asked softly.

She blinked at him. "Ah, yes, I'd nearly forgotten." She sighed. "Your shadow will be returned upon the death of the one who stole it from you. It is by the magic of the caster that you remain separated from your own magic."

He furrowed his brows. "It is not magic."

"Think what you wish, Gray Lord," she said tiredly. "But I assure you, your shadow is the magic of the in-between. It is the magic I desire above all else. Why else would I have kept you alive for so long?"

He took a step forward. "You mean to tell me you actually wish for my shadow to be returned?"

She sighed, placing her head back in her hands. "Truly, I do not really care anymore. If you were to regain your shadow now, you would be of little use at this late hour."

He blinked at her, wondering about her attitude. Did she truly think herself entirely doomed? She had been utterly confident before facing Ealasaid.

Desperation emboldened him. He took another step forward, then pulled out a seat at the table, directly across from her. "What have you learned that has defeated you?"

She lifted wide eyes to him. "You would dare speak to me in such a tone?"

He tilted his head. "If you wish to be spoken to like a queen, you should act like one."

Her eyes widened further. He knew he was risking life and limb in antagonizing her, but he saw no other choice. He needed her help.

To his surprise, she sighed, then produced a slip of paper

in her hand, as if by magic. Slowly, she set it down and pushed it across the table.

Óengus fought to hide his anticipation as he retrieved the paper and lifted it from the table. It read:

You have broken the treaty. Consider this your cordial invitation to the battle at Garenoch. Come, so that your people might perish with dignity.

Frowning, he set the paper back on the table. "What does it mean?"

"It means," she said tiredly, "that the Cavari believe they will return to their full power, if they have not already. It means that Finnur will be their queen in truth. They travel toward Garenoch, whether to take the burgh, or ally themselves with the human queen, it does not matter. Together with Finnur and my mother's shroud, they will be unstoppable. May the gods have mercy on any who would dare stand in their way."

"And what of this treaty?" he pressed.

She placed her head back in her hands. "Centuries ago, they tricked me. I wanted only to save my people, so I agreed to limit my magic. Little did I know they would use the agreement to force me into my long slumber. Because of that, my brave Aos Sí faded away. All but the lesser Faie became a thing of myth."

"*That* was what ended the Faie War?" he balked.

She nodded. "The lesser Faie live off the magic of the land, but greater beings must have a source of power."

"But why?" he questioned. "Why would the Cavari care to limit you?"

"They seek only power," she muttered. "And they shall have it. None will stand against them at their full strength, with their queen wearing my mother's shroud."

He stared at her for a long while, committing everything she'd said to memory. He now knew a history most would never comprehend.

Eventually, she lifted her gaze once more. "Was there something else, Gray Lord?"

"Yes," he answered, meeting her glittering eyes. "I want you to rally your warriors to fight."

She glared at him, but with little malice. She simply seemed . . . tired. "To what end? Without my mother's shroud, or an ally like the Queen of Wands, I cannot defeat Finnur, not now that she has claimed her true title, and stolen away so many of my Faie."

"You prepare yourself," he advised, rising from his seat, "and I will fetch your shroud."

"Oh?" she questioned, her tone clearly mocking. "And what would you hope to gain? Do not tell me you have fallen in love with me."

Ignoring her comments, he smiled. "All I ask in return is that when the time comes, you kill the sorceress. Kill Keiren Deasmhumhain, and return my shadow."

She stared at him for several seconds, *calculating*, then a small smile crossed her lips, letting him know he'd finally gained her interest. "And how do you intend to steal away the shroud, when not even I could do so?"

He straightened his winter cloak and the sword at his hip, fully prepared to leave right that moment. "You struck at Finnur's physical form, but that is not the way to beat her. To defeat someone like her, you must strike at the heart. She cares deeply for her friends."

Oighear tilted her head. "Use her beloved mortals against her?"

He nodded.

Her smile widened. "You will take my leon gheimhridh. She is far faster than any horse."

Óengus shivered at the thought of the creature, a massive white cat, big enough for riding, but he would not refuse it. He needed to reach Finn while there were still humans nearby to be used against her. If there was anything he'd learned in his time spent watching the tree girl, it was that she was loyal to a fault, and while Óengus respected such qualities, he would also gladly use them to his advantage.

Once the ceremony was finished, Ealasaid, Maarav, and Kai retreated to the shelter of Ealasaid's chamber. She would have preferred to go to bed with her husband, but the duties of a queen never ended. With her growing suspicions about Keiren's true plans, she wanted to meet with Finn before Keiren found out. *If* she found out. Keiren usually made an effort to interact with her frequently, but perhaps she was just tired from her travels. Surely she'd see more of the sorceress tomorrow. There would be questions. *Many* questions.

She wanted to enact her current plan before Keiren could try to stop her. She would attempt to take Kai to the in-between while Maarav watched over them. She wasn't even sure if it could be done, or if they'd be able to locate Finn, but if everything worked, she wanted Kai there. Finn would trust him more than Ealasaid. He could bridge the gap between them. If she wasn't there . . . then perhaps her mother, the woman who looked so much like her, could help.

"Is it really necessary for me to lie on the bed with you," Kai asked, already seated on the mattress as he tugged off his left boot, then his right. Though candles and a roaring fire lit the room, the shadows of night gave the situation an air of intimacy.

"Trust me," Maarav muttered, leaning his back against the closed door, "if there were any other way, I'd be the one in bed with my *wife*."

Ealasaid smirked, her eyes lingering on the extra weapons Maarav had donned to protect them, then advanced toward the bed. "Yes, I'll admit it's not my preference either, but I need to be touching you. It's either that, or we both lie on the floor."

"Fine," Kai sighed, then swung his legs up, settling his head on one of two pillows.

Holding her chin high to bely the fact that she was feeling just as embarrassed as Kai, Ealasaid climbed onto the bed beside him. Lying on her back, she tugged her long blonde curls out from under her, then situated her head on her pillow. She took Kai's hand, holding it tightly.

"What happens if you accidentally let go?" he asked, his voice wary.

She was glad he wasn't looking at her, and therefore couldn't see her startled expression. She'd hoped to at least appear like she knew what she was doing. Keiren hadn't let her go when she brought her to the in-between, but also had not seemed worried about the possibility. Perhaps it had not been a risk since Ealasaid had magic of her own.

"Maarav?" she called out.

A moment later, he appeared beside the bed.

"Could you perhaps bind our hands together?"

He raised a dark brow at her. "Are you marrying him now too?" Despite his quip, he turned to the wardrobe to fetch a length of green ribbon meant for belting one of Ealasaid's dresses. Running the soft ribbon once through his hands, he began binding their wrists together.

Ealasaid met Maarav's eyes as he finished, conveying her worry.

He gave her a wink, then stepped back.

Trying to remain calm, she shut her eyes. "You'll need to do your best to sleep," she instructed Kai. "Hopefully with you this close, I'll be able to take you to the Gray Place with me."

"Might you accidentally take me one of these days?" Maarav asked curiously. "When *I'm* the one sleeping next to you."

She shook her head against her pillow. "I wouldn't try to go if you were lying next to me. You needn't worry. Now be quiet, we are trying to sleep."

Maarav muttered under his breath, but he obeyed. She listened as his footsteps receded to a chair, then the wood creaked as he sat.

It was a good thing she was exhausted, else she never would have been able to sleep in such an odd situation. As it was, weariness soon took her, and when she opened her eyes, she was in a land shrouded with mist.

Kai cursed every god, king, and queen he could think of as he opened his eyes to find himself in a strange land. It had actually worked. Ealasaid had brought him to the Gray Place, and he was conscious for the experience, unlike the last time.

He looked to his left to find Ealasaid standing there, peering around, but not touching him.

"We're no longer holding hands," he observed, "yet I'm still here?"

She turned to look up at him. "Our bodies are still touching, we're only here in mind. As I understand, when you came here before, it was in mind and body. This is more akin to a dream."

He exhaled a sigh of relief. He far preferred to be in this strange land only in his mind.

"We should start searching," she urged. "Hopefully Finn will be here in her dreams, or perhaps someone else . . . " she trailed off. She started walking, leaving Kai with little choice but to follow.

"Someone else?" he questioned as he caught up to her, stepping around low brambles shrouded in mist. It was nighttime in this realm too, making it difficult to see their footing.

Ealasaid nodded distantly, her attention on their surroundings. "I met a woman here the other night who looked almost exactly like Finn, except with long brown hair, and more angular features. She claimed to be her mother."

"Ah," he observed, "that would be Móirne. She is indeed Finn's mother. What did she say to you?"

Ealasaid halted in her tracks, then slowly turned toward him, her eyes wide. "You mean you've met her, have you met the other Cavari?"

Kai raised a brow at her. "I've personally met only her, but she's one of the good ones as far as I'm concerned. She protected Finn from the Cavari until she could remember who she was."

Ealasaid pursed her lips in thought. After a moment, she asked, "Do you think I can trust what she told me? I was unsure of her motives, especially since what she said was in alignment with what . . . someone else wants."

Kai wasn't quite sure what she was talking about, but he shrugged. "Yes and no. I'd guess that whatever Móirne wants is something that will help Finn, but that might not necessarily be something that will help *you*, and it surely isn't what Finn actually *wants*."

"I thought I sensed you here," a voice said from behind them.

Kai turned. "Ah," he observed, looking Móirne up and down, "we were just talking about you."

Ealasaid stepped in front of Kai. "What do you want?" she demanded of Móirne.

Móirne smirked at her with a cold, calculating expression they'd likely never see on Finn's face. Without answering, she turned her attention back to Kai. "You have my daughter's blood in your veins. I sensed you. She's very upset that you left. In fact, your shortsightedness may have doomed us all."

"What do you mean?" he hissed, stepping around Ealasaid. He'd left to *save* Finn.

Móirne's shoulders slumped with a heavy sigh. "Truly, you mortals are tiresome. As her *friend*, you should have seen that she was teetering on the brink as it was. You and your other companions served to keep her humanity in place. Without you, she is too susceptible to her magical nature. It will overcome her, making her as she once was."

Kai shook his head in disbelief. "She was going to give me another part of her immortality. I could not let her weaken herself, and she still has other humans near her."

Móirne shook her head. "The others have departed. She has only Iseult, her last remaining link to the world of man. Can you not understand that you would have given her as much as she would have given you. Humanity in exchange for immortality?" Her blue eyes beseeched him to understand.

His heart sank. He'd never considered that humanity could be *good* for Finn. He'd considered it a weakness, nothing more.

"What does any of this have to do with what you told me to do?" Ealasaid interrupted. "We came here in hopes of finding Finn, of ending this feud, and we end up with you, *again*."

Móirne snorted. "You are too late. The Oak Queen goes to war. Not against you, fortunately. She hopes to save you both, and it will be her undoing."

"Can you bring her here?" Kai asked, desperation constricting his chest. "If we could speak with her—"

Móirne shook her head. "It will do you no good. Her mind is made up to save you all." She turned her attention to Ealasaid. "I will at least offer you a warning, for other messengers may not arrive in time. An army of men is on the march. They intend to destroy you. I would prepare your mages, because Finnur and her Faie will not reach you before they do."

"An army?" Ealasaid hissed. "An Fiach?"

Móirne nodded. "I imagine your scouts will be reporting to you soon enough. They likely formed far to the west, in Sormyr, to escape your notice."

"We need to get to Finn," Kai muttered in disbelief.

Móirne shook her head. "I told you, it will do no good. She will find you soon enough. For now, I must go before my people realize with whom I meet."

"Wait," Ealasaid demanded. "First tell me why you want to break the barrier to the in-between."

"A mother would do much for her daughter," she replied as she turned away. "Especially having failed her once before." She started walking, then faded from sight.

Kai watched her go, his mind racing. He needed to speak with Finn, to tell her that Ealasaid was firmly on her side. That *he* was still on her side. He'd left to protect her, not to push her into joining the war.

He'd almost forgotten about Ealasaid standing beside him until she spoke. "We need to wake up and warn my people that war is upon us. An army of men can only mean An Fiach. They may have been unprepared last time, but now they're well aware of what they face. They would not march upon us if they did not think they could win."

Kai's entire body was tense. He felt prepared to snap any

moment. He'd gone to Garenoch to help Finn, and now he would be trapped in the middle of a war of which he should have no part. He was no mage, nor was he entirely human.

He would have liked to flee the moment he awoke, but he could not. He could not run when Finn was coming right toward him, with an army of Faie at her heels.

CHAPTER NINE

*A*nna, Eywen, Bedelia, and Àed stood on the road leading to the newly constructed gates of Garenoch, their horses steaming in the cold air from the arduous ride. They'd had to press on despite weariness to reach the burgh before the army of men.

Peering at the burgh, Anna felt hollow. They hadn't seen any signs of Kai, nor had the Pixies. He might be within the burgh, but she doubted it. Now she was here with no purpose, and Eywen would need to continue on his own.

"Do you think she's in there?" Bedelia asked cryptically, staring down the road toward the gates.

"I dinnae know, lass," Àed replied, seeming to know to whom she referred.

Anna turned away from them, not particularly caring what they were talking about. Instead, she looked up at Eywen.

"Are you sure?" she asked.

With a small smile, he nodded. His black hair fell

forward to obscure half his face. "I will not deliberately take you into the realm of the Snow Queen and the Aos Sí. I will not risk it. You should stay here. I will try to return with help before An Fiach arrives."

Though she was standing utterly still, her heart was racing. She didn't quite understand the emotions he had awoken in her, but she was reluctant to let them go. Reluctant to let *him* go.

"Promise me," she began, her voice quivering, "promise me you *will* return. I feel like if you leave now, I will never see you again."

Holding his reins in one hand, he used the other to pull her against his chest. She tensed, uncomfortable with Bedelia and Àed so near, then forced herself to relax into his partial embrace.

"You are a Gray Lady of Clan Liath," Eywen muttered above her. "If I am unable to return, I have faith that you will find me."

She pulled away enough to look up at him. "You bet your hind end I'll find you, then I'll wallop you for not returning on your own."

He smiled, then kissed her forehead. "Go to the burgh with your friends," he murmured. "Perhaps there you will find Kai. If the threat of An Fiach appears too great, slip through the woods and back to Finnur's fortress."

She nodded, then pulled away, refusing the cry. He was right, if he did not return, she would find him. She felt quite certain she could track his energy to the ends of the earth.

His fingers stroked through her hair, lingering a moment, then he turned away. He gracefully mounted his horse, gave her a final wave, then galloped off toward the Snow Queen's domain.

A hand alighted on Anna's shoulder, drawing her gaze away from Eywen's fast-shrinking form.

"You'll see him again," Bedelia comforted.

Anna glared at her. "Who says I want to?" she snapped, then stalked away, leading her horse behind her.

She held her breath as she picked up her pace, unwilling to allow Àed or Bedelia to see the tears she wiped from her eyes.

Bedelia waited a moment before starting forward, giving Anna the space she so clearly desired. She wasn't offended by her behavior. In fact, she knew the sort of woman Anna was all too well. She was like Keiren in many ways. She'd cut out her own heart before allowing anyone to learn she had one to begin with.

Bedelia glanced at Àed, leading his horse silently beside her. He too knew what kind of woman Keiren was, yet he thought they could save her. They were perhaps the only two people Keiren had ever loved, besides her mother. While her mother's death had been accidental, what she'd done to her father had been entirely intentional. What she'd done to *her* . . . she shook her head, unwilling to dwell on it. She would never love Keiren again, but she felt it her duty to prevent her from hurting anyone else, especially a sweet girl like Ealasaid.

She turned her gaze forward, watching as Anna reached the gates ahead of them. She seemed to be speaking to the guards atop the wall, though Bedelia was too far away to make out what was said. After a moment of conversation, Anna began gesturing angrily at them. A few choice expletives caught on the wind to be carried back to Bedelia's ears.

"She willnae be gettin' into the burgh speakin' like that," Àed grumbled. "Fool girl will get us all locked out."

By the time they caught up to Anna, she'd turned her back to the gate. Her face was beet red with anger.

Bedelia reached her, careful to keep her expression impassive. "What did they say?"

Anna pouted. "We're too late. They already know about the army headed this way. No one is to come in or out of the burgh."

Bedelia raised an eyebrow at her. "Did you tell them we are friends of Ealasaid? If she has taken charge of Garenoch, surely she could persuade the guards to let us in."

Anna scowled, "I tried to tell them," she hesitated, "though it was after I told them that they should stop trying to wear their backsides as helmets."

It took Bedelia a moment to realize what Anna meant, then she laughed. "Perhaps I should try speaking with them."

She turned away from Anna and looked up to the guards. "Greetings!" she called up to them. "We are close friends of Lady Ealasaid's. I assure you, she will want to see us!"

One of the guards who looked suspiciously like one of Slàine's assassins leaned over the parapet. He stared at her for several seconds, then said, "Wait there a moment! We'll fetch someone to verify your tale!"

Bedelia waved to him, then turned back to Anna, who

crossed her arms and pouted. Àed stared at his feet, grumbling to himself.

It was a sad day when Bedelia, a seasoned warrior more accustomed to killing than social niceties, was the most pleasant companion of the group.

Before long, the gates creaked open just enough for one person to fit through. A black-cowled man stepped out, followed by Maarav. It took Bedelia a moment to realize the black-cowled man was Kai, not one of the assassins who usually wore such a head-covering.

Bedelia watched as Anna blinked at Kai in surprise. Her expression went from excitement, to anger. With a growl, she marched right up to Kai and slapped him across the face, the action dulled by his protective fabric.

"What was that for!" he exclaimed, lifting a hand to his face and stepping back.

"For running off like a fool!" Anna snarled.

Bedelia was about to intervene, but Maarav stepped forward instead. "Not that I'm not thrilled to see you all, but let us retreat within the burgh. The mages are preparing for war."

Bedelia exhaled a sigh of relief as Maarav gestured to the men at the gates, then escorted them inside.

Kai sidled up to her, avoiding Anna as Maarav led them down the wide dirt road leading into town. "What are you doing here?" he muttered, darting his gaze around. His eyes were red-rimmed, and what she could see of his face was unnaturally pale.

She glanced to Anna, very intentionally ignoring them both, then back to Kai. "Anna came to find you," she explained. "Àed and I came to find . . . someone else."

"Keiren?" Kai questioned. "You're welcome to her. That cursed sorceress seems to be a thorn in everyone's side."

Bedelia blinked at him in surprise, stumbling, then jumping out of the way before her horse could step on her.

Kai watched her curiously as she regained her composure. "I'm not that *dense*," he chided. "If you weren't sent here by Finn to speak with Ealasaid, I can see only one other reason why you'd come."

Bedelia let out a shaky breath. "Yes," she admitted, "Àed and I would like to speak with her. We—" she hesitated. "We understand her motives more than most."

Kai snorted. "At least someone does."

They spent the rest of the walk in silence, though Bedelia was burning with questions. Instead of asking them, she occupied herself with observing the rest of the burgh as they passed through. It had changed a great deal since they'd left. The once somber main street was now decorated with freshly constructed buildings, and the population seemed to have tripled. Whereas once the townsfolk would have mostly had the tanned skin and sandy hair of the South, now there were many with the red and white-blond hair of the Northeast, and some with the black hair and paler complexions of the Northwest.

Eventually, they reached a second pair of gates, leading to the estate at the southern end of the burgh. Maarav once again gestured up to the guards, and was admitted without question.

They walked through the gates into an expansive grassy courtyard, dotted with guards, assassins, and other less conspicuous forms hurrying to and fro.

"I'm afraid you've come at a bad time as we're about to

be attacked," Maarav explained to the group as they walked across the center of the courtyard. "Though I can show you a way out into the forest bordering the burgh if you'd like to flee during the attack."

Having never been one to flee during an attack, Bedelia stiffened, then had to remind herself that wasn't why they were there. They were there to see Keiren, a fate far more frightening than battle.

Anna and Kai began quietly arguing amongst themselves as two men came and took their three horses away. Seeming to grow quite agitated, Kai took hold of Anna's sleeve and dragged her off toward the western side of the estate.

Left with just Maarav and Àed, Bedelia turned her attention to the former. "While I would love to see Ealasaid, I must admit why we came here. We would like to speak with Keiren."

"Oh?" Maarav questioned. "Would you first care to share any valuable information on our jolly sorceress?"

Bedelia eyed him coolly. *Of course* he'd want something in return for escorting them. He was Maarav, after all. She'd had dealings with him long before either of them had met Finn.

Maarav raised his hands in surrender with a laugh. "Calm down, huntress, I'll escort you to her chamber, then I'll have to be off. I hope you'll at least stay for an evening meal so Ealasaid might see you."

She watched in shock as he turned and led the way, then glanced over to Àed, who'd been observing the whole scene none-too-curiously.

"Ye better follow, lass," he grumbled, nodding toward Maarav's back.

With a quick nod, she followed. It seemed Maarav had changed for the better. She could only hope the same could be said for Keiren.

Maarav led them around the main estate, then through a massive garden in the back, eventually leading to one of the many outbuildings. Climbing a set of exterior stone stairs to the second floor, they entered through a heavy wooden door into a long hall. No one bothered them along the way, except for the occasional wave of greeting to Maarav. They all seemed to trust that he would not bring dangerous guests into the estate.

Bedelia felt as if she were walking in slow motion down the long hall toward Keiren's room. When she'd escaped from Keiren's fortress in the marshlands, she'd been thinking only of survival, not the next time she'd see her ex-lover. Keiren had finally confided in her about her mission to free her mother from the in-between, and Bedelia had thrown it in her face by running away.

Of course, Keiren had taken her against her will. She couldn't really blame her for running . . . though she undoubtedly would.

They reached a heavy wooden door at the end of the hall. Bedelia glanced at Àed, wondering if he was as nervous as she, or as *angry*. While Keiren had locked her away in a room with a cushy bed, he had been rotting in a barred cell with no comforts and little food.

Maarav knocked on the door, then waited for a response.

Nothing.

He knocked again.

When he was once again met with silence, he turned

toward them with a shrug. "I was not alerted of her departure, but she tends to come and go as she pleases."

Muttering to himself, Àed skirted past Maarav and pushed on the door handle. The door swung inward freely, and he did not wait before barging inside.

With a deep breath, Bedelia aimed an apologetic look at Maarav, then followed.

The room inside was clean and sparse. Just a bed piled high with blankets and pillows, a wardrobe, a washbasin, a cushy chair, and a floor-length mirror. Spotting something white on the burgundy-draped bed, Bedelia stepped forward while Àed rummaged through the drawers of the wardrobe.

She reached the bed and lifted a perfectly folded note. Ealasaid's name was scrawled on the front of the paper. Before Maarav, who'd stepped into the room with them, could see it, she quickly unfolded the note.

It read:

Urgent business has taken me away. Please forgive my abrupt departure. When you are ready to consider your true options, meet me in the in-between.

Bedelia stared down at the note, wondering what it might mean. What true options? What was she trying to manipulate Ealasaid into doing?

She sensed a presence at her back, then turned to see Maarav hovering over her shoulder, reading the note.

Finished, he sighed. "She wants Ealasaid to help her

destroy the barrier to the in-between. We suspect that has been her intent from the start."

Bedelia lowered the note, then let it flutter to the bed. "Yes," she muttered distantly, "that is indeed her intent, but for reasons other than what you may think."

"Which are?" he questioned.

She turned to face him, then shook her head. "That is a secret I'm unwilling to divulge, though I know my loyalties are displaced in the matter."

He stared at her for a moment, then nodded. "You must be tired. I'll find someone to prepare rooms for you both, though it may not be wise to stay for long with an army on the way. I imagine Kai will see to Anna."

Bedelia nodded her thanks, having already forgotten about Kai and Anna. Kai was likely receiving the tongue-lashing of a lifetime right that moment, especially with Anna already emotional from parting ways with Eywen.

"We should speak further before we rest," she sighed. "There is much we must tell you."

With a nod, Maarav led the way out of the room. At least they were able to carry out Finn's wishes as messengers, even if they were late with the direly needed information, but Bedelia couldn't quite bring herself to care. She'd thought she'd been finished with Keiren many times over, but she realized in that moment that perhaps the struggle had only just begun. She'd told Ealasaid to meet her in the in-between. She knew there would be no other way to find her. She'd never been to the in-between herself, but if Keiren did not return, she'd follow her even there.

Kai darted out of the way as a well-aimed book hurtled through the space where his head had been just seconds before. It was lucky his reflexes had improved, else Anna would have knocked him unconscious by now. He'd taken her to his rooms in hopes of discussing things more calmly, but her ire had only increased with the privacy.

"You mud-brained fool!" she growled, retrieving a pitcher from beside his washbasin and chucking it toward his face.

His hands darted up reflexively to catch the pitcher, but this only seemed to make Anna even *more* angry.

"You should have told me!" she hissed, her face pink with rage. "Instead you ran off like a coward! Until today, I didn't even know if you were alive or dead!"

Another projectile whizzed his way, which he deftly caught and set aside. "And you shouldn't have schemed with Finn to help me," he countered calmly. "I was entitled to make my own choice, and I did the only thing I could think of to keep you women from attacking me and forcing another sliver of Finn's immortality down my throat."

"We would have given you a choice," she snarled, but he'd already noted a moment of hesitation in her ire. There would have been no choice.

He crossed his arms, hoping she would not throw something else while he was unprepared. "There would have been no choice, and as you can see, I'm not *dying*."

Anna looked him up and down. "No, not dying, but you forget I can see more than what meets the eye. You're turning into one of them, one of the Dearg Due."

He rolled his eyes, wishing he felt as confident inside as he was trying to be outside. "Male Dearg Due do not exist, and I highly doubt I can fully turn into one when I was not born that way. Finn's blood likely saved me from the worst of it."

Her shoulders fell as the last of her anger seemed to seep away. She slumped onto his unmade bed. "Perhaps not, but we do not know what you might turn into. Eywen believes the Dair cannot become Dearg Due, and humans turn into rotting thralls."

He shook his head. "Bitten *humans* turn into rotting thralls. I was not only bitten, but given the blood of the Dearg Due to heal me." He waited for her outrage, but she showed none.

"Finn told you everything then," he sighed.

She looked up to steadily meet his gaze, her dark eyes full of judgement. "Yes, and she told me of the changes you were experiencing. And you're still changing, aren't you? Do not lie to me."

He frowned, knowing she'd see through any lie he tried to tell. "Yes," he replied, moving to sit on the bed beside her, their shoulders touching. "At first I was so ill with fever I thought I was going to die, then things began to change. I only felt weak and ill during the day, at night I felt incredible. I've become more agile and quick, even during the day now, though the sun stings my skin and eyes like fire."

She turned her dark eyes to him, her gaze knowing. "Their blood gave you some of their magic, just like Finn's blood. Blood from two different immortal races now runs through your veins."

He nodded. "Yes, and there's nothing I could do about that. All I could do was prevent Finn from weakening herself further in an attempt to help me."

Anna sighed, then leaned her head on his shoulder. "I understand."

Tension he didn't know he'd been holding leaked out of him. It was nice to have a friend simply *understand* . . . finally.

"What will you do when the army arrives?" she questioned tiredly.

He shrugged, keeping the movement small to not push her off his shoulder. "I never intended to stay here in the first place, but Ealasaid and Maarav insisted. Eala managed to take me with her to the Gray Place last night, and Móirne found us there. She believes our departure has doomed Finn, that we were the reason she was holding onto her humanity. She claimed that Finn giving me more of her blood would have been a good thing for us both. So basically, I have messed everything up yet again."

Anna took his hand and gave it a squeeze. "There is still time for things to turn out alright."

He wanted to just believe her, but too much had happened for him to be so naive. "Finn is marching with the Faie to prevent An Fiach from harming Ealasaid. No one knows what Oighear is planning, but I doubt she'll let the opportunity of a battle weakening her enemies pass. As far as I'm concerned, everyone is about to collide, and there's no saying who will live to tell the tale."

She was silent for a moment, then replied, "Eywen is on his way toward Oighear's domain to see if any more Aos Sí would like to declare Finn their new queen, and there are still the Travelers to be concerned about. No one knows what role the Ceàrdaman might hope to play, but I doubt it will be in our favor."

Kai soaked in the additional news. With all that was happening, he hadn't even thought of the Travelers. He gave Anna's hand another squeeze. "At least you're here."

She laughed. "Yes, surely together we can survive this latest disaster?"

He chuckled. "The disaster to end all disasters as far as I'm concerned."

"That it is," she sighed. "That it is."

Kai smiled. While he still felt the end was near for them all, at least he'd go out fighting with his best friend by his side, just like she always had been.

Iseult had sensed someone watching them all day, though he did not think it was Sugn. Sugn had said what he'd needed to say, there was no need for him to spy now. No, someone *else* watched them from within the cover of the dense forest, though he had not alerted Finn of his suspicions. She had enough to worry about.

Sparing a brief glance at her, riding at his side, he turned his gaze outward. They were roughly another day and a half away from Garenoch, judging by the changing trees and vegetation. Far behind them now was the mud and coarse grass of the marshlands, traded in for dense fir trees, brambles, and other deep green foliage.

He sensed something again. Someone was definitely watching, yet he could not spot them. Various Faie flitted and scurried around in the periphery, but it was not their magic he sensed.

"I'll scout ahead," he muttered to Finn. "I'll return shortly."

She nodded, her expression still trapped in some distant thought.

Reluctantly, he urged his horse to a trot and rode away. He hated leaving her alone, but he could admit she could probably take care of herself. If not, she had Loinnir and the surrounding Faie to protect her.

Focusing on his senses, he veered his horse to the right, toward where he'd sensed eyes on them. Seeing nothing out of the ordinary, he rode on. Soon enough he bordered on a distance he no longer felt comfortable traveling from Finn. He halted his horse and scanned the quiet woods. He still sensed a presence, but could see nothing.

"Your senses are better than I'd given you credit for," a female voice purred from behind him.

He tugged his horse's reins to turn toward the woman. "Keiren," he observed.

She arched a red brow at him. "Have we met?"

He eyed her cooly. "Fiery haired woman in the middle of the woods, wearing silks instead of traveling clothes with no horse or provisions. Forgive me for reaching my own conclusions."

She laughed. "Very well, I suppose it's only fair you know who I am."

"What do you want?" he growled. As far as he was concerned, this woman was the enemy.

She began to pace across the dry needles littering the forest floor, though her feet made no sound. "I want to help you."

"By trapping Finn in the in-between?" he questioned,

rage bubbling up at the memory. "Or will you try to steal her immortality in this realm now?"

Keiren stopped her pacing to glare at him. "I gave up on that plan as soon as I learned she'd shared her immortality with another." She looked him up and down, not including his horse in the gesture. "Though I see she did not give it to *you*. What a shame."

Iseult's feet itched to urge his horse forward, past the sorceress and back to Finn. This could merely be a distraction while Keiren had her attacked.

He forced his nerves to still. "Say what you must, then be on your way."

She sighed. "You're far less fun than your brother. As I said before, I want to help you. I've learned that I will personally benefit from Finnur winning this war. I need her to be the surviving queen."

His hands flexed on his reins. "Why?"

Keiren took a step toward him. "Let's just say that I've learned some new information on the prophecy. There are three possible fates for us all. I would like the fate that Finnur would bring about."

"Which is?" he questioned.

"Now, now," she chided. "I cannot tell you everything until you have accepted my help."

He knew this was likely a trick, but what if she really did have information on the prophecy? "Speak your terms," he said evenly.

Keiren smiled. "I want you to arrange for me to speak with Finn the morning after next, but not with the Cavari around. They cannot be trusted."

It rankled that they actually agreed on something. "And

how do I know this is not just another ploy to pull her back into the in-between?"

"You have my word," she offered.

"Not good enough," he growled.

Her cornflower blue eyes narrowed. "Then name *your* terms."

"The only way I can ensure the Cavari are not present is to meet with them myself," he explained. "And I cannot allow you near Finn when I am unsure of your intent. Prove to me that a meeting with you would be to her benefit."

Keiren seemed to think about what he'd said, then smiled. "Tell her to wear the ring Niklas gave her. It will grant her in-between magic, making her even more powerful than she is now. She will have nothing to fear from a meeting with me. If I prove trustworthy, I will find you on the second morning from now. You will not need to seek me out. Now you should run off to find her. The Cavari have moved in during your absence."

Cursing under his breath, he kicked his horse into a gallop, rushing past the sorceress without another word.

Finn glared down at Sugn, walking on foot beside her unicorn with a pleasant smile on his face. He'd shown up mere seconds after Iseult had ridden off, proving he'd been watching all along. She wished Naoki was there to bite him, but she hadn't seen her little dragon for quite some time. Long enough that she was beginning to grow worried.

She pushed thoughts of her lost friend away. "I do not

require an escort," she said for what felt like the hundredth time.

"A queen should not be left unattended," Sugn replied, aiming a wry look at her. "I am simply doing my duty as your loyal subject."

His words dripped with sarcasm, and she knew he was far from loyal, so what was he playing at? Was he there just to irritate her?

"What do you want, Sugn?" she asked tiredly.

"I want to know what my future holds," he replied. "Surely that is not too much to ask. I was a mere ghost in the night for one hundred years because of you. You cannot blame me for fearing such a fate might befall me once more."

"I have no intention of becoming a tree again," she snapped.

"That I believe," he replied. "You seem to have developed a fondness for the world of man. One *man* in particular. Funny, considering what they did to you." He aimed a knowing smile at her, then added, "and what you did to *them*."

"That is the past," she muttered. "It does not concern me now."

"Doesn't it?" he questioned. "Do you no longer care what happened to our daughter?"

"She was never yours," she hissed. "Do not pretend to care for her." Where in the gods was Iseult?

"You know the humans will turn on you eventually," he continued as if she hadn't spoken. "They fear what they can never understand. You will use your power to save them, then they will destroy you. The human queen will drive a dagger straight through your heart."

Her magic suddenly surged through her, making Loinnir prance nervously.

"Finn," Iseult's voice called out.

She turned to see him riding toward her, but her magic was like water rushing across her ears. She had barely even heard his voice. She ached to lash out at Sugn.

Taking a deep breath, she aimed a glare at him instead.

Unfazed, Sugn flicked his gaze to Iseult as he reached them, then back to Finn. "Or perhaps *he'll* kill you first," he whispered. "Who wouldn't want to avenge their kin against a monster like you?"

Iseult's horse stomped between Loinnir and Sugn. All Finn could see was his back, but she knew the sort of gaze Iseult now aimed at Sugn.

With a laugh, Sugn turned and walked off.

Iseult turned his attention to her. "Are you well?"

She fought the tears stinging her eyes. Her magic still thrummed through her body, pushing for release. She was determined to use it for good, to help her friends, even if, perhaps, she did not deserve them.

Iseult leaned over, bridging the gap between their mounts to place his hand on her shoulder. "Let us take a moment to rest."

She shook her head, still fighting tears. "Time is short. We must make it to Garenoch."

"A few minutes will not make a difference," he countered, then dismounted his horse before she could argue.

With his reins looped around his elbow, he loosely held onto her waist to help her down.

She grasped his arms as her feet hit the ground. Her

magic was beginning to rescind into the depths from which it came, and it left her feeling unbearably tired. Perhaps that had been Sugn's intent, just to make her even more miserable.

They stood staring at each other for a moment, then Iseult pulled away, guiding his horse toward a nearby tree.

Finn watched him, then a warm force pushed against her back. She turned to observe Loinnir, poised to nudge her again, as if encouraging her to near Iseult. Suddenly she felt awkward. The wall between her and Iseult had finally toppled down, yet, now she wasn't quite sure how to act.

She stroked Loinnir's nose, then turned her attention to the surrounding woods, wanting to ensure that Sugn had truly gone. The thought of him *watching* her with Iseult made her ill. She stroked the gold locket at her neck, thinking of her daughter, and the sad memories Sugn inspired.

Finished with his horse, Iseult turned to her. "I wanted to ask you about the ring Niklas gave you," he said, surprising her.

She stared at him, trying to determine his intent. "It's in my saddlebag. Whenever I throw it away it ends up back on my finger, so that's the best I could do to part myself with it."

He closed the distance between them. "Why do you think he gave it to you?"

She shook her head. "You know as well as I that the Travelers never divulge their plans, especially Niklas. At times, he has claimed allegiance to me, yet he also helped Keiren trap me in the in-between."

He nodded. "I think this is something we need to figure out. It could be useful."

She watched his gray-green eyes for any hint he might be joking, though he was not the joking type. "You hate the Travelers," she pressed. "I'd think you'd want nothing to do with that ring. Why are you pushing this *now*?"

His expression crumpled, just for a moment, a small chink in his seemingly impenetrable armor. "Finn," he began, extending his hands to gently hold her upper arms. "I don't want you to die. If there is a single straw to grasp that could tip the odds in your favor, can you blame me for grasping at it?"

The muscles in her clenched jaw softened. "Tell me what has happened to make you press this issue now? Is it Sugn?"

He sighed, his gaze flicking around nervously. "In part." He seemed to think for a moment, then sighed again. "Keiren wants to meet with you. I asked her for proof she actually intended to aid you, and she claimed the ring would grant you great power. I didn't want to bring it up at all. I didn't want you to—"

She raised her hand to cut him off. "You met with Keiren?"

He nodded. "I sensed her. That was the only reason I was willing to leave you alone, where Sugn might . . . pester you."

She shook her head, astonished. "What of Àed and Bedelia. They're trying to find her. Has she eluded them?"

"I do not know," he replied. "She asked to meet with you . . . *alone*. Far from prying ears."

Her thoughts slowly caught up with her. "And you

wanted to see if she told the truth about the ring, to see if you could trust her?"

He nodded, his expression unreadable.

"But why?" she pressed. "Why would you want me to meet with her after all she has done?"

His hands dropped from her arms. He sighed, "Because she seems to value your life more than you do."

Her jaw dropped. When she could find the words to speak, she blurted, "You don't know what you're talking about! Of course I value my life."

He shook his head. "You will lose yourself to your magic just to defeat Oighear and An Fiach. You would rather die than have the same fate befall Ealasaid. Everyone else has left us, and I feel I am the only one to ensure your survival, yet I am not a powerful sorceress. Nor am I the Ceàrdaman. If powerful forces want to keep you alive, then I can no longer consider them enemies."

Her heart ached with betrayal. Did he trust her so little? She wanted to argue with him, to tell him she would never be so foolish as to sacrifice herself . . . but . . . could she truly argue? She knew the Cavari would not follow her indefinitely. She knew once she granted them their full magic, they would find a way to kill her without losing it again. Yet, she was willing to do it to save her friends, even if it meant her demise.

"I will meet with Keiren," she breathed, "if only to learn her intent, and encourage her to meet with Bedelia and Àed."

His shoulders slumped in relief. "I will try to arrange for you to have . . . privacy."

She nodded, her chest welling with mixed emotions.

Truly, she would have wanted to meet with Keiren in any circumstance. She wanted to ask her *why*. Why had she tried forcing her to share her immortality? Why had she turned Ealasaid against her? It was time for answers, and she finally felt confident she could persuade Keiren to give them to her.

Though her emotions were still conflicted, she knew something else for sure. Iseult loved her too much to let her make the decisions that needed to be made. He was right, though she desired life, she would gladly sacrifice herself to ensure the safety of those she cared about. She had accepted long ago that the only way to eliminate the Cavari would be to seal away both her magic, and theirs, before they could kill her. She might well die in the process, or she might die in the coming battle, but she would not allow others to die in her stead.

Iseult loved her too much to accept that, and so, she would have to enact her plans without him.

He watched her face as she reached her conclusion, though what his thoughts were, she did not know. She stood up on her toes, leaning her palms against his chest to kiss his cheek.

She would keep him safe, no matter the cost.

CHAPTER TEN

*A*fter an evening meal with Ealasaid and the others, and a long discussion where information had been freely exchanged, Anna had finally been allowed to rest. Unfortunately, sleep had eluded her. She rose with the sun, unable to remain cooped up with her thoughts.

She emerged from her foreign room and headed toward the courtyard to witness preparations. As she entered the grassy expanse, she could not believe how many mages Ealasaid had gathered. Had they been hiding in the country-side all along, or had many experienced a wakening of power once magic returned along with Finn?

She walked through the damp grass, supposing it didn't matter. Things would continue to happen with or without explanation, and as always, she seemed to be caught in the middle. If Kai intended to stay and fight, and wait for Finn, then she would too.

She could also admit, if only to herself, that Kai was not the only reason she remained. This was the first place

Eywen would look for her upon his return, though she knew she shouldn't concern herself with such thoughts. Even if they'd formed some sort of strange bond, he was an immortal Faie warrior, and she was human. At least she wouldn't have to worry about him outliving her since they'd probably both die within the next few days.

She caught sight of a fluffy blonde head of hair and changed her course. While she'd never been close to Ealasaid, a friendly face was better than none.

Ealasaid spotted her as she approached, offering a wave before turning back to her conversation with a dark-haired mage. As Anna reached them, the mage gave her a polite nod, then hurried away.

Ealasaid turned toward her, her face, hair, and heavy purple cloak glistening with morning mist, making it clear she'd been outside since dawn. "My scouts have returned with information on An Fiach's position," she explained before Anna could question her, then turned to walk toward the gates, gesturing for Anna to walk by her side. "They believe they will reach us tomorrow evening, or perhaps the next morning. If you intend to return to Finn, you should leave today."

Anna shook her head, taking a deep breath of rain-scented air. "We're staying here. There's no reason for us to leave when Finn already intends on coming here to protect you from An Fiach."

Anna noted the momentary slump in Ealasaid's shoulders before she forced her back to straighten. "I'm such a fool," she admitted. "I knew how Keiren had used Bedelia, and I allowed her to use me as well. I should have never told Finn to stay away."

Anna shrugged, unsure of why Ealasaid would confide in her of all people. "You cannot be blamed. You are a part of that cursed prophecy, after all. Three queens, one will live, two must die." She waggled her fingers in the air with a flourish. "You're just trying not to die."

Ealasaid stopped walking, turned, and stared up at her.

Anna shifted uncomfortably. *"What?"*

Ealasaid shook her head, a small smile forming on her lips. "Nothing, it's just that no one else has managed to put it so succinctly. I don't want to die, and I don't want my mages to die simply for being what they are. It's quite simple when you think of it that way."

Anna nodded. "Yes, and Finn doesn't want to die, nor does she want any of us to die. Funny, so many of us do not want to die or kill, yet we are all going to war."

Ealasaid sighed, then started walking again. "Sometimes war is needed for change, and it has little to do with a prophecy."

Anna followed at her side, but did not speak. She'd always cared little for war, or the fate of the land at large. As long as she could earn enough coin and have a bit of adventure while she was at it, she didn't care if the rest of the world burned. It made her current situation seem all the more ridiculous.

Ealasaid stopped at the gates, then waved up to a gray-haired woman standing atop the adjoining parapet. It took Anna a moment to realize it was Slàine, the assassin who'd informed them of the prophecy in the first place.

"Surprised to see her still around," Anna muttered as Slàine waved back, then headed toward wall's edge into an internal tower, where stairs led down to the courtyard.

Ealasaid turned to Anna with mischief glittering in her eyes. "Well she's technically my mother by way of marriage now, so I believe I'm stuck with her."

Anna's jaw dropped. She hadn't thought of it that way. Ealasaid, sweet, soft-spoken Ealasaid, had officially married into a guild of ruthless assassins.

Having descended the tower, Slàine reached them. "Nothing new to report," she informed, "the army still marches in our direction. Have you managed any contact with Finnur?"

Anna watched the conversation curiously, surprised Slàine would encourage Ealasaid to contact the woman who might mean her end, if the prophecy were to be believed.

Ealasaid shook her head. "No, not yet."

Slàine cast Anna a wary look, then turned back to Ealasaid. "When will you try again? We must know what she plans. I do not want to be surprised during the battle with An Fiach."

Ah, Anna thought, now Slàine's concern made more sense. "I might have a way to contact her," she stated, hoping it would not be a mistake to share information in front of Slàine.

Both women turned their eyes to her.

"The Pixies," she explained. "If I leave the burgh, I may be able to locate a flock. They will carry word to Finn."

Slàine sucked her teeth. "So the Faie truly obey her command?"

Anna nodded, nearly mentioning what Eywen had said about the Faie drawing power from Finn. She bit her tongue. She might be willing to relay such information to Ealasaid, but not in front of Slàine.

"Why didn't Kai mention this sooner?" Ealasaid interjected.

"He wouldn't have known where to find them," she explained. "The Pixies followed Eywen and I here while we searched for Kai so that we might communicate with Finn if need be."

"Eywen?" Slàine questioned suspiciously.

Anna held back. There was no good way of telling Ealasaid she'd . . . *befriended* one of the Aos Sí. Not when others had killed so many of her mages. "A friend," she explained. "He moved on to other business once we reached the burgh."

Seeming to accept her answer, Slàine turned her attention to Ealasaid. "It is your choice on the . . . Pixes," she said like the word was foreign to her tongue, "but I would advise against sharing any of *your* plans with Finn." She turned to Anna, "If the Pixies will report back to you, however, they might be of more use."

"Do it," Ealasaid decided, her gray eyes intent on Anna. "Even if they have no information to share, I'd like to call a truce between Finn and I. Can you go now? I'll find you an escort so the guards do not question you at the gates."

Anna nodded. "I'd like to bring Kai with me. I believe there are some . . . *things*, he'd like to say to Finn."

"I'll go with them," Slàine interrupted, then turned her attention to Anna. "Are you ready? We can fetch Kai on the way."

Anna raised a brow at her. "You're not just going to take us out into the woods and kill us, are you?"

Slàine didn't smile. "Not unless you mean harm toward my new daughter."

Anna's eyes widened. She was a skilled fighter, but she'd seen Slàine in battle. They were at the very least evenly matched.

"I wouldn't touch a hair on her precious head," she assured with a smirk, patting Ealasaid's curls for emphasis.

Ealasaid sighed. "Something tells me I'll regret putting you two together." She turned to Anna. "Please tell Finn I desire to rebuild our friendship. She is welcome here."

"I'll tell her," she assured. She turned to Slàine. "It may take time to locate the Pixies, just so you are aware. You may want to make preparations while I rouse Kai."

Slàine nodded. "My people are properly trained. They will continue battle preparations without me."

Anna had no doubt that was the truth. "In that case, I will try to rouse Kai quickly. We'll meet you at the gates."

Slàine smirked. "I'll come with you, otherwise I'll just be standing around."

Anna sighed, gave a final nod to the clearly worried Ealasaid, then led the way toward the lodgings with Slàine in tow.

Once Ealasaid was out of sight, Anna whispered, "It seems you do not trust me."

Slàine smiled, walking casually at Anna's side. "And do you trust me?"

She frowned. "I suppose not."

Slàine continued to smile. "Then we're even, you and I. So show me these Pixies, show me that you do not mean to betray Ealasaid, and I'll make sure you do not die in the battle to come."

Anna's face reddened at the subtle threat. She resisted a clever retort. Slàine did command the assassins after all. It would not be difficult to end Anna's life in the fray of battle. She knew when situations warranted caution, and this was one of them. Fortunately, she had no intent of betraying Ealasaid, at least not currently. Now, if it came to choosing between Eala and Kai, or Eywen, or even Finn, well, then she and Slàine might have some issues to work out.

———

Óengus sat in an expansive field, halfway between Oighear's domain and Finnur's. He ate a fresh apple he'd plucked from a nearby orchard, though the fruit was small and bitter, a testament to the poor harvest this season.

Beside him waited the leon gheimhridh, Oihear's prized mount, who had indeed carried him faster than any horse ever could. He'd be able to reach Finnur the next day, using the creature's instincts to track her.

He moved to take another bite of his apple, then something thrummed in his satchel. Curious, he tossed the apple aside, then sifted through his few belongings to find one of two crystals that resided there. Instead of the crystal which linked him to Oighear, like expected, his fingers found the one linking him to Keiren. He withdrew it, then peered down at its translucent surface, thrumming with magical energy.

He lifted it to his lips. "Have you reconsidered Oighear's offer?" he questioned.

"Hardly," Keiren's voice replied.

"Then what do you want?" he growled. Truly, he could not wait for the day when Oighear ended Keiren's miserable existence.

"I want to finally give you that which you seek," her voice answered. "We are very close to having both our wishes fulfilled."

He smiled. So Keiren wanted to help him after all. Unfortunately for her, he preferred the option of Oighear killing her. Of course, if he met with her now, he could learn whatever information she had, then he might try killing her himself.

"Where shall we meet?" he inquired.

He could practically *feel* her gloating smile hovering over the crystal he'd given her. "Continue on your course. I'll find you at dusk." The magic seeped out of the crystal, turning it into a benign object once more.

He turned to find Oighear's leon gheimhridh watching him, as if it had understood every word.

"Do not worry," he said to the beast, "I will not betray your mistress." He chuckled to himself. "Far from it."

Keiren waited right where she knew Óengus would end up. Her sight might fail her when it came to the Ceàrdaman, but mortal men like Óengus were as predictable as they came.

It also did not pass her notice, as she lounged with her back against a large oak tree, that she had not needed to venture far from where she met Iseult. Óengus was coming to offer either Finn or Iseult a deal. She needed to see to it that his plan did not interfere with hers.

She sensed the massive cat-like creature a moment before it appeared, with Óengus atop its back, his silver hair coordinating nicely with the creature's silvery white coat.

She did not rise as the creature scented the air, then turned and stalked toward her. She would not show fear in the face of such a beast, simply because she could not stand granting Óengus the satisfaction.

Reaching her, Óengus smirked, then deftly dismounted the beast.

Finally, Keiren stood, refusing to cast a wary glance at the giant white cat.

"What do you want?" Óengus questioned. "I haven't much time to spare you."

"Off to speak with Finnur?" she questioned. "Don't tell me Oighear actually hopes to make an alliance with *her* now."

Óengus' nearly white eyes did not give his intentions away, not even with the slightest flicker. "What do you want?" he asked again.

She smiled, hoping the expression appeared pleasant and not like a snarl. "I had a visit with one of the Ceàrdaman," she explained, gliding forward to close the distance between them. "I learned some highly interesting information about who must win this war."

Óengus raised a silver brow at her. "Oh? Do continue."

"You see," she smoothly continued, resisting her urge to pace. If she started pacing, he'd know just how agitated she was. "The Travelers and I have been sharing information because we want the same thing. This thing will help you too, though you may not believe me at this point."

His cool expression did not falter. "And why would I trust a single thing the Travelers say?"

"The Travelers cannot lie," she reminded him. *Though I can*, she added in her mind.

He sighed. "Speak your information woman, so that I might be on my way."

"Oighear must win this war," she stated.

"Do you think me such a fool?" he scoffed.

The great cat turned its head toward them at Óengus' tone, blinking glittering blue-gray eyes curiously.

"I do not," she replied, "and that is why I'm telling you this now. Oighear must attack Ealasaid *now*, before she and Finnur can band together. If Finnur reaches Garenoch before Oighear, your beloved Snow Queen will not stand a chance."

He watched her cautiously. "Why tell me this? Why support Ealasaid all this time, only to betray her?"

Keiren rolled her eyes. "I was wrong. I thought Ealasaid would bring about the end I desired, but that will not be the case. It is Oighear who must triumph."

"And what will you gain?" he questioned.

"If Oighear succeeds, the barrier to the in-between will be destroyed," she lied. "I will have what I want, and your shadow will be returned."

He stroked his silver beard in thought. "And all I need to do is get Oighear to Garenoch?"

She nodded, keeping her expression even to hide her inner triumph. If Oighear attacked Ealasaid right after An Fiach, Ealasaid would be killed. Then Finnur, grief-stricken, would surely kill Oighear. Finn had the Cavari and the Faie Queen's shroud. If her companion motivated her to use Niklas' ring, she could not lose.

"I'll think on it," Óengus decided, then added, "That is, of course, after I have ensured that Oighear will not be defeated."

"And how will you do that?" she asked, unable to hide her irritation.

He walked back to Oighear's giant cat and climbed atop its back. "You'll see," he said, just seconds before the cat bounded away.

Keiren scowled after him. She would *see* indeed. If Óengus thought he could somehow ensure Oighear's victory by meeting with Finn, she'd be there to stop him.

She sighed at her own thoughts. *Protecting* Finn. She'd spent all her time hoping to use Finn's immortality to destroy the barrier, when all along the answer had been far more simple. She did not need to threaten Finn, or manipulate her. She simply needed to help her win. To gain her trust enough to make her believe her daughter was only a realm away, waiting for her. Just like Keiren's mother.

She stalked through the trees in the direction Óengus had gone. She'd let him get a head start for now, though his intent was likely to harm Finn in some way, he would not succeed.

When the time came, and Finn needed a savior, *she* would be the one to protect her.

The words of both Sugn and Keiren lay heavy on Iseult's mind as he and Finn shared a fire to ward away the darkness. They sat in silence, deep in their individual thoughts.

Iseult resisted the urge to sigh. If not for Sugn's threat, he might not have listened to Keiren, but now . . . If it was true the ring would grant Finn greater power, he should persuade her to use it. Yet, greater power was a double-edged sword. He knew she struggled enough with what she had. With every passing day, her physical body seemed to be wilting away.

He tensed at a fluttering sound, then relaxed as a Pixie landed on a rotted stump beside Finn. The Pixie's name was Miaella, and she'd become their primary messenger.

"What is it?" Finn asked with a yawn.

"Word from Garenoch, my queen," Miaella buzzed. "Anna and Kai found us in the woods to the west of the burgh, along with another woman."

"Kai?" Finn gasped. "Anna found him?"

The little Pixie nodded, bobbing her frizzy purple hair, its normal vibrancy dulled by the darkness. Iseult watched on silently, wondering what Anna might have to say about how they'd ended up in Garenoch.

"Anna carried a message from Lady Ealasaid," Miaella explained. "She wishes you to join her in Garenoch. She and Kai attempted to find you in the in-between to tell you as much."

Finn whipped her gaze to Iseult, who shrugged. Perhaps it was a good sign, perhaps not.

"She also wishes you to know that Bedelia and Àed are well," Miaella continued. "They made it to Garenoch with Anna."

"And Kai?" Finn asked, relief clear in her tone. "Did he have anything to say?"

Miaella glanced at Iseult, her tiny features tense. She hesitantly turned her attention back to Finn. "He wished for me to relay his message to you, and you alone."

Iseult stood and walked away without Finn needing to ask. Now there would be no chance of stopping her course. Everyone she cared about was in Garenoch, and an army was heading their way. He needed to find Keiren. If she could help keep Finn safe, he had to take that chance.

He stalked into the darkness, thinking over her proposal. If she'd told him the truth, the ring would bring Finn great power, yet something still nagged at him. He could persuade her to wear the ring to protect herself, and they could take Keiren's help, but at what cost? He was beginning to learn that magic always had a price. Those who wielded it often seemed to lose themselves in the process. Had Keiren once been someone entirely different from what she was now? Had Sugn?

He couldn't bear to see Finn warp herself into someone different. He could already see the world chipping away at her kind, giving heart.

Still, he knew it was the only choice to be made. He just hoped she'd actually make it.

It was dark by the time Óengus reached the forest, which was fortunate. He didn't want to risk being spotted by Finnur or Iseult. They were not his quarry. The ones he sought would be a little harder to find.

He dismounted the leon gheimhridh, leaving the massive cat to walk behind him. He knew there were many Faie in the forest surrounding Finnur. They would likely report his presence before long, so he would have to be quick.

He started to sweat despite the icy air. This mission was

his last chance. He didn't believe for a second Keiren actually wanted Oighear to survive. He needed to counteract whatever plan the sorceress had set in motion.

He was just about to remount the leon gheimhridh to ride further from where Finn and Iseult rested, then he saw them in the pale dark. Three cloaked forms standing not twenty paces away, watching him.

"There you are," he commented, feigning bravery. Oighear had told him tales of the Cavari, he knew of what they were capable.

The cloaked forms did not reply. Instead, one lifted its arm.

Óengus felt a ripple of magic. "Wait!" he hissed, sensing he was about to meet his end. "You do not want to kill me. Not until you've heard what I have to say."

The center form stepped forward, then removed its cloak, revealing masculine cheekbones and golden hair, the rest of his features obscured by darkness. "Bold for a mortal," the man said. "Speak, and I will make your death quick. You must be punished for seeking out the Cavari."

So they knew he was searching for them, Óengus thought with a shiver. Perhaps they already knew what he had to say, but it seemed there was little choice now but to say it. "I've come for the Faie Queen's shroud."

The golden haired man walked forward, closing the distance between them.

Óengus resisted the urge to step back out of reach, near the protective leon gheimhridh waiting calmly behind him.

The man's eyes sharpened. "You're aware you're asking the wrong person?" He gestured down to his loosely flowing cloak. "Cleary, I do not have it."

"Clearly," Óengus replied, "else you would have used it to steal magic away from all others."

The man smirked. "Clever, for a mortal, but that still doesn't explain why you sought out our clan, and why you're accompanied by a beast belonging to Oighear the White." He glanced past Óengus to the leon gheimhridh.

"How did you know I was looking for you?" Óengus questioned, since clearly this man did not know *everything*.

The man tilted his head. "We know when we are sought. Now spit out what you have to say before our queen comes to kill you herself."

Óengus snorted. "That girl wouldn't harm a gnat."

Genuine surprise crossed the man's face, exactly what Óengus was going for. "And how do you know anything about our queen?"

"People tend to talk. I tend to listen," he said casually. It was not a lie. He'd spent much time listening to Keiren talk about Finnur. He knew her entire history, and he knew that she'd been *running* from the Cavari. Yet, here they were, calling her *queen*.

"Is that your offer then?" the man asked. "We give you the shroud, and what? You tell us of Finnur's deepest desires? That's hardly an offer. I've known her since she was a girl. I know her in ways no one else *ever* has."

That wasn't what he'd been expecting. She'd been separated from the Cavari for over a century, until now. Perhaps he'd misjudged the situation.

"Now," the man began, stroking his chin in thought, "if you could tell us more of her human influencers, information that might actually be of value to us, then perhaps we might not kill you. Not right away, at least."

Óengus stiffened at the leon gheimhridh's low growl. "And what of the shroud?" he questioned.

The man snorted. "The shroud is of little consequence. Shroud or no, Oighear will be put to rest once again, and there she will remain. Now come," he gestured for Óengus to walk toward the other two cloaked forms, still shielded by their hoods. "We have much to discuss."

His jaw clenched, Óengus followed. He had stepped right into the spider's web. Fortunately, that was exactly where he wanted to be.

Ealasaid shuffled through her wardrobe, searching for the appropriate apparel for battle. She wanted to finish her search before Maarav came to find her. She didn't need him knowing just how nervous and flustered she was, nervous enough to plan her clothing at least a full day in advance. Witnessing her fear, he'd tell her to hide within the estate. Yet, it wasn't fear for her own life that had taken hold.

Tossing a pair of thick wool breeches onto her bed beside a dark blue tunic, she slammed her wardrobe doors shut with a huff, then marched over to her bed. She peered down at an odd lump beneath the mattress, then knelt and lifted up the edge of her blanket, revealing the edge of a black velvet box. She'd nearly forgotten about it in all the excitement.

Holding her breath, she tugged on the box, withdrawing it fully. She glanced at the closed door behind her, then set the box on her knees. She slowly lifted the lid, revealing the wand gifted to her by Clan Solas Na Réaltaí. The imperfect clear gem at the wand's tip stared back at her like a captive eyeball, or at least, that's what it felt like. She hadn't noticed it before, but the wand thrummed with electric currents of magic.

With one trembling hand, she withdrew the wand, setting the box on the floor before standing.

She hefted the wand in her hand, wondering at its purpose. Some queens carried scepters, but the wand was too short for that. Not really thinking about what she was doing, she wrapped her fingers firmly around the jewel-encrusted rod, then sliced it in a well-practiced arc, just like Slàine had taught her with a sword.

Magic tingled down her spine, accompanied by a cadence of thunder outside her window. Lowering the wand to her side, she rushed across the room to peer out into the night. At first she saw only darkness, then lightning cut across the sky, one thundering bolt after another. The wand felt alive in her hand.

Her breath caught in her throat as she watched the lightning. Had she . . . She shook her head. It wasn't possible. She could call lightning, yes, but not like this. Not to light up the entire night sky.

She heaved a sigh of relief as the smell of ozone hit her, seconds later accompanied by the gentle patter of raindrops. She most certainly couldn't call rain. It was just a normal storm, nothing more.

A knock sounded at her door, prompting her to quickly hide the wand within her wardrobe. On her way to the door, she kicked the velvet box beneath her bed. When she finally answered, Maarav waited on the other side.

"Quite a storm," he observed, peering past her toward

her window. He turned his gray-green eyes down to her, lifting one black brow mischievously. "If you're scared, we could hide beneath your blankets."

She scowled at him, but stood aside to let him enter. There was no way she could have caused the storm. It absolutely wasn't possible . . . but she'd be cursed before she was left alone with that wand that night, while the thunder and lightning still raged outside.

CHAPTER ELEVEN

*F*inn watched as Iseult kicked dirt over the remaining embers of their fire. The morning sun shone strongly above them, its warmth pleasant on her already hot cheeks. Not hot from exertion, but anxiety.

She was finally going to meet with Keiren on even ground. She might even find out just why the sorceress has plagued her since her branches rescinded, leaving her naked and alone in a meadow.

Iseult approached her. His short sword hung at his hip, and the hilt of another blade peeked out of his boot. She hoped to the gods he would not have to use them.

He reached out, taking both her arms in his hands. "I will not be far," he assured. "Just far . . . enough."

She nodded. While she was nervous to meet with Keiren, her real fear lay in the fact that Iseult would be endangering himself by serving as distraction to Sugn and the other Cavari. She trusted they'd not kill him, as they would not so brazenly incur her wrath, but there were other ways to harm. Insidious ways to plant the idea in Iseult's mind that she was a monster, and would turn on him eventually.

In her past lifetime, that was exactly what she had become, but she would not let it happen again. She was different now, wiser.

Their eyes met, a silent exchange of words that needn't be spoken. Then he pulled away. She watched him retreat, trying not to focus on the desperation constricting her chest. She'd need her energy for her meeting with Keiren.

Once he was out of sight, she sat crosslegged in the dry grass, her breeches already too dirty for her to care about soiling them further. Iseult's horse snuffled behind her, clearly displeased to be tethered to a tree while Loinnir was allowed to graze freely.

She turned her gaze over her shoulder, searching for the unicorn, then relaxed upon spotting her just a few paces away. Perhaps she relied too heavily on the beast for a sense of security, but there was no arguing with the fact that the unicorn's presence cut her nerves in half.

She turned forward again, wondering how long she'd need to wait. Keiren had informed Iseult that she would find them two mornings after she'd made her offer. This was that morning, but she felt doubtful Keiren would actually show. Perhaps it was all just a scheme to isolate Iseult amongst the Cavari. Perhaps Keiren was working with *them*.

Her heart suddenly pounding, she stood, prepared to race off after them.

"Have you changed your mind so quickly?" a woman's voice called out.

Finn whipped her head around, peering in the direction of the voice.

Keiren stepped out of the trees on the opposite side of their campsite. She wore black today, the silky fabric hugging her tall, willowy frame provocatively. Her crimson hair fell in glossy tendrils across the shoulders of her fine dress.

Finn suddenly wished she had dressed for the meeting, though she had little else to wear. She at least could have combed her hair and donned clean breeches.

"No," she replied. "I have not changed my mind. I wish to know why you have plagued me so."

Keiren continued her approach, stopping just on the other side of the deadened fire. "And all shall be revealed," she said with a smirk. "Even my foolishness at not realizing that my destiny awaited with you all along."

Finn tilted her head, waiting for Keiren to continue.

Instead, Keiren glanced at Finn's finger. "I see you decided to wear the ring after all. Wise choice."

She frowned, once again wondering if the ring was another trick, and wouldn't actually make her magic stronger. Iseult had insisted she wear it, to protect herself in case Keiren attacked her.

"I'll wear what I please," she said out loud. "Now tell me what you mean about your destiny. What end did you hope to achieve with all your scheming?"

Keiren seated herself upon a fallen log, the movement somehow graceful despite the constricting layers of her gown. She gestured for Finn to sit . . . in the dirt.

Scowling, she crossed her arms and remained standing.

Keiren sighed. "I was born with many gifts, but my

strongest is my *sight*. I can sense hidden intentions, and can sometimes see what will come to pass. I knew you would be returning to this land, but could see little else."

Her expression softening, Finn nodded for her to continue.

Keiren shifted, searching for a more comfortable position. "An immortal being had not been seen in this land for many, *many* years, except, perhaps, the Ceàrdaman. For some reason though, I saw you coming. I knew it must be the fate I'd been waiting for."

Sensing a long story was about to ensue, Finn reluctantly sat on a nearby boulder.

"I sought you out," Keiren continued, "but something obscured you from my sight. Because of this, I soon enlisted others. First Bedelia, then Óengus."

The mention of Bedelia made anger flare within her. Keiren had *used* her more than any other. "My mother protected me," Finn said honestly, willing to share a small parcel of information now that Keiren seemed to be doing the same. Of course, it might all be lies, but she didn't think so.

Keiren nodded, accepting the information without comment. "Even though I could not see you, I had to find you. There was a ritual I heard of once, long ago. It takes someone with immortal blood to break the barrier to the in-between."

Finn inhaled sharply through her teeth. "So that is your aim? *Why?*"

Keiren glared at her. "I am not foolish enough to believe Bedelia did not divulge my secrets to you."

She blinked at her. "Secrets? Bedelia said nothing of secrets."

Keiren tilted her head, now seeming to share in Finn's confusion. "I held her captive in the marshlands until she escaped with my father and that filthy Faie-infected sailor to run back to *you*."

Finn shook her head. "Àed told me—" she cut herself off, realizing they had lied to her. Àed hadn't found Bedelia wandering the marshlands. He'd found her within Keiren's fortress, or perhaps it was the other way around. And the sailor . . . could she mean Sativola? Bedelia had claimed no knowledge of his fate.

"She truly did not tell you?" Keiren asked.

She shook her head again, wondering why Bedelia had lied.

Keiren chuckled. "Foolish girl. She should never have been loyal to me from the start." She sighed. "While Bedelia was with me, I confided to her my plan. I want to break the barrier to the in-between to find my dead mother. When I was a child, I cursed my mother. Not on purpose, mind you, but she still died because of it. She is now trapped in the in-between, much like the souls you stole, and much like your daughter."

All of Finn's thoughts came to a crashing halt, like waves breaking on the shore. "What—" she gasped, "what did you say?"

"Your daughter," Keiren said again as if she weren't currently shattering Finn's heart into a million pieces, "Niklas told me she's there."

Finn shook her head. "That cannot be. She died a natural death, she should have moved on."

Keiren's sad eyes seemed to reflect a measure of Finn's pain. "Great magics always require a price. You cursed the people of Uí Néid because they killed your daughter. Her loss anchored the curse. When their souls fled their bodies for the in-between, hers went with them."

Finn gripped her stomach, nausea coursing through her. Her baby, her little Niamh, she'd . . . cursed her? She fell to her side and vomited in the grass.

Moments later, a cool hand alighted on her shoulder. She tugged away, then blinked through teary eyes to see Keiren hovering over her.

"You're lying," Finn hissed. "It cannot be so."

Keiren stared down at her. "You know the Travelers cannot lie. This is what they told me."

Finn forced her weakened arms to push her up off the ground, away from the mess she'd made. She hunched forward, tucking her knees to her chest. "What exactly did they tell you?"

Keiren sat beside her, tarnishing her silken dress with dirt. "I only recently learned this, mind you, but Niklas confided that he too wants to break the barrier to the in-between. The Ceàrdaman originated there, but curious, came to this land to play with the lives of mortals. When too many of them came through, they left a hole in the barrier, seeping magic into this land. Eventually the hole plugged, and they were trapped here. For centuries they have endeavored to return."

"Then this is all a ruse to trick us into helping them," Finn decided. Niamh couldn't be stuck, she *couldn't*. Finn had been to the in-between many times, but she'd never seen her daughter there.

"I do not believe that to be the case," Keiren said softly.

Overcome with emotion, Finn glared at her. "The Travelers do nothing for others. They have tricked you. If my daughter and your mother were there, we would have *seen* them."

Keiren shook her head. "I believe they are some place those from this realm cannot go. A place where only denizens of the in-between can venture."

Finn took a long, shaky breath. "So if what you say is true, breaking the barrier will release them? It will allow their spirits to move on?"

Keiren nodded. "Or, it will bring them back."

Finn's jaw fell. "You cannot bring back the dead!" she gasped.

Keiren turned her startling blue eyes to her, her face impassive. "Magic can do many things. If a soul exists, flesh can be created around it."

Tears streaked down Finn's face. "As much as I'd like to believe that, I cannot. My daughter is dead."

Keiren raised a red brow at her. "You would leave her trapped then? I have underestimated your compassion."

Finn shook her head. "No, if she is there, I will free her, but only so she can move on. I will free her in the same way I will free Iseult's ancestors. I will use this." She tugged at the ragged white swath of fabric tied around her waist.

Keiren's eyebrows lifted. "The Faie Queen's shroud? It can do many things, but it cannot free souls from the in-between. It is filled with magic of the Faie, magic of *this* realm, not of that one."

Finn's face crumpled. She'd been sure that the shroud

would grant her enough power to free them. It could take magic away, and souls. Could it not return them?

"The only way to free them is to break the barrier," Keiren pressed. "What you do with their souls after that is up to you. They are anchored to this land by your curse, and my mother by mine, yet because they are dead, they are in the in-between. Normal spirits would move on, but they cannot. The only way to sever that anchor is to break the barrier."

"I will think on this," Finn breathed, surprised at her words. This was what the Travelers wanted, what Keiren wanted. Both were her enemies, but were they truly? Her thoughts darted to Branwen. Niklas had sent her to Finn for a reason. She'd need Branwen's in-between energy to break the barrier, but she hadn't seen her in days.

"What is it?" Keiren asked.

"I have lost the wraith Niklas sent me," she sighed. "I could not break the barrier, even if I wanted to."

"There are other ways," Keiren assured. "I know the ritual, I just need you to perform it. Plus, you have this." She tapped the ring on Finn's finger. "It is a relic of the in-between. It can serve as a connection."

Finn was barely able to nod. She felt utterly numb. She wanted to break the barrier right that minute, but, "I have to make it to Garenoch first. An Fiach will attack there. They may need my help."

"You will aid Ealasaid, even after she turned you away?" Keiren questioned.

Finn glared at her. "Do not think me naive enough to believe she reached that point on her own. I seem to recall *you* standing at her side when we met in the in-between."

Keiren had the grace to blush. "Yes, forgive me, I'd hoped to use her as a pawn against you, to force you to break the barrier. Little did I know, I simply could have asked."

Finn snorted, still feeling numb. "Yes, your manipulations were for naught. Now you'll have to feel quite uncomfortable when you help me protect Garenoch."

Keiren leaned away from her. "You cannot be serious," she balked. "Ealasaid wants nothing to do with me. She doesn't trust me."

"And why should she?" Finn questioned. "You just openly admitted you were using her to manipulate me. You owe her an apology, at the very least."

Keiren blinked at her. "An apology? Most certainly not."

"Oh most certainly," Finn argued. "We are all going to help each other, it is only by standing together that we may survive."

Keiren primly plucked at her skirts, though the effort was in vain, as it only shifted more dirt onto them. "And what of the prophecy? You know both you and she cannot survive."

"If that is truly the case, then it shall be her," Finn sighed, and she meant it. She knew Iseult would try to stop her, but he could not. She would free her daughter, and they would both move on together. It would be as it should have been, over a century ago, if that was the only way.

Keiren shook her head. "No, you have to be the remaining queen if the barrier is to be broken."

Finn furrowed her brow. "Is there something else you're not telling me?"

Keiren scowled. "Niklas claims that the barrier will be broken once you are the remaining queen. If Ealasaid survives, she will start an even larger war to protect the mages. If Oighear lives, she will wrap the land in eternal winter."

Finn stood, having heard enough. She still felt ill, and not entirely present in her body, but she knew she must hold herself together for just a little while longer. "I'll prove the Travelers wrong," she decided. "I will help Ealasaid, then I will break the barrier, even if it kills me."

Still seated on the ground, Keiren turned wide eyes up to her. "You know, I can finally see why so many follow you. You truly put their lives before your own. Perhaps you do deserve to be queen of all the land."

"I do not want to be queen," Finn muttered. "I only want to right the wrongs I committed. I want to ensure the peace and safety of my friends, even if such a fate is not a possible end for me."

Keiren stood, brushing the dirt from her skirts.

"We cannot let you do that," a voice said from behind them, sending a shiver up Finn's spine.

She turned to see what Sugn wanted, then her heart fell to her feet. He was not alone. Sugn held a dagger to Iseult's throat, though Iseult seemed to be barely maintaining consciousness. Beside him stood Óengus.

"How dare you," she growled, stepping toward them. She'd been sure they wouldn't harm him, not when she'd proven she could *destroy* them.

Keiren grabbed her wrist before she could advance. "I'd be cautious, if I were you," she whispered.

Finn halted. Keiren was right. Loinnir stomped her hooves on the ground, but Finn raised a hand to calm her. She could sense the Faie in the surrounding forest too, but she could not call to them. Just one wrong move, and Iseult would die.

"I did not want to believe the mortal," Sugn explained, nodding toward Óengus, "but it seems he spoke true. You will use the power of the Faie Queen's shroud to assist you in breaking the barrier to the in-between. We cannot let that happen, and so, that power must be taken away."

"What do you want?" Finn hissed, her eyes glued to the dagger at Iseult's throat. His eyes had fluttered shut, but Sugn easily held him aloft.

Sugn tilted his head. "Give the shroud to the mortal," he instructed, "and your lover shall live."

Finn clenched her fists. If she gave the shroud away, she might not be able to free her daughter. "And what will he do with it?" she asked evenly.

Sugn smiled. "He will deliver it to Oighear the White. It is hers, after all."

Finn's jaw tightened. "You'll doom us all?"

Sugn smirked. "Hardly. We do not fear the Snow Queen. When you grant us our full power, none shall defeat us. It shall be as it was before. She will tremble in our presence."

She cringed slightly as the dagger pressed into Iseult's flesh, drawing blood. Summoning strength, she shot back, "*We* had the shroud back then. Oighear signed the treaty because she was weakened."

"Yes," Sugn agreed, "but you were just a girl at the time, not the woman you have become. Oighear is losing followers every day. What is a queen without an empire? Let her have the shroud. She'll need it to crush the human queen."

Rage curled within her. First they'd harmed Iseult, now

they would threaten Ealasaid? "But why?" she questioned, her body aching to lash out. "Why not just take the shroud for yourselves? Why even follow me this far if your only intent is to sabotage my plans?"

"This is not sabotage, my dear," he replied. "You do not have the will to kill the human queen, and so we will grant Oighear the power to do it for you. These mortals hold you back. Now give the shroud to the mortal, or I will kill your beloved here and now."

"If you do that, she will kill you," Keiren growled, stepping forward.

Sugn tilted his head. "Yes, but he will still be dead." He turned back to Finn. "And we all know what type of monster she becomes when those she loves are killed."

"What is to stop her from killing you after he is safe?" Keiren pressed.

Sugn grinned. "Without the shroud, she is not strong enough. She will not be able to resist us. To resist what she truly is. We, the Dair, were created to rule over this land, and so we shall."

Finn was surprised when Keiren's hand wrapped around hers, until she realized what the sorceress was doing. She subtly pressed on Finn's green-stoned ring. "I advise you to give them the shroud," she said calmly. "There are other ways to move forward."

Finn took a shaky breath. She was the Oaken Queen, and she still held a powerful relic. She did not need the shroud to end them. She could save Iseult, then stop Oighear when the time came.

"Fine," she agreed, stepping away from Keiren. She

lowered her hands to untie the shroud from her waist. "Take it, but free Iseult first."

Sugn turned to Óengus. "Retrieve the shroud, then step away. I will protect you from her." He turned his gaze back to Finn. "Once you've released the shroud, I will release your lover."

Glancing at the blood trickling down Iseult's neck, she knew she had no choice, despite knowing he would not want her to succumb, not for him.

With trembling hands she unknotted the shroud, then stepped forward as Óengus moved to meet her.

She met his icy gaze as she handed it to him. "Do not run away too quickly, I will be retrieving this from you later."

Óengus smiled. "You shall try."

She turned back to Sugn. "Now let him go."

"With pleasure," Sugn replied. He withdrew the dagger from Iseult's throat, then jammed it violently into his gut.

Everything blurred around Finn as she screamed. Iseult fell to the ground, with Sugn hovering over him, bloody dagger in hand. Finn willed her feet to move toward Iseult.

In an instant, she was at his side. Blood welled from his wound. She tore her shirt off, not even considering it left her bare save for her underpinnings, and held it to his wound. Sugn could well have stabbed her in the back at that moment, but the blow never came.

Keiren focused on Finn's sobbing form, creating a protective barrier around her since the Cavari man still held his knife.

Seeming to sense this, Sugn met her gaze. "Foolish girl, you know little of the matters in which you interfere." He turned and stalked away, clearly never having intended to harm Finn.

Remembering Óengus and the shroud, Keiren scanned the area for him and Oighear's giant cat, which was likely near, but he had fled. She almost debated going after him, but if the man that Finn loved were to die, much more than the shroud would be lost, and her own plans might be thwarted.

With a frustrated growl, she hurried to Finn's side, keeping a watchful eye out for the return of the Cavari.

Deeming the area clear, she knelt beside Finn, looking down at the injured man. If they did not stop the bleeding, the wound would prove fatal.

"I can alter the air around him to slow the bleeding," she explained, "but healing magic is beyond me."

"Do it," Finn ordered.

She shooed Finn away, focusing on the wound. With her mind, she solidified the air around the puncture, placing pressure on it.

She turned to see Finn wipe a bloody hand across her tear-stained cheek. "I can heal him," she gasped desperately. "I've done it once before." Kneeling toward Iseult, she withdrew a blade from her belt.

Realizing her intent, Keiren shook her head. "Your immortality? You cannot! If you share it again, it will weaken you further. This may be exactly what your people want."

"I don't care," Finn growled. She sliced Iseult's limp palm with the dagger, then sliced her own before sealing the wounds against each other. She trembled as she leaned forward to kiss his pale brow.

Keiren could feel the magic pulsing between the pair. Finn had already tainted her immortality once, and now she'd taint it further. Would she even be immortal enough to use the ritual to break the barrier? Would she have enough power without the shroud?

Keiren cursed herself for letting it all happen. If she'd have known Óengus' intent, she would have killed him when they met the previous day.

Now, all she could do was keep pressure on this worthless mortal's wound while all hope of saving her mother left her.

She'd known her life was cursed from a very early age, but this had finally proven it.

Iseult's thoughts were a blur. The last thing he remembered was meeting with Sugn. He'd announced that he'd thought about his plan, and would aid him, if only to keep Finn safe, then things had gone horribly awry, all because of Óengus.

Óengus, somehow miraculously still alive and with the Cavari, had divulged that Keiren was meeting with Finn to sway her on another course.

Then everything had gone black. He might even be dead. All he knew was that he'd failed.

Suddenly his recollection halted, and he was overwhelmed with something like fire coursing through his veins. He gasped, choking on the intake of breath. Managing another painful breath, he sat up.

His eyes fluttered open. Finn was inches from his face, and behind her, Keiren.

"How?" he rasped, then noticed his hand joined with Finn's, and the tired look on her face.

"It was the only way," she replied breathlessly, releasing his hand.

Tendrils of hair floated around her face. He realized distantly they were floating on waves of her magic. It surrounded them both.

"I told you," he groaned, "never to weaken yourself for me." He could feel where the wound had been in his gut, though he was not sure how he'd incurred it. Probably Sugn . . . or Óengus.

He squinted against the brightness of the sun, trying to raise his head to peer around them. "Where are they?" he hissed.

Finn moved to brace him with her shoulder so he could remain partially upright.

It was Keiren who answered, "Gone, for now, and Óengus has the shroud." She glared at him. "I hope your life was worth it."

He realized blearily that Keiren had not betrayed him as he'd originally thought. She'd had no idea that he'd be attacked while she met with Finn.

"It was not," he muttered.

He forced his thudding heart to quiet, focusing on his breathing. Finn had given him a slice of her immortality, just like she had with Kai, weakening herself further. *He* would be the one to cause her demise.

"We must go after Óengus," he growled. "We must regain the shroud."

"The shroud is lost to us for now," Keiren muttered. "Óengus had Oighear's giant cat. Not even I could hope to catch him if he does not wish to be caught."

"Then Sugn," he grumbled, unable to finish his thought.

"Sugn has what he wants too," Keiren finished for him. "Finn has been weakened, both by the loss of the shroud and from saving *you*. She may not be able to defeat the Cavari on her own, and they do not want such a conflict."

Iseult watched as Finn turned wide eyes to her. "Why do you believe that?"

Keiren sighed, rolling her eyes at Finn. "Sugn could have tried to kill you when you ran to Iseult," she pursed her lips, "though I would have protected you, of course. I imagine they simply want you weak enough to control. They believe they can defeat Oighear, even with your powers lessened."

"Oighear," Finn muttered at his side. "I still don't under-stand why they'd give her the shroud. Why not take it for themselves?"

"To kill Ealasaid," Keiren answered. "They know you will not kill her, and they want you to be the remaining queen, to rule over all the land. They know if Oighear kills Eala-said, you will kill Oighear. Or at least, you will try."

Slowly, Iseult regained his composure, though he felt weaker than he ever had before, despite the immortal blood now running through his veins. "If that is the case, we must make for Garenoch at once."

"Yes," Keiren grumbled, "if the Cavari let us. They will likely interfere if we try to save Ealasaid."

"We?" Finn questioned. "You still intend to help?"

Keiren sighed. "What I told you was the truth. I want to

free my mother's soul, and you are still my best hope of doing so."

Iseult watched her, wondering if her motives were genuine. Regardless, he would not turn her away now. It was clear she could better protect Finn than he ever could.

While the thought stung, he was not prideful enough for it to matter.

Sugn returned to the Cavari camp, a triumphant smile on his face. *Everything* was going exactly as planned. The mortal, Óengus, had simply made things a little more convenient. Now Finnur would be weak enough to control. Oighear would be strong enough to defeat the human queen, but not strong enough to defeat Finn, not when her people would be there to support her.

He'd boasted he could replace her, but that was not the case. She'd been born under the correct alignment of the stars. Her return had given them life. If she died while they were in their weakened state, she would take much of their magic with her. He had to force her to return it, but that moment would come in time.

For now, he'd wait while Óengus returned the shroud to Oighear. Finnur would try to reach her friends. Perhaps she'd even make it in time, but with Oighear there, they'd have the war of a lifetime regardless. Finnur would be left with no other choice but to strengthen them, else everyone she loved would die. The human queen could die during the battle, or after, it did not matter, but she *would* die.

Sugn walked through the ranks of the waiting Cavari as

each dropped to their knees before him. Well, all except Móirne, who was already on her knees, bound and gagged. She'd need to remain under heavy guard. She'd been spying on him long enough to learn the truth, that he'd killed his own daughter. She'd been such a weak little thing, unfit to call him *father*. It had been so easy to blame it on the powerless sailors of Uí Néid.

Yes, it had been oh so easy to turn Finnur into a monster over a century ago. He had no doubt he'd be able to do it again, and this time, she would not escape him.

Óengus rode on well into the night, atop the leon gheimhridh. The cool wind whipped his face, carrying him back toward Oighear.

It had all been too easy. He'd persuaded the Cavari to use Iseult against Finn, but they'd been far too eager to accept. Far too eager to allow him to take the shroud. He could understand them wanting to weaken Finn, but to strengthen Oighear? It made no sense. It could not be to simply kill Ealasaid. They could do that themselves.

Leaning forward, close to the leon gheimhridh's soft white fur, he shook his head. The Cavari had faith that Finn could defeat Oighear, even without the shroud. If they had wanted Finn killed, Sugn could have succeeded as she rushed to Iseult. No, they didn't want her dead.

He sat up, signaling the leon gheimhridh to slow. He needed time to think this through. If returning the shroud to Oighear was a trap laid by the Cavari, he could not continue with his plan. He could not risk his only hope at reclaiming his shadow before he died. He could not risk his soul being unable to move on.

The leon gheimhridh slowed to a walk, and Óengus deftly dismounted to stride beside it. He tugged at the shroud he'd tied around his waist, wondering at its power. Would such power be Oighear's and in effect, *his* undoing?

He supposed it could not be enough to dissuade him. Without it, Oighear would likely perish regardless. With it, at least she stood a chance. He could always tell her he suspected the Cavari of duplicity. She would readily believe him. They had been her enemies for centuries.

His resolve strengthening, he walked onward. The Cavari might be laying a trap, so he'd just have to make sure to lay a better one.

As night closed in, Finn lay beside Iseult, near their campfire. For once, he actually seemed to rest. She'd never seen him in so deep a slumber. Even with magical aid, healing such an extensive wound had taken much of his, and *her*, energy. Sugn had not bothered them again, but they would need to remain wary. Keiren remained on watch, and beyond her were the droves of Faie that Finn had called near.

No one would be bothering them that night. Not with the Pixies on watch, and the Trow forming a protective barrier around them. Not with Finn, however weakened, ready to kill any who would dare threaten them again.

She twisted the ring on her finger, sensing a tickle of power from the cool metal. Even weakened, she still had something to give her power that perhaps the Cavari did not know about.

"Do you think we should try to contact Ealasaid?" she questioned. She's already sent word with the Pixies about Oighear, but what if they could not reach anyone within the burgh?

Keiren turned at the sound of her voice, the firelight illuminating half her angular face. "You said you sent your Pixies back to them. What more could you need to say?"

Finn sighed, pulling her bedroll up over her shoulder. "What if they Pixies cannot reach them? They must be warned that Oighear will soon have the shroud. She will be more powerful an adversary now."

"I do not think that should be our primary concern," Keiren replied. "Your people are the ones spinning a web to catch us all. I can see that clearly, though their plans are beyond me. However, they do not fear Oighear possessing the shroud."

"And they don't want us to break the barrier," Finn added. "I wonder why."

Keiren shrugged. "None can say what will happen when it breaks, except perhaps Niklas. If I knew where he was, I would ask him."

"Isn't it strange that he would be the one to bring us together?" Finn questioned distantly, not really expecting an answer.

"Not really strange at all," Keiren muttered. "We all want the same thing."

She watched Keiren's face for several moments. When she did not continue, Finn asked, "Which is?"

With elbow on upward bent knee, and chin in her palm,

Keiren sighed. "To reclaim the last thing that truly felt like home, the thing that landed us on this course to begin with."

"My daughter," Finn observed.

"And my mother," Keiren murmured, then added, "and for Niklas, everything else."

CHAPTER TWELVE

*J*seult forced his eyes open, then winced at the early morning sun. He was wrapped in his bedroll, though he didn't remember getting there.

His mind clearing, he bolted upright. How had he allowed himself such a deep sleep when the Cavari still lurked? His hands reflexively found the wound in his gut, now just a sore lump of scar tissue.

"It's about time," a woman's voice snarled.

His bleary eyes found Keiren sitting on a nearby rock, perusing an ancient tome.

"Thank you for perhaps ruining our chances of conducting my ritual," she added with a quick flip of the page.

He wasn't sure what she was talking about, and he didn't care. "Where is Finn?"

"Speaking with her Pixies," she said tersely.

He forced his weary legs out of his bedroll and stood, though he felt unsteady. How could he have let this happen?

He peered around for Finn, unable to fully focus.

Her gaze still on her book, Keiren pointed a finger behind him.

He turned, finally spotting Finn some distance away. Beside her stood Loinnir, flashes of color around them signaling the presence of Pixies, though he was too far to see them clearly.

Not bothering to thank Keiren for pointing her out—he wouldn't be thanking that cursed sorceress for *anything*—he strode toward Finn.

Seeming to sense him, she turned, her hand resting comfortably on Loinnir's white neck. "Oh good, you're awake," she said breathlessly. "We must hurry. An Fiach is nearly upon the burgh."

"Do you feel well enough to face them?" he questioned, closing the distance between them. He wasn't sure just what toll saving him had taken on her. She couldn't die because of him. He wouldn't let her.

The Pixies buzzed around, watching him curiously. Did they know what had happened?

Finn pushed a long strand of hair behind her ear. She didn't appear any weaker than before. In fact, she seemed somehow more . . . *real*. "I must," she replied. "Ealasaid, Kai, and all the others are there. I will aid them if I can."

"What of the Cavari?" he questioned.

She continued to stroke Loinnir, as if drawing comfort from the animal. "I cannot waste my energy searching for them. They have not returned to bother us, so they must be waiting for me to act. *We'll* be safer in Garenoch too."

"Not with an army heading that way," Keiren scoffed from behind them.

Iseult turned to see her walking their way. Her book was nowhere to be seen.

"We already agreed—" Finn began, but Keiren raised a hand to cut her off.

"Yes, we agreed," Keiren sighed upon reaching them. "We will go to Garenoch, and I will help as I can, then you and I will figure out how to enact *our* plan."

She spared a brief, indecipherable glare for Iseult, then turned back to Finn.

Finn's shoulders rose and fell with a heavy sigh, her fingers absentmindedly stroking her unicorn's mane. "Then we should start moving." Her gaze on Keiren, she asked. "Will you be," she hesitated, glancing at Loinnir, then beyond her to Iseult's mount, "meeting us there?"

Keiren rolled her cornflower blue eyes. "Hardly. I'm not going to leave you unprotected while the Cavari yet lurk. We will travel together."

Finn nodded, seeming relieved. Iseult could admit, if only to himself, that he was relieved too. In his weakened state, he'd do Finn little good if the Cavari attacked.

Keiren turned her attention to Loinnir, then back to Finn. "Will she allow me to ride with you?"

Finn's eyes widened. "Oh, um, I don't think she'd mind . . ."

In the silence that ensued, Keiren smirked. "Now, now, don't look so stunned. I can better protect you if we're touching."

Iseult sighed, unable to argue, and Finn seemed too stunned to do so.

"Well then," Keiren announced, "let us be off. We've a battle to attend."

Ealasaid shifted her weight from foot to foot, feeling uncomfortable with her tight breeches and the leather breastplate over her dark blue tunic, all topped with a cloak to ward away the cold. The breastplate had been a final concession to the demands of both Slàine and Maarav. Ealasaid would stand on the parapet of the outer wall with her archers, but only on the condition that she'd at least take a slight bit of protection from the arrows that might fly back at them.

To her left was Maarav, and to her right stood Sage, neither one armored beyond their simple clothes, Maarav's all done in shades of black. Maarav had a bow in his hands, though he was no skilled archer, just as Ealasaid had a thin sword strapped across her back beneath her cloak, though she was no skilled swordswoman.

"We should see them soon," Sage muttered, his eyes narrowed toward the west where the Sand Road wove along all the way to Sormyr.

Ealasaid's teeth clenched. According to her scouts, the army was massive. They had likely begun gathering forces not long after the last battle in Garenoch, far enough away that Ealasaid's scouts could not see.

She shivered, thinking of the previous battle. While those men had only been partially successful due to Keiren's help, this new force would not need such aid. There were six times as many men marching toward them, if her scouts were to be believed.

As fear settled into her bones, she wished she'd never

ordered Finn to stay away. With Finn there, the entire weight of the battle would not be solely on her shoulders.

"We are well prepared," Maarav comforted, warily watching her strained expression. "We'll send them away before they can even breach the outer wall."

"But how many will die in the process?" she asked. She knew she should be putting on a brave face for those close enough to hear her, but she could not help her dark thoughts.

"We all knew what we risked in joining you," Sage interrupted. "Do not fear for us. If we die, we will die proud of what we are. We will die fighting."

She offered him a weak smile, though his words only made her feel worse. *She* had inspired them to fight. To *die*.

"Look," Maarav pointed west.

She strained her eyes to see what he'd noticed just as shouts erupted from the other end of the wall. An Fiach had been spotted.

Maarav took her hand and squeezed it, drawing her nervous gaze up to his. "No unnecessary risks," he cautioned.

She nodded. "You either."

He smiled. "I love you, wife."

Her heart fluttered at the word. "And I you, husband."

The shouts grew in intensity as the archers and mages dotting the walls put themselves into position. They would all do their best to turn An Fiach back, but in all likelihood they would still breach the other wall.

She reminded herself that they were prepared for that too. There were the assassins waiting within, along with the human guards that had protected the burgh long before Ealasaid came along. There were also more mages, more mages than non-magical humans. They were positioned on nearly every rooftop, and many were in the streets. More still were ready to protect the inner wall of the estate, where those who could not fight had been herded. She'd done the best she could do, now all that was left was to fight for what she believed in.

Kai and Anna both waited in the street within the burgh, ready to fight, though the murky sun stung Kai's eyes despite his black cowl. No one looked at him oddly for wearing it. They'd all become used to the assassins' all black garb, and likely just thought him one of them.

"Are we sure about this?" Anna asked, her dark eyes shifting around them. "Do we truly want to risk ourselves for someone else's cause?"

Kai nodded, though he wasn't entirely sure. Part of him wanted to escape the burgh to find Finn, to make sure his words had reached her. Móirne's warning had not left his mind. If Finn lost her grip on her humanity because of him . . . he shook his head. There was no use thinking about it at this point. If he survived this battle, he would see her soon enough. Shouts had rung out from the walls above, and he could hear the men marching in the distance. He needed to focus on the here and now.

His body tensed, preparing for action. He was so focused, he almost didn't notice the sudden weight on his shoulder until something climbed into his cowl.

"Do not acknowledge me," a voice buzzed in his ear. "I fear what the humans might do if they see me."

"Miaelle?" he questioned, barely moving his lips. He hadn't expected the Pixies' lead scout to return to him in the middle of the burgh.

Anna turned to him, her eyebrow raised.

He held up his hand to stall her forthcoming question.

"Yes, it is I," Miaelle hummed. "My queen wished me to tell you that she is coming. You may share this information as you see fit. She trusts your judgement."

"She is well?" he muttered, barely moving his lips.

Anna scanned his face, then raised both brows, seeming to have spotted Miaelle huddling in his cowl. She fully turned toward Kai, pretending converse with him so his words would not draw attention.

"She is well," Miaelle explained.

"And what of my message?" he pressed, speaking more freely now that it would appear as if he was just speaking to Anna.

"She wished me to tell you that she is stronger than you think," Miaelle replied cryptically. "Now, I must go. Our queen will help you as she can, but the rest of us cannot be seen. The humans would think us attackers. You must know, Oighear may now possess the Faie Queen's shroud. There is no saying how great her magic may be."

Kai nodded, though ice lanced through his gut at the information. "How will you escape without being spotted?"

"I am dressed in black," she explained. "Those who see me will think me a bird." With that, the weight lifted from his shoulder and buzzed upward.

Anna's gaze darted up after Miaelle, then back to Kai. "Well?"

He moved closer to her, leaning in so his words would not be heard. "Finn is coming. She will help as she can, but the Faie will remain hidden."

Anna nodded. "I'd say that's wise. The mages would likely try to kill them."

"Yes," he replied distantly, turning his attention back to the wall and the increasing shouts.

He could see Sage standing beside Maarav and Ealasaid. Sage lifted his arm, and the archers along the parapet readied their bows. The shouts of men could be heard just outside the wall. There was a brief moment of stillness, then the battle began. All Kai could do was wait with bated breath for the gates to fall.

Maarav tensed as Ealasaid raised her arms to the sky, raining lightning like he'd never seen down upon the soldiers below. Though many had already fallen, a group of men had reached the gates with a battering ram. More men shielded those hefting the ram with massive iron shields, deflecting magic and arrows alike.

Maarav stood ready to take an arrow for Ealasaid if need be, but the army was focused primarily on defending themselves while they worked on the gates. It was a sound plan, given they would be more difficult to target once they were amongst Ealasaid's people within the burgh.

The men below shouted orders. The battering ram

swung back, then propelled forward, striking the gates with such force that the wall trembled beneath their feet.

Sage lunged forward, extending his hands to spew flames onto the men battering the gate. A few screamed, but the shields deflected most of the attack.

"They'll break through before long!" one of the archers shouted before loosing an arrow at the unprotected men further back.

Maarav scanned the massive army. The men might not have magic on their side, but they had the numbers, enough to possibly overwhelm the mages within the burgh.

"We should retreat to the estate," he urged, watching Ealasaid as she rained more lighting down upon the men.

She lowered her arms. "We will do more good out here!" He only then noticed the silver wand slung through her belt on her hip, previously hidden beneath her cloak. He recognized it as the wand presented to her by the Ceàrdaman.

She spared a quick glance for him as the gates shook again, accompanied by a loud crack of the massive wooden bar within splintering. If the bar gave way, so would the other latches. An Fiach would be upon them soon.

Noticing his glance, she shouted over the noise, "I do not know what purpose it serves! But I can sense its magic. It might prove useful if the situation grows dire!"

Maarav thought the situation already was dire, but he kept his mouth shut, then flinched as the gates gave way. The men flooded into the burgh. Maarav set his bow aside and reached for his sword, then followed Ealasaid as she darted toward the stairs leading down into the chaos below.

Bedelia's sword collided with the soldier's. The attackers, with their red-crested uniforms, were easy to pick out from the mages and other fighters of the burgh. Their skill was also evident. She'd felled two men, but she was an adept swordswoman. The assassins were an easy match for the soldiers, but the other burghsfolk, those without magic . . . not so much.

Bedelia flinched as a woman screamed beside her, then focused on her opponent, parrying his next swipe before deftly slicing her sword across his belly. He fell with a sickening gurgle. She wiped a splatter of blood from her face, then moved on, finally in her element.

Magics coursed around her as she retreated from the broken gates, knowing she'd do more harm than good there. The mages needed a clear path to hit the men with their magics, keeping them outside the wall, though not entirely.

Something wet hit her cheek, cold instead of warm like blood. She stepped back into an alleyway where the fighting had not yet reached and peered up. *Snow.* Her fingers flexed around her sword. If Oighear attacked now . . .

They could not shrug off the possibility of Oighear waiting for An Fiach to weaken the burgh before she swept in to end them all. According to Ealasaid, she'd used this method before.

Bedelia took a steadying breath. Ealasaid had faced her once and survived. She'd do so again. For now, the focus had to be on defeating An Fiach.

With a final prayer, she darted back into battle, forcing away thoughts of the Aos Sí, unbelievably skilled warriors that had once bested both her and Iseult.

All she could do now was fight, and hope that Finn would come before it was too late.

"Snow!" Ealasaid gasped, pausing at the top of the stairs.

A moment later, she was thrown to the stones of the parapet. Her breath fled from her body painfully, panic coursing through her until she realized it was Maarav on top of her.

"We need to leave the wall," he groaned. "They've focused their archers on the mages."

She would have kissed him in gratitude if she could move, or *breathe*. If it weren't for his lightning fast reflexes, she might have been skewered by an arrow whizzing by.

Before she had fully recovered, Maarav lifted her to her feet and rushed her down the stairs leading down into the burgh below.

"Clear a path!" Maarav hissed, "I'll find you a better vantage point."

Unable to reply, Ealasaid called her lightning, blasting aside the men who'd neared the base of the stairs to cut them off. The brilliant light illuminating snowflakes would have been beautiful if she wasn't on the verge of terror.

The men she'd hit fell aside screaming. She fought back her tears. They were her enemy, but it still hurt her to maim them. Before she could look too closely at the destruction she'd caused, Maarav swept her aside, protecting her with his body as he half-shoved, half-carried her down the nearest alley. All she could do was allow herself to be pushed along. It was utter chaos with such a large battle occurring within the tight quarters of the burgh.

Once relatively safe in the alley, Maarav growled, "You *must* go back to the estate. If Oighear is coming, you need to be ready."

The clang of steel and screams of the dying nearly drowned out his words. She'd thought she'd been ready for this battle, no longer naive to the ways of war, but every scream tore at her heart. She could not hide. Her chest ached with magic, ready to be released.

"No," she hissed, pulling away from him to retreat further down the alley. "If we do not fight An Fiach now, we will stand no chance against the Aos Sí."

An electric spark stung her hand as she retreated. She stopped and looked down, realizing she'd brushed against the wand fastened at her hip. She still didn't know its purpose, or why the Travelers had given it to her, but she'd brought it along in case things grew desperate. As far as she was concerned, they were at that point.

"Ealasaid—" Maarav began.

Before he could finish, she turned and fled toward the back of one of the buildings yet shielding them from the battle. Skidding to halt, she looked both directions, then turned right and ran to a stack of empty crates piled high against a wall. Scanning the crates doubtfully, she gripped the edge of the nearest, which came up to her stomach, and began to pull herself up.

A hand gripped her arm.

She turned frantic eyes back toward Maarav.

He looked at her for several heartbeats, sighed, then put his hands around her waist and boosted her up onto the first crate. He climbed up behind her, then helped her finish her ascent. Soon they both stood on the rooftop, peering at the battle beyond.

"The gates," Maarav gestured. "If you can stop them from coming through, we can overwhelm those already within."

She nodded, then withdrew the wand from her belt. She felt cool air, not against her skin, but *inside* of her. She knew in that moment that she *had* caused that storm outside her window. Something about the wand amplified her power.

Focusing on the broken gates, she called to her magic. She wasn't entirely sure what she was trying to do, she just knew she needed to stop the rest of the army from coming in. The sky grew dark, casting the errant snowflakes in shadow. Lightning shot down in front of the gates. The soldiers coming through screamed. Those nearest to the bolts were thrown aside, their blackened corpses unmoving as they landed.

She fought through tears, still focusing on the opening as the stones sparked from her magic. All at once, her lightning snapped into place, forming an animate grid across the opening.

Realizing what had happened, her mages cheered, then attacked the soldiers now trapped within while the rest of their regiment shouted outside the wall.

Ealasaid lowered the wand. Her hands trembled so violently that it was hard to keep hold of it. She wasn't even sure she *wanted* to. If it weren't for the rapidly increasing snowfall, she would have dropped it to the roof beneath her feet.

"Ealasaid," Maarav said, his hands outstretched, but not quite touching her. "Are you well?"

She nodded, but it was as if she was seeing him through gauze. In that moment, they were not entirely within the same reality.

"Ealasaid!" another voice said from behind them.

She turned to see Kai climbing onto the roof, followed by Anna. Suddenly she snapped back into action. She glanced over her shoulder at the gates, wondering if her magic would now falter, but the lightning held true, keeping the additional men outside.

Reaching them, Kai looked Ealasaid up and down, his gaze shielded by his cowl. Shaking his head, he explained, "Finn is on her way."

Ealasaid heaved a sigh of relief. Once Finn was here to help, she wouldn't need to access the wand's frightening magic. They could work together to protect the burgh. As for the prophecy . . . they could work that out later. For now, they just needed to survive Oighear's attack.

"The Aos Sí!" someone shouted.

Ealasaid whipped her gaze toward the wall where her archers crouched behind the parapet. The shout had come from their direction, so one of them must have spotted the Aos Sí, though her vantage point was too low for her to see herself.

Maarav turned to Kai. "How will we know when Finn arrives?"

Ealasaid watched as Kai shook his head. "Perhaps one of the Pixies will find us. All I know is that she's coming, and that Oighear has the Faie Queen's shroud."

She turned her gaze back to the snowflakes eddying

around those still fighting. She didn't know much about the shroud, except that Finn had labored greatly to obtain it, and that it was a powerful object. Perhaps it even rivaled the wand still grasped in her trembling hand.

The last time she'd faced Oighear the White, their power had been evenly matched. Now the odds had been tipped on both sides, and there was no saying with whom their favor might lay.

Àed stood alone in his daughter's vacated room within the estate. No one had cared to involve him in battle preparations, and that was just how he liked it. He was far too old to care which way any war went. Ealasaid had become a strong woman in her own right. She no longer needed him, nor did Finn.

He stared at the floor-length mirror, sensing the residual magic on its surface. He knew his daughter's gifts well. Just who had she been talking to through the reflective glass?

He thought of his long dead wife, and what she'd want him to do for their troubled girl. Truly, even now, he wasn't sure what he should do. Save everyone from her, or try to save her from herself.

Of course, whatever he intended, he'd have to find her first. For now, he would wait. He knew Finn would come, as would Oighear, and so, Keiren would not be far behind.

He'd waited his whole life to save her, but after seeing the twisted woman she'd become . . . he was no longer sure what that meant.

CHAPTER THIRTEEN

*L*oinnir raced through the trees, just a blur of white amongst the green bows. Finn clung to her reins, leaning low over Loinnir's neck with Keiren a warm weight at her back. Iseult raced his horse at their side, not yet fully recovered, but stubbornly refusing to remain behind.

Finn worried for him, but what could she do? Battle sounds rang out in the distance, and she feared they were already too late.

"Slow down!" Keiren called out. "We do not want to ride in blindly!"

Loinnir obeyed without Finn tugging the reins.

Iseult slowed his horse alongside Loinnir, then stopped. His keen eyes scanned the distance, though trees obscured their view of the burgh. "The battle is well underway," he muttered.

"Head toward the road," Keiren instructed, "but stay near enough the trees should we need to quickly conceal ourselves. If it looks like we cannot reach the gates, I know another way in."

Finn nodded, meeting Iseult's gaze as their mounts resumed a more leisurely pace. With reins yet in hand, she twisted the ring on her finger, hoping Keiren was right about its purpose.

As they reached the edge of the trees, Keiren hissed through her teeth.

Finn did not have to ask why. Snow had begun to coat the road leading toward the burgh. In the distance they could see the walls, and a massive army. Radiant light flickered where the gates should have been, keeping the men back, but they had begun tossing heavy hooks adorned with lengths of rope up toward the parapets. They would scale the walls, despite the arrows and magic raining down upon them in waves.

Finn tore her eyes away from the men, searching for the source of the snow.

"There," Iseult pointed. "Aos Sí."

Her eyes followed his outstretched finger toward where the Sand Road veered north. The snow was denser there, but through it she could see the unusual armor of the Aos Sí. Light glinted dully off artful curves like ocean waves.

"What do we do?" she muttered.

"We must face Oighear," Keiren replied. "Let Ealasaid deal with An Fiach."

Finn began to shake her head, wishing to help her friend more directly, then stopped, sealing her lips into a firm line. Keiren was right. Ealasaid seemed to be handling An Fiach. Oighear was the greater threat to them all.

"How will we find her amongst her soldiers?" she

questioned.

"She will find us," Keiren breathed. "She knows you're here."

Finn glanced over her shoulder to meet her gaze, but Keiren's eyes were closed. She realized she was using her *sight* to seek out Oighear.

She faced forward, scanning the waiting Aos Sí. A massive white cat emerged ahead of them, with Oighear on its back. Her cloak of white feathers rippled in currents of snow. Though she was some distance away, Finn could feel it when Oighear's eyes landed upon her. She spotted Òengus not far behind her, standing with the Aos Sí. She still could not imagine what had motivated him to help the Snow Queen, someone who held little love for mortals, but there he was.

Leaving her men and Òengus further behind, Oighear's cat carried her toward Finn.

Finn steeled her gaze. Without looking back, she said to Keiren, "You must continue on foot. Go into the burgh and find Ealasaid. Tell her to remain behind her walls with her mages. I must face Oighear alone."

"I will not argue," Keiren replied, slipping down from Loinnir's saddle with feline grace.

Finn watched her stalk off into the trees, then turned to Iseult. "Forgive me," she said. She lifted her ring-clad hand, summoning the earth around him and his mount.

"Finn, no!" he growled. He tried to leap away as massive roots shot up around his airborne form, but they quickly ensnared him, pulling him back into the trees. Terrified, his horse sped off into the forest.

She willed the roots to encase him within the forest's

edge, keeping him unseen and safe.

"I must face her alone," she muttered to the now empty space. Her heart ached that she might never see him again, but at least this way, he might survive. If she died, the roots would release him.

She urged Loinnir forward, out onto the Sand Road. Oighear's cat made a direct line toward her. The Aos Sí remained immobile on the northern end of the Sand Road. Finn knew in her bones that Oighear had only brought an army in case she tried to hide. Sending Óengus to steal the shroud had been her invitation to this battle of queens. Because of this, she did not summon forth her Faie. This was not like facing the Cavari or An Fiach. This was *personal*. It would be just she and Oighear.

They neared each other, both on their white mounts, far out of reach of the burgh.

When Oighear had nearly reached her, she climbed down from her cat's back. A glittering tiara rested atop her white tresses, and underneath her feathered cloak was the Faie Queen's shroud, tethered around her slender waist.

Finn dismounted Loinnir and moved forward bravely, gesturing for the unicorn to stay behind. She spun the ring on her finger, the metal slick with sweat from her palms. It would have to be enough.

"I'm surprised you would face me on your own, Finnur," Oighear called out. "And here I came fully prepared for war."

"I am no coward," Finn replied evenly, though her insides trembled with fear.

"Not like the Cavari, then," Oighear hissed. "It is a shame you must die."

They both stopped within ten paces of each other. Finn felt diminished by Oighear's height and flowing white regalia. She resisted the urge to dust her breeches. "I will not be afraid," she muttered under her breath.

Though her muttering was not meant to be heard by Oighear, she replied, "We'll see about that." Her hand shot forth, sending a torrent of ice toward Finn.

The ice hit her, stinging her skin. Drawing on the ring, she summoned just enough magic to protect herself. *This is how it must end,* she thought. *I will not be afraid.*

Thinking of her daughter, she struggled through the current of ice until she stood directly in front of Oighear's outstretched palm.

Oighear's eyes widened as Finn's nearness forced her to lower her arm, ceasing her ineffective magic. "What are you doing?" she hissed. "Fight me!"

"Finn!" a familiar voice called.

Finn cursed under her breath, turning to see Ealasaid running toward her from within the trees, Maarav, Kai, and Anna hot on her heels. Keiren must have fetched them. She was *supposed* to keep them safe within the burgh.

Not thinking, Finn used the distraction to launch herself at Oighear. Her fingers wrapped around the shroud at Oighear's waist as she summoned every shred of power she had. The ring on her finger sang with earth magic.

Oighear struggled, but with Finn clinging to her, should could not strike her with magic.

Finn slipped her arms further around Oighear's waist, gripping the shroud, wrapping them in magic. Oighear's body began to grow cold, stinging Finn where skin touched skin.

Finn held on. Niklas had sent her Branwen to help break the barrier to the in-between, but he'd also given her another option. The ring on her finger was composed of in-between magic, linking her to that realm. She sensed more magic being added to the mix, and realized Oighear's tiara was an artifact of similar origins. She would break the barrier here and now. Perhaps it would kill them both, but her daughter's soul would be freed.

"She's going to use their magic to break the barrier!" Ealasaid shouted, her voice seeming distant.

Finn realized how *not* distant the voice was when a weight thudded into her, then began prying her and Oighear apart. "I will not allow you to do this," Ealasaid growled.

Finn caught sight of something twinkling at Ealasaid's belt seconds before more power surged around them. Reality seemed to shift. There was the pressure of an ocean above them, its massive weight being held by a thin sheet of oiled canvas.

"No!" Oighear screeched, but it was too late. Their combined magic shot upward, seeming to pierce the sky.

All at once, the canvas gave way, and magic came crashing down.

Ealasaid groaned, then opened her eyes. She was flat on her back in a grassy meadow, at the edge of a forest. She sat up, blinking against bright sun. To one side sprawled Oighear, and to the other, Finn. Had this been Keiren's plan all along? When Keiren had suddenly appeared at her side within the burgh, she'd been shocked, but after hearing the usually stoic sorceress hurriedly explain that Finn needed her help, she'd snapped into action. Anna, Kai, and Maarav had refused to stay behind, but where were they now?

Oighear stirred first, grunting as she pushed herself into a seated position. Her feathered cloak and glittering tiara seemed somehow less regal now that her rump was on the ground. Seeming to slowly regain focus, Oighear blinked at her. "What have you done, Queen of Wands?"

Ealasaid's mouth fell open. She was accusing *her*? "I just tried to pry the two of you apart. *I* didn't bring us here."

They both turned to look at Finn as she sat up.

She peered around, her long hair flecked with strands of yellow grass. "The in-between?" Finn questioned. "How are we here? The barrier should have been destroyed."

"You did destroy it," a voice said from behind Ealasaid.

She turned to see a red-haired woman stepping out of the trees with Naoki at her side. The white dragon had nearly doubled in size since Ealasaid had last seen her.

"Branwen?" Finn questioned. "What has happened? How are you here?"

The woman, Branwen, turned honey colored eyes toward Finn. "None of us will be here for long. Your magic destroyed the barrier, but Druantia holds this place together . . . for now."

Ealasaid watched as Finn slowly climbed to her feet, then, realizing her own rump was still on the ground, she quickly did the same. She'd heard mention of Branwen before, though she'd never met her.

Glaring at everyone, Oighear stood.

"Druantia is here?" Finn questioned.

Branwen nodded. "It is by her doing that you have come here. This is the place the dead go before they move on. Sometimes trapped souls come here too."

"What is this nonsense?" Oighear hissed, stepping forward. "Why can I not summon my magic?"

Ealasaid inhaled sharply, then tested her own magic, realizing just then that it had left her.

Branwen cleared her throat. "As I said, this is a realm where only the dead and familiars can enter. This is a neutral place where none hold power. Druantia would like to speak with Finn."

"What about *me*?" Oighear growled, flicking her feathered cloak aside.

Branwen raised a red brow at her. "You've longed to reach the in-between for all this time. This may be your last chance to explore what is left of it."

Ealasaid frowned. "If the barrier is broken, and this is all that remains of the Gray Place, what is happening to those we've left behind?"

"They suffer the consequences of *your* actions," Branwen chided. Turning back to Finn, she held out an arm. "Now come. Time is short."

Ealasaid watched as Finn stepped forward, placing her hand on Naoki's head. "Is this where you've been all this time?" she asked the dragon.

"Naoki brought me here," Branwen explained, somewhat bitterly.

Finn nodded, as if that somehow made sense. She turned to Branwen. "May Ealasaid come with us? I'd rather not leave her with—" she subtly nodded in Oighear's direction.

"I saw that," Oighear grumbled, crossing her white clad

arms. "And if she's going, *I'm* going. I'll not stand idly by while you trap me here."

With a heavy sigh, Finn turned back to Branwen.

Branwen shrugged. "Fine." With that, she turned back toward the forest and walked into the shadows.

Naoki tugged at Finn's tunic, urging her to follow.

With a worried glance at Ealasaid, Finn obeyed.

Ealasaid quickly followed, leaving Oighear to trudge behind them.

Finn wiped her trembling hands on her breeches, nervous to face Druantia, if the Druid Goddess truly dwelt in this place. The last she'd heard from her had been outside the Druid fortress, back in their realm. She would not be surprised if some other phantom had tricked Branwen, keeping her in the realm of the dead.

Regardless, she'd meet this being, if only to learn why they'd been brought there. She followed Branwen as she picked her way through the trees that seemed to go on forever.

She occasionally glanced back at Oighear, just to ensure she wasn't about to drive a dagger into her back, or Ealasaid's. She worried for the health of those they'd left behind too, but there was little she could do about it now. She'd chosen to break the barrier despite the consequences, to free her daughter's soul, and Iseult's. It was odd that the two souls she cherished the most had been trapped together all along.

Eventually they reached a small, shimmering pond.

Branwen approached the water's edge, gesturing for Finn to do the same.

Finn stepped forward, sensing immense power radiating from the pond.

"A true goddess," Oighear muttered behind her, disbelief clear in her tone.

"Yes," a voice burbled from within the water, "we *do* still exist, though our followers have abandoned us."

Finn fidgeted, realizing Druantia was the water itself. She wondered to what followers the goddess referred, as her true followers, the Druids, had not abandoned her. They had been slaughtered for having magic.

"Why have you brought us here?" she questioned.

"I brought *you* here," Druantia corrected. "The other two clung along for the ride. You have destroyed the in-between barrier. This place now exists by my magic alone, though I cannot sustain it indefinitely. You have gone against nature using your magic in such a way," she sighed, "though I cannot say I am surprised."

"You know I had no choice," Finn replied. While she felt guilt for what she had done, if her daughter's soul was freed, she'd do it one hundred times over.

"Yes," Druantia sighed, "your daughter. She is here with me."

Finn's heart seemed to stop beating. Niamh was here? Even now? She'd expected her soul to be freed, but had not hoped she'd actually see her again.

"Where is she?" Finn boldly demanded. "Reveal her to me."

"She will reveal herself if she so chooses," Druantia burbled back.

Finn resisted the urge to kick the water's surface. Someone took her hand. She turned to see Ealasaid standing at her side, sympathy in her gray eyes.

She forced her breathing to slow. Ealasaid's entire family had been slaughtered, and *she* wasn't acting like a spoiled child. If Ealasaid could remain composed, she could too.

"Is—" a hesitant voice began from behind them.

Finn turned to see Oighear waiting several paces away. Unshed tears rimmed her eyes.

She bit her pale lip, then continued, gazing not at Finn, but at the pond, "Is my mother here as well?"

"Your mother was Faie," the pond sighed. "She belonged to the earth, and it is there her soul lives on forever."

Finn watched as glittering tears fell down Oighear's white cheeks. "All along?" she breathed, then hung her head.

"Yes, child," Druantia replied.

Suddenly, Finn understood. Oighear was not so different from her after all. She'd worried for her mother's soul all these years. Yet, unlike Niamh, her mother's soul was never cursed.

"Immortal beings hold memories more dear than mortals," Druantia sighed. "Mortals learn to move on, to let go, because their time is short. Those with longer lives know they have centuries, perhaps longer, to search for a way to erase their pain. To bring back the dead, or at the very least, to learn where their beloved dead have gone."

"Mother?" a small voice questioned.

Finn whipped around, dropping Ealasaid's hand. Her eyes darted across the pond to a small form now standing on the other side. She still wore the white funeral dress she'd been buried in.

Finn fell to her knees, overcome with emotion. "Niamh?" she sobbed in disbelief.

The little girl pushed a golden tendril of hair behind her perfect little ear, just as Finn recalled doing for her each night when she moved to kiss her daughter's cheek.

Feeling hardly capable of standing, Finn forced herself to her feet, then raced around the pond, forgetting about those she left on the other side.

She reached her daughter, then fell back to her knees, wrapping Niamh tightly in her arms. She felt *real*, not a ghost, but her flesh and blood child.

Niamh trembled, then pushed Finn away.

Finn cried, reaching out for her.

Niamh stepped back, shaking her head. "You should not have done what you did, mother. You should not have upset the natural balance, just to free me. Your dragon found me. I think she wanted me to tell you, but I was not strong enough to reach you."

"The child can only venture as far as the meadow's edge," Druantia explained. "The dragon pulled the wraith into this realm, I believe hoping the wraith could explain, not knowing that she would become trapped here as well."

"Yes," Branwen seconded, "once I was brought here, I could not leave. Although now . . . "

The pond sighed heavily. "Yes, child, now that the barrier has been broken, you may return to your realm without death as the consequence."

Shaking away their words, Finn turned back to Niamh. She reached for her again, and this time Niamh allowed her to place her hands gently on her shoulders. "What would you have me do, Niamh?"

"I would have you move on with your life, mother," she answered. "I remain trapped with those you cursed not through the power of your magic, but through the power of your heart. We all remain trapped because you will not release you grief, nor your guilt. Your magic placed us here, but it is not what keeps us here."

Finn trembled, tears streaming freely down her face. "I have done this to you? I have tormented you all this time?"

Niamh shook her head. "Druantia has cared for me here. The others that you trapped . . . they wander. Even now, they are held in place as the rest of the in-between melts into your realm."

Finn turned her glare toward the pond. "You knew she was here, and you did not tell me?" she hissed. She'd encountered Druantia before, the goddess could have saved her so much time . . .

"You made your choice that day," the pond sighed. "It was not my place to sway you."

Finn stifled a shiver. She could not blame the goddess. *She* was the one who'd trapped her daughter here, and now the in-between would be no more, simply because she could not let go.

"You said this place will not hold together indefinitely," she began, her gaze on the pond. "What will happen to Niamh?"

"Once you release her," the pond burbled, "she will be able to move on. But you must let her go. You have upset the natural order enough. The dead must not come back to life."

"Must not?" Finn questioned, "not *cannot*?" Perhaps Keiren had been right all along. She'd thought she'd been prepared to let her daughter go, but when faced with the option . . .

"You would raise yourself to the level of goddess then?" Druantia hissed. "You use your power so that your friends may live, while others must die. *Everyone* loses loved ones. It is the way of life. You think you desire a human life, but your sight is clouded. Humans must deal with their pain. They must move on. They do not have centuries to grieve."

Finn wiped the tears from her cheeks, one hand still on Niamh's shoulder. She peered past the pond to where Ealasaid, Branwen, and Oighear stood with Naoki. The three women were wildly different, yet also, the same.

She turned back to Niamh, laying a gentle kiss on her cheek for the last time. "I only held on because I love you so much," she breathed.

Niamh hugged her. "I know, but you must let go. It is only once you let go, that my soul can someday find its way back to you."

Finn sobbed, sealing her eyes shut as she held tight to her daughter. She had destroyed the natural order searching for her, only to realize that all she had to do was let go, and Niamh would come back to her, whether in this life, or another.

Reluctantly, she loosened her arms and let go. When she opened her eyes, Niamh was gone.

She stood. Her legs trembled, but held. "We must set things right," she stated.

"We must see the prophecy through," Oighear countered from the other side of the pond.

Finn shook her head. "Don't you understand? In-between magic is now part of our land. We are the greatest forces in existence no longer. We are nothing. No more, and no less, than any mortal or Faie in the land."

Oighear's eyes widened. She looked first to Ealasaid, then to Branwen, as if expecting one of them to say otherwise.

Both women shrugged.

"The dragon can return you to your realm," Druantia interrupted.

"And what of you?" Finn asked, turning her gaze down to the pond.

"I am the trees, the earth, and the water flowing across the land," Druantia answered. "Wherever they exist, so do I, in one way or another." The pond went still as the shimmering light on its surface went dark.

Finn looked to the place where Niamh had stood, saying one last silent goodbye to her daughter. Her heart felt torn to shreds, but her work was not done. She would set things right, for Niamh.

Steeling herself, she marched around the pond, then stroked a hand on Naoki's feathered head.

"You will *not* leave me here," Oighear stated.

Finn lifted her free arm toward her. "Then you'd better take my hand."

Ealasaid and Branwen both walked forward without needing to be asked. Each touched Naoki.

Finally, Oighear trudged toward them, then took Finn's hand.

Finn knew she might regret bringing Oighear back with them, but she wouldn't upset the fates any further than she already had. She'd caused enough damage with her selfishness already.

CHAPTER FOURTEEN

*B*edelia's sword hand trembled. She'd backed away from the dead, the fighting now ceased with the rest of An Fiach held back by Ealasaid's lightning barrier. She'd not seen where Ealasaid and the others had gone, but the mages were beginning to grow restless.

Murmurs occasionally cut through the silence. She could see the men outside the wall, but they had frozen too. It seemed all had felt the massive crash of . . . something.

She needed to reach the wall. From there she would be able to see what was happening beyond the burgh.

She was about to head off when she spotted Àed cutting through the muttering crowd toward her, skirting around the corpses at their feet.

"Ye need to come with me," he said upon reaching her. "I know where she is."

She didn't have to ask who *she* was. She followed Àed through the burgh, back toward the estate. He must have found a route of escape there, because she knew whatever was happening outside the burgh, Keiren was likely at the center of it.

***

Anna struggled to right herself. They'd been hit by a wave of . . . something. Something that felt like the in-between, cool and warm all at once.

Finn, Ealasaid, and Oighear had disappeared, but An Fiach still remained by the burgh, and the Aos Sí beyond them. Yet, all fighting had ceased. The soldiers of An Fiach peered around themselves, clearly stunned. They no longer tried to climb the high walls of Garenoch.

Though Anna could hardly see the Aos Sí in the distance, she imagined they were in a similar state.

Stepping up beside her, Maarav rubbed his eyes. "I think they destroyed the barrier to the in-between. It's the only explanation for what just happened. But then, where are they? Where is Ealasaid?"

"Great magic drew them away," Keiren said.

Anna whipped her gaze to Keiren, just as Kai side-stepped away from her.

She supposed she should be grateful that Keiren had found them, revealing Finn was near and needed aid, but she still didn't trust the woman. "But the barrier is in fact destroyed?" she questioned.

Keiren narrowed her eyes toward the road where Finn, Oighear, and Ealasaid had stood. "It has, " she answered, her gaze scanning their surroundings as if searching for something. She shook her head. "We should return to the burgh. An Fiach will not remain stunned for long, and who is to say what the Aos Sí will do without their queen?"

Anna shivered, wondering if Eywen had felt the release of magic wherever he was.

"Look there," Kai pointed, stepping up to her other side.

She followed his gaze west down the Sand Road. White forms swayed in the distance. "Travelers," she grumbled. "What could *they* want?" She hadn't forgotten what Eywen had told her, that someplace far back in her ancestry she might have Faie *or* Traveler blood.

"The Ceàrdaman have achieved their ultimate goal," Keiren stated. "Only time will tell what they will do now that they have been reconnected with the magic of their homeland."

Anna turned to balk at her. "You would have us believe they came from the in-between?"

Keiren's eyes remained on the distant forms. "Believe it, or do not, it does not matter now."

"Well if this is what *they* wanted," Kai interrupted, "perhaps they know where Finn and Ealasaid have gone."

Something moved behind them. Anna whipped around, then groaned.

One of the Trow blinked back at her. "What has happened to our queen?"

She heard the gasps of her companions as they all turned to face the Trow. A Pixie flitted overhead, then a Bucca scrambled near before quickly darting back behind the Trow.

"Get back," Keiren demanded, herding Anna away a

moment before a golden haired man stepped out of the forest.

Anna knew instantly he was Cavari, though now instead of shapeless robes he wore leather breeches, a silken blue tunic, and a golden breastplate. Behind him appeared others dressed in a similar fashion, though she did not see Móirne among them.

"Your queen will return soon," the man explained to the Trow. "Until she does, I, as the leader of her tribe, will guide you."

"What are you doing here?" Anna asked.

At the same time, Keiren growled, "This was what you wanted all along, wasn't it? You *did* want her to break the barrier."

The man snorted. "Hardly. I did not think her capable without the shroud, but I will take advantage as I see fit. I feel my bindings unraveling. With this new magic, we are no longer dependent on Finnur to sustain us. We are free to do as we please. I could never have planned such a perfect fate as this."

Kai stepped around Anna, looking between Keiren and the golden-haired man. "What in the name of the gods is going on?" he demanded.

Keiren's glare remained on the golden haired man. "This man's name is Sugn. He is the leader of the Cavari, who have been restored to their full power."

Anna's body tensed as she took a closer look at the Cavari. They did appear more solid, more *real*. They were terrifying to begin with. What sort of power might they wield *now*?

"Finnur's magics are unraveling," Sugn explained. "*All*

magic is unraveling. All curses. All long-standing treaties. It will be interesting to see who will come to lead in this new world."

Sugn lifted his gaze past them, inciting Anna to glance over her shoulder. The Travelers neared, and An Fiach had resumed their senses enough to be aware of them.

Anna could sense in her bones that what Sugn said was true. Magic was unraveling, the bounds of reality were shifting. With a start, she realized something else. *Her* magic had changed. She could feel in-between magic pulsing around her.

Sugn quirked an eyebrow at her. "One of Clan Liath?" he questioned with a laugh. He glanced at the magic flowing around them, as if he could actually see it, and not just feel it. He turned his gaze back to Anna. "Welcome home, I suppose."

Iseult struggled within his prison. He should have seen this coming. Finn was willing to sacrifice her life, and knew he would die with her if she tried. He'd almost given up, then something had changed. The roots around him grew brittle and weak . . . though they still trapped him entirely.

He shifted his shoulders, barely able to move. Though the roots did not continue to constrict, they had little give. There were so many of them he was left in utter darkness.

Suddenly, the unyielding roots shifted. Iseult froze, focusing his senses on his surroundings. He sensed magic, but not Faie.

The shift happened again, almost as if someone, or *something*, was pushing against the roots.

Light shot through his prison, stinging his eyes. The bonds around him began to loosen, creaking as they gave way. One by one, the roots snapped. When he could move, he climbed the rest of the way out, then hopped to the forest floor, short sword in hand.

Facing him was Loinnir, her glittering horn shining with magic. Had she nullified Finn's magic, or had it been something else?

The unicorn stepped toward him, then bent its front knees.

Not questioning the invitation, Iseult climbed atop the unicorn's back, hoping the beast's presence meant he was not too late.

Finn exhaled as her feet touched down on solid ground. They were back. *Niamh*. She was truly gone now, and she had to let her go.

Her hand still resting atop Naoki's head, she peered past Oighear, Ealasaid, and Branwen, her entire body tense to learn what had transpired while they were away.

Some distance off, the ranks of An Fiach had edged past the burgh, almost as if retreating? She saw the Aos Sí, waiting where Oighear had left them.

"Look," Ealasaid said.

Finn turned.

Behind them, the Ceàrdaman approached. More of them

than she'd ever seen. She recalled Druantia's words, that the Ceàrdaman had been reconnected with their magic. The only question was, what did they plan to do with it?

Oighear inhaled sharply at her side, turning Finn's gaze southeast. *Sugn.* She knew he'd be waiting when she returned. It was time to find out what he truly wanted.

He approached her confidently, not once glancing at the hoard of Ceàrdaman. Behind him were more of the Cavari, more than she'd seen gathered together in a long while, all wearing fine silks and leather.

She glanced at Oighear as she backed away.

"Do not leave us quite yet, Snow Queen," Sugn called out. "We must thank you for undoing Finnur's magic and returning our full power."

"No," Oighear gasped, pure terror in her voice.

"And you as well, Queen of Wands," Sugn said, nodding to Ealasaid as he neared.

"I wasn't planning on going anywhere," Ealasaid said boldly.

Naoki let out a low growl, but held fast at Finn's side.

Finn stepped forward, ready to protect Ealasaid, and even Oighear. "Was this your plan all along? You hoped we'd break the barrier?"

He smirked. "Truly, I had other plans entirely. I'd never hoped to be entirely free of you, but in breaking the barrier, you cut our long standing ties. We no longer need your magic. All I'd hoped to do was drive you mad again with grief, just like before. Of course, you turning into a tree was not the end I'd expected."

"Not what you'd expected?" she questioned. "How could

you have expected anything at all? You could not have predicted our daughter's death, the reason I turned into such a monster."

His eyes widened, then he quickly schooled his expression to cover his gaffe.

It was a vain effort. She should have suspected this sooner. Her daughter's death had given Sugn what he'd wanted, a *strong* queen, willing to decimate entire clans. She took another step forward, rage thrumming through her. She no longer cared that she broken the barrier, that she had freed the Cavari.

She took another staggering step. "Did you know our daughter would die?" she snarled.

The women behind her stood silent, as did the other Cavari, though they did not appear surprised. They had known too. They *all* had known. She focused on Sugn, willing away all else.

He sighed, then met her gaze.

Her entire world came crashing down with the subtle affirmation. She'd hated Sugn. He'd never deserved the title of father, but he couldn't have . . . she shook her head. He didn't just know that her daughter would die. He had—

"Sugn," she began, her voice trembling. "Did you kill my child? Did you kill her and blame the sailors of Uí Néid?"

He sighed again. "I hadn't wanted you to find out this way, but I suppose it doesn't matter now. Now that our full power has been returned, we will not let you take it from us again."

It was all she could do to not fall to her knees. "How could you!" she growled, charging toward him.

He lifted his hand, flicking his wrist toward her feet.

The earth rumbled beneath her. She was airborne for a moment, then landed hard on her side, groaning in pain.

Sucking in an agonizing breath, she called her magic. Roots shot up around Sugn, but the Cavari standing near him lifted their hands, forcing them back into the earth.

With a scream of rage, she forced herself to her feet, slipping on the loose earth below her. She reached for the power of her ring, then nearly screamed again when she realized it was gone. She'd had it while in the in-between, but it must not have traveled back with her.

She summoned her power in spite of her weaknesses, knowing that with mortal blood running through her veins, it might not be enough. She didn't care. She didn't need to beat him, she only needed to take him down with her.

She was about to throw everything she had at Sugn and the other Cavari, then someone took her hand. She felt Ealasaid's magic coursing through her to join with her own.

Someone took her other hand. Cool, icy magic crept up her arm. She turned wide eyes to Oighear.

"Do not think this a truce," the Snow Queen growled, "but they will put me back to sleep again, and my people will cease to exist. I will not allow it."

Finn turned her attention back toward Sugn.

A new emotion had entered his eyes, something she'd never seen there before. *Fear*. He might have planned her downfall time and again, but he could have never expected this. He never could have expected the three fated queens to band together against him.

Drawing on the power coursing into her from either side, Finn focused on Sugn and the Cavari, forcing every bit of magic she could summon at them. She thought of the earth from which they came, and what they were meant to be. They were not meant to use nature's power, but to simply coexist with it. Cursed they once were, and cursed they must be again.

"Don't you dare!" Sugn snarled. The Cavari backed away behind him.

Finn smiled. Her smile would be the last thing Sugn would experience.

Everything became bright, blinding light. Finn lost her grip on the two women's hands as she was propelled backward, landing hard on her back.

Pain sang through her, leaving her unable to move for several seconds.

When she finally sat up, before her stood a gathering of saplings. The Cavari were gone, and in their place were young trees. She knew deep down that this new curse had affected all Cavari, not just those standing in front of her, including her mother.

Ealasaid approached her side, then helped her to her feet. "Should we cut them down?" she asked, staring at the small trees.

Finn shook her head, then wiped tears from her eyes. It had been Sugn all along. She'd cursed Iseult's people for no reason. They'd likely never been able to figure out who among them had killed her child, because none of them had.

She heard hoofbeats galloping up behind her. She turned, but was too late. Oighear held a gleaming dagger, and now it sped toward Finn's heart.

A flash of white, and Finn fell aside. Loinnir stood above her, and Ealasaid at her back, but she could not see what had happened. She frantically scrambled to her feet, bracing herself against the unicorn.

She peered around the beast, and there stood Iseult, his back to her. His sword gleamed crimson with fresh blood.

She rushed past him, falling to Oighear's side. Blood soaked through the chest of her white gown, and onto the shroud around her waist.

Miraculously, Oighear sat up. She coughed, spewing more blood down her chest. She lifted her hand, dabbing at the blood then raising it to her eyeline. Her hand dropped. "This will not kill me," she rasped. "What will you do? Will you prove to be just like your people?"

Finn stared at her. She could sense Iseult and Ealasaid at her back, allowing her the final decision. She'd thought she'd killed Oighear once, but she had indeed survived a mortal wound. She would likely survive.

"Why?" Finn asked. "Why attack me *now*?"

Oighear glared at her. "You are the only person left with the power to seal me away."

Finn shook her head. Oighear would never trust her, and the feeling was mutual. She leaned forward and tugged the blood-stained shroud from Oighear's waist.

Oighear did not fight her, she simply stared at Finn with accusing eyes.

"The leader of my people murdered my daughter," Finn breathed. "I will not be like them. There has been enough death already." She stood. "But know this, if you seek to harm anyone again, I will end you."

Oighear laughed, sputtering up more blood. "You are no queen to be making such threats. You've turned your most powerful allies into *trees*, not that I mind *that* part."

Clutching the shroud, Finn retreated to Iseult's side. "No," she replied, "I am not a queen, nor are you any longer. I do not know what type of world we have created, but it is likely a world with greater powers than you or I. We do not matter. Perhaps we never did."

"The prophecy?" Ealasaid questioned.

Finn glanced at her. She'd nearly forgotten she was there. "I don't think the prophecy matters any longer." She turned her gaze to the Ceàrdaman, who'd stopped not far away to wait patiently. Spotting Niklas at the forefront, she raised her voice to ask, "Does it?"

Niklas smiled and walked toward them. "It never really did. Just as you gave power to the curse you cast, so too did your focus on the prophecy." He stopped beside Oighear and glanced down at her. "*Some* perhaps gave it more power than others."

Finn opened her mouth to ask more, then Keiren appeared, huffing as if she'd greatly exerted herself in getting there. "Where is my mother?" she demanded, glancing between Niklas and Finn. "The barrier is broken, so where is she?"

Niklas' smile faltered. "Your mother moved on long ago, child. You have made others your pawns for decades. Could you not realize when the same was done to you?"

Even after all Keiren had done, Finn's heart went out to her. Unfortunately, there was little time for consoling her. The distant soldiers of An Fiach watched, and Oighear's Aos Sí had closed in, likely intent on rescuing their queen.

Finn watched as Òengus left their ranks and hurried

toward Oighear. He knelt and cradled her in his arms, almost . . . lovingly?

She raised her eyes to the Aos Sí, then gasped as the soldier standing front and center raised the faceplate of his helmet. "Eywen?" she questioned. "Have you betrayed me?"

Eywen, once again dressed in the unusual armor of his people, stepped forward from his ranks. "No, my queen. I have brought you an army, as promised." He gestured to the Aos Sí behind him.

"Traitors!" Oighear hissed, still cradled in Óengus' arms.

"Perhaps," Eywen replied, tilting his head, "but I will not suffer my people to live in darkness out of loyalty to a tyrant. Not anymore."

"You will all die without me!" Oighear growled.

Eywen shook his head. "Do you not feel the magic in the land?" He raised his hands to his sides, as if capturing raindrops. "We no longer require your magic to sustain us." His eyes met Finn's. "Nor yours, my queen."

"How curious," Niklas commented. "I had thought the Ceàrdaman to be the only victors in this new land." He smiled up at the sky. "It feels as if we've been returned home."

Finn sensed Keiren's magic at her side a moment before the sorceress raged forward. "You lying, snake-tongued, sharp toothed coward!" she shouted. "Where is my mother!" A dagger appeared in her hand as if by magic as she rushed forward.

"Yer mother didnae die of a curse!" a voice shouted behind them.

Finn's shoulders slumped in relief to see Àed hobbling

toward them from the direction of the woods bordering the burgh. Bedelia kept pace at his side.

Keiren turned toward him, her ire-filled expression frozen. Seeming to recover, she lowered her dagger and stepped away from Niklas. "Do not lie to me, father. I've had enough lies."

She glared at Niklas, who didn't seem the least bit frightened of her dagger.

"Yer mother died a normal, mortal death," Àed sighed, halting a few paces from Keiren. "Ye couldnae accept that me magic couldnae save her, nor could yers, but that doesn't change the fact that she was never cursed, even though you couldnae let her go."

Keiren's lip trembled. She shook her head, tossing her fiery hair from side to side. "You're wrong," she breathed, but there was no fight in her words.

More movement behind them signaled the arrival of the rest of Finn's friends. She nearly collapsed in relief at the sight of Kai, Anna, and Maarav, the latter muttering about Keiren trapping them in place while she ran off. Finn smiled at them, but Anna's eyes were all for Eywen, and Maarav's for Ealasaid.

Only Kai looked Finn's way, an apologetic smile on his lips. She nodded to him, accepting the unsaid apology for leaving.

She turned her attention back to Niklas. "Why did you come here? The barrier is broken, what else do you want?"

Niklas bowed his bald head, and the cloaked Travelers behind him did the same. "We came to give thanks, Oaken Queen. Though the prophecy means nothing, if a time would have come where we had to choose a queen, it would be you."

Though she mostly hated the Travelers, she couldn't help but smile. The war was far from over, but this seeming peace between races was a start.

A throat cleared.

Finn turned to see Óengus, now standing with Oighear in his arms. Two more beings she rather detested, but hatred was no reason to punish.

"If you do not mind, we will take our leave of you," Óengus announced.

Oighear clung to him, a willing captive.

Finn almost laughed, the sight was so ridiculous. Instead she asked, "Where will you go?"

Óengus smirked. "I've finally been granted what I was searching for. We will go somewhere far from fiery sorceresses and naive little tree girls, I assure you."

Finn nodded.

The Aos Sí behind them parted to let them pass as Oighear's massive white cat joined them, ready to carry the fallen Snow Queen and Óengus away.

Once Oighear and Óengus were out of sight, Ealasaid announced, "I must see to my mages. They do not know what has transpired." She watched the Aos Sí warily.

Maarav took her hand. "Are you sure you want to let Oighear go? Your parents—"

She raised her free hand to cut him off. "She has lost her kingdom, and kin of her own. It is enough." She glanced again at the Aos Sí, then back to Finn. "They are under your command now, correct? My mages will likely attack them on sight."

Finn nodded. "They will not approach the burgh if you don't think it wise, though I would like for Eywen to remain with us."

Ealasaid glanced at Maarav, then replied, "One Aos Sí will be acceptable."

Finn nodded, agreeing, then took a deep breath. As the Travelers slowly retreated, she finally turned to Iseult. Her hero, even after she'd trapped him in roots. She didn't need to ask how he'd escaped. She'd known all along, that despite any odds, he would always be there to save her.

Anna knew she should be focused on the waiting force of An Fiach, but Eywen was watching her with a small knowing smile and she couldn't seem to look away.

Her friends were all watching, as were the waiting Aos Sí, and Keiren was crying while her father and Bedelia consoled her . . . but curse the gods, she didn't care about any of it.

She marched up to Eywen while his curious men watched on. She stopped within reach and peered up into his strange sapphire eyes.

He raised a dark brow at her. "I told you I'd return for you."

She snorted. "I'm not fool enough to believe you returned just for me."

He snaked a hand around her waist and pulled her closer. "Perhaps not, but you will be the reason for everything else I do, from this point forward."

She wanted to kiss him more than anything, but the

blasted Trow had come out of the forest, and the Pixies were now darting overhead.

She sighed, then stood on her toes and kissed him.

He wrapped his arms around her and returned the kiss, pressing her against his cool armor.

Though she felt stunned eyes on her, she did not pull away. Any who questioned her later could answer to her daggers, or Eywen's army. This moment was hers.

CHAPTER FIFTEEN

inn rode atop Loinnir, leading the way toward
An Fiach. She had a feeling the sight of Aos Sí
would have made them retreat, but they had nowhere to go.
North was the direction from which the Aos Sí had come,
west were the retreating Travelers, Finn, and everyone else,
and south was the burgh filled with mages. To the east lay
dense forests and insurmountable rocky escarpments.

On one side of her walked Iseult, and the other Eywen.
She itched to ask Iseult if his soul had been returned. With
the barrier broken, it should have, but there really was no
saying what should and would happen now that the in-
between and their known reality were intermingled. She
wanted to right the destructive wrongs she'd committed,
but was it even possible? She glanced back at Branwen,
walking near Naoki. She had many questions for *her* as well.

"Do not venture too near," Iseult warned. "They may still
attack."

She scanned the line of men with shields raised defensively, some facing the burgh, some facing her and the Aos Sí.

She shook her head. "I want to find out just who organized them, and why. I must know why they hate the mages so much."

"They fear them," Keiren said, speeding up on foot to push herself between Loinnir's flank and Eywen. "It made their smaller groups rather easy to manipulate in the past, though I never found their leader."

"Then it's time we faced them, once and for all," Finn decided.

They reached the first line of men, though Iseult placed a hand on Loinnir's reins before she could venture close enough that a released arrow might strike her. The men stood eerily silent, *waiting*. They knew they were outnumbered and outclassed by the mighty Aos Sí.

"We would speak with your Captain!" Eywen called out.

There were murmurs amongst the men, then the shields at the forefront parted. A lone man walked through, marching toward them bravely. His close cropped hair was an uncommon sight, but it was barely noticeable within his air of confidence. His gaze shifted past Finn to Naoki, likely quite a sight for one who'd never seen a dragon.

He stopped roughly twenty paces away, his eyes once more on Finn. "I am the Captain of this contingent!" he called out. "What do your people want!"

Finn looked to Ealasaid, standing with Maarav, intentionally far from Eywen, untrusting of the Aos Sí in general. Some here now might have been present during the first attack on the burgh. Naming them as allies might take some time, but . . .

"We've come to protect those within the burgh!" Finn called out. "Surrender your attack, or we will be forced to advance!"

"We fight for Migris!" the man shouted, "and those lost in the burghs of the countryside! We will *not* relent until those deaths have been avenged! Advance on us if you must!"

Ealasaid let out a loud sigh, then advanced toward the man, heedless of the army waiting behind him.

Maarav cursed under his breath, then followed.

"Should we stop them?" Eywen questioned.

Finn shook her head. "This is her battle. Let her do as she must."

She glanced at Iseult as he let out a visible sigh of relief.

She smiled softly at him. She'd put him through quite a lot, but she was finally ready to stop fighting everyone's battles. She was even ready to stop fighting her own.

The war might be far from over, but her part in it, finally, was at an end.

"What are you doing you fool woman?" Maarav hissed, catching up to Ealasaid's side as she approached the lone man whose eyes were set in determination

"This hatred will never end with fighting," she growled, intent on her task. Stopping just a few paces away, she stared down the muscular man before her, more determined than he.

"What is your name?" she demanded.

The man eyed her cautiously. "Radley," he replied curtly. "And you are?"

"I am the leader of An Solas," she announced, "and I would like to tell you my story."

Radley's eyes narrowed, but he nodded for her to go on.

"I grew up in a small burgh in the Northeast," she began. "My family had a small farm. Life was simple. Then we began to hear reports of men terrorizing villages. They called themselves An Fiach . . . "

She continued her story, every painful detail, even including how Oighear had used An Fiach to torture those she cared about. By the time she finished, Radley was blinking at her in shock.

"That cannot be true," he muttered. "My men are good men. We fight to protect innocent people from the Faie, and from mages who would see them harmed. Mages destroyed Migris."

Ealasaid shook her head. "Oighear destroyed Migris. It was the Faie."

Radley sucked his teeth, then shook his head. "Even if that is true, we cannot allow the mages to gather like this. We cannot allow such a threat to exist."

Ealasaid sighed. "You know this *threat*," she gestured toward the burgh, spotting a few mages watching them from the wall, "exists because your people forced us into this position, do you not? Our only choices were to band together, or to die."

It was Radley's turn to sigh. "For that, I apologize, my lady, but it does not change where we are at now. I must protect my people, just as you must protect yours."

"So we'll kill each other for no reason?" she asked with an eyebrow raised.

He glanced past her toward the waiting Aos Sí, then shook his head. "I know when I am outmatched, and I will not sacrifice my men in vain. If you will allow our retreat, we will leave you."

She tilted her head. "You will leave us, only to attack again in the future, despite the risks?"

Radley nodded. "Perhaps."

Maarav leaned toward her shoulder. "It may not be wise to let them go," he whispered. "You will always be waiting for another attack."

Ealasaid turned slightly to look up at him. "And I will always be ready for it. I will not be like the men who devastated my village, or any other village for that matter. I will not lash out at that which frightens me. I will simply grow stronger to rise above it." She turned back to Radley. "You may retreat, but be warned. This land has been claimed in the name of the mages. You may not understand it yet, but a barrier has been broken this day. Magic will likely only increase. You may find that one day, your supposed enemy will be the man looking back at you in the mirror."

Radley bowed his head. "And just so you know, my lady, there are reports of Reivers gathering in the far North. They will take advantage of this war." With that, he retreated to rejoin his men.

She had wondered what Conall had been up to since taking advantage of the mages in the North, but that was a problem for another time.

Maarav placed a hand gently on her shoulder. "Woman, you never cease to amaze me."

"Why thank you," she replied with a smirk, then turned to rejoin Finn and the others.

She knew her fight was far from over, but finally, for once, she was not afraid.

The Aos Sí, An Fiach . . . Keiren watched it all numbly. Her father and Bedelia remained with her, *why*, she did not know. She did not deserve their sympathy.

She'd been such a fool. A scared little girl, unwilling to let go of her long dead mother.

Ealasaid didn't so much as glance at her when she and Maarav passed by to rejoin Finn and their other companions.

"What will you do now?" Bedelia asked, startling her out of her revelry.

She shrugged. "Oh, the usual. I'll likely lock myself away in a tower for some time, planning my vengeance upon Niklas for using me."

Bedelia snorted. "You know, Ealasaid will need help in the time to come. You could consider it your penance."

Keiren laughed bitterly, finally turning to look at her one-time lover. "She likely wishes me dead."

"Not everyone is like you," Bedelia said hotly, the blood stains on her face and clothing giving her a wild appearance. "*Some* of us," she gestured to herself, then to Àed, "are capable of forgiveness. This bitterness you hold so dear will slowly turn your heart to ice."

Àed eyed his feet through the entire conversation, just as unable to discuss emotions as she.

She raked a finger through her hair, wishing her cheeks weren't burning for all to see. "Bitterness is all I know. It's all I've ever had."

Bedelia sighed. "You've had love, you were just too blinded by hatred to see it."

Her shoulders slumped. She felt absolutely ridiculous standing there, near two mighty armies, with droves of Faie lurking in the nearby forest, arguing about *feelings*.

"I suppose I could help her deal with the Faie nuisance that's soon to come," she muttered. "If the Aos Sí no longer need a queen, the other greater Faie will likely be free as well. It will be utter chaos before long."

"Now that's more like it," Bedelia said smugly.

Keiren snorted. "When did you become so confident?"

Bedelia smiled. "When you forced me to stand up for myself. It gets easier the more I do it."

Keiren rolled her eyes, then looked down to her father. "And you? What do you have to say about this."

"I'd say I need a dram of whiskey, or six," he grumbled. "Let's get to the inn. I'm sure the mages will be celebratin'."

She couldn't help but laugh. She knew there would be a great deal more penance for her crimes, but buying a dram of whiskey for Bedelia and her father was a good place to start.

With An Fiach retreating, and Ealasaid, Maarav, Bedelia, and Àed returning to the burgh, it was time for Finn to see to the Faie. They waited for her near the forest, just past the new saplings that were once the Cavari.

Accompanied by Iseult, Kai, Anna, and Eywen, she stopped in front of the lead sapling, Sugn.

She looked down at its delicate branches, resisting the urge to snap them off.

"He killed my daughter," she said to no one in particular. "All this time . . . " she trailed off, shaking her head. She turned to Iseult. "Your people never committed the grave crime of which they were accused. Sugn cast the blame upon them, and I blindly believed him."

Iseult placed a hand on her shoulder, with a soft, sad smile on his face. "You have set things as right as they can be. My people are free."

She wiped a tear from her eye. "And you?"

He nodded, a new sense of light shining behind his normally cool gaze.

Anna, Kai, and Eywen stood back silently, watching the exchange.

Finn smiled up at Iseult, then lifted her hands to remove the gold locket from around her neck. With trembling fingers, she stood on tip toe and fastened it beneath the curtain of Iseult's hair.

He lifted the locket, running a finger across its gilded surface.

"It was meant for my daughter," she explained, "but I must let go of the dead. If I wish to live, then I must learn to let go."

He nodded. "I will keep it for now. Perhaps, someday, you will know just what to do with it."

She smiled, then turned back to the others. "Shall we see to the Faie?"

Kai nodded, though he watched the saplings warily. "Are we sure we don't want to cut them down?"

She reached out to Sugn's sapling, sensing none of his malicious power. "Their power has been returned to the earth. They will watch this land grow and change, uncontrolled by them. It is a fitting fate."

"Good point," Kai agreed.

Her heart feeling lighter than it had in over one hundred years, Finn turned and led the way toward the forest and the waiting Faie.

Anna stuck to Kai's side as they journeyed toward the forest, while Finn, Iseult, and Eywen walked ahead.

"Do you feel any different?" Anna whispered, leaning near his shoulder. "I mean, since the barrier broke?"

He shook his head. "I don't think so. I felt the shift, but I don't think it's changed anything for me."

Anna let out a heavy sigh. "So it's just me then, and the Aos Sí. I feel . . . " she trailed off, glancing at him. "Well for instance, I can *see* the difference in you now, beyond the physical. I can sense Finn's blood, and the Dearg Due's."

"Can you perhaps tell me what will happen to me in the end?" he questioned.

Anna shook her head, then faced forward. She stopped walking. "No, but maybe *they* can."

Ahead of them, Finn and the others had nearly reached the tree line. Within the tree shadows waited the Trow, Pixies, and other strange Faie. Not far off were three of the

Dearg Due, huddled within the shadows, their eyes squinted against the sun.

His heart stopped. The last time he'd encountered them, they had tried to kill him.

Anna gripped his arm. "We must ask them what's happening to you. Perhaps there is a cure."

He shook his head. "I'd rather light them all on fire."

The decision was made for them both when Finn veered off course, straight toward the Dearg Due.

"Blasted woman can't keep to herself," Kai muttered, then jogged toward her. He knew Finn had veered to address the Dearg Due on his behalf, but as always, it was not her issue to bear.

Reaching her, he turned to face the monsters in the trees. He immediately recognized the one who'd bitten him, held him hostage, and fed him blood to save him. All the while thinking he was Dair, and therefore worth saving.

Glancing at him, Finn took his hand, then turned toward the Dearg Due. Iseult and Eywen waited patiently as Anna caught up and walked on the other side of Kai.

"Why have you come here?" Finn asked, raising her voice to be heard across the distance. "You have gravely injured my friend. I fear you are my enemies."

The three white haired women each lowered to one knee, though their backs remained erect, submissive, yet still proud. "We have come to thank the Oaken Queen for freeing us from servitude. The other Faie told us what occurred. We no longer need swear fealty to the Snow Queen, nor any other."

"So now they're monsters without a leash," Kai muttered. "Lovely."

"As for your friend," the lead woman began, rising. "He is not injured. He has been granted a great gift, one normally forbidden amongst my people."

Kai snorted. "Hardly."

Though his words had been quiet, the Dearg Due whipped her gaze to him. "You are a liar. You told us you were Dair. I never would have given you my blood otherwise. For a male to be granted our gifts," she shook her head, tossing spider silk hair from side to side. "You should be honored."

"So he will not die?" Anna asked, having reached his side.

The Dearg Due addressed her. "No, he will not die, Gray Lady. He will live longer than his mortal life would have allowed, with gifts no mortal should have. Normally, we would eliminate such a mistake, but as thanks to the Oaken Queen, he shall not be pursued." She turned her gaze back to Finn. "That is all we have come to say. May we be free now?"

Kai watched as Finn bit her lip. The Dearg Due were dangerous predators. She would not want them roaming free to hurt others.

"You may," she replied. "But keep to the borders of the Marshlands, and never enter Garenoch."

The woman bowed her head. "It will be as you say. The marshes shall become the Realm of the Faie." She and her sisters turned and stalked off into the woods.

Kai shook his head in disbelief. How could she let them go? He turned toward Finn. "They will kill again. You know this?"

Finn nodded, her gaze distant. "I have destroyed the balance of this land, freeing the greater Faie and allowing magics to run rampant. This is all I can do to bring a new balance into being. There must be light and dark. Life and death. It can be no other way." She turned to smile at him. "Just not *your* death. I have not given up my selfish ways entirely."

He laughed, feeling sick and dizzy, but also relieved. He didn't know what the future held for him, but at least it wasn't a dark descent into the life of a blood-thirsty Faie.

"There are more Faie to address," Finn said with a sigh. "They will all be freed with a request to keep to the Marshlands and forests. That will at least give An Fiach pause if they ever decide to travel east again."

"And if they revolt," Anna added. "There're plenty of mages around to put them down."

Kai shook his head. Both women seemed to have gone a bit mad, but they were right. The Faie might have magics, but so too did the humans. It was a new, magical world. Surely more wars would come about, but the dwellers of Garenoch would not be the ones to submit, at least not as long as they had Ealasaid at their head.

Later that evening, Finn rested within the grand estate in Garenoch. Sitting in a cushy chair with her legs curled about her, she sipped a pewter mug of wine by the fire. In the chair next to her sat Àed, and at his feet snored Naoki. Loinnir had accepted a place in the estate's stables, far finer than where she'd been housed at the old Druid fortress.

Most had retired, but Finn knew Iseult would be lurking somewhere nearby. The return of his soul hadn't outwardly changed him much. His heart seemed lighter, and he smiled a bit more, but he was still silent, brooding, and overprotective to a fault . . . and he was still *hers*.

"What will you do now?" she asked distantly.

Àed sipped his whiskey. "I imagine I'll stay here for a time, make sure me daughter willnae get herself into any more trouble."

Finn smirked, knowing that's exactly what Keiren would do. Bedelia had opted to stay behind as well, though she and Finn had sat down for a long talk about plans to meet in the future.

"Ye know," Àed began, seeming uncomfortable, "It's not me secret to tell, but the girl, Bedelia, suffers from a Faie bite. It's slowly killin' her."

Finn smiled. "I know. She'd been trying to hide it from me." She looked at him pointedly. "She also admitted what happened with Sativola. Though you were both foolish to hide such truths from me, I gladly healed her."

He raised a bushy brow at her.

She grinned wider. "I cannot shed my past without shedding what I was. I give my immortality freely, to care for those I love." She had not hesitated in the choice. She'd shared her magic with Kai, Iseult, and now Bedelia. She was more human now than she'd ever hoped, though her natural gifts were unlikely to leave her.

"I'd like to make the same offer to you," she added. "I know Keiren crippled you long ago. I can likely fix the damage."

He waved her off with his hand not holding the whiskey. "Don't ye dare lass. I've lived a long life, and I have all that I want now. Me girls are all safe. That's good enough for me."

"Girls?" she questioned.

He sighed, blushing beneath his heavy brows and bushy hair. "Ye know what I mean, lass. I'm glad to see ye all safe, and movin' on with yer lives."

She laughed, more than ready to do just as Àed wanted. It was time to move on. She ran her fingers across the piece of tattered fabric in her lap. With a heavy sigh, she lifted the Faie Queen's shroud, the last relic of power from an era coming to a close. She'd been unsure of what to do with it, but now she knew. She may have disrupted the balance in the land, but a new balance would be found. *True* balance. She tossed the shroud into the fire. There was a brilliant flash of light, then the fabric burned, turning to ash along with its dark past.

Àed sipped his whiskey, not bothering to comment.

She settled back against her chair, turning a warm smile to her friend, her *family*. She'd never really considered that Àed might understand the loss she felt for her daughter. He'd lost one too, after all, even though he had her back now. In some ways, Finn felt like she had Niamh back too. Her spirit was free, and would return to her in some shape or form, in this life, or the next. The pleasant scent of woodsmoke curled around them, soothing her further.

"Of course," Àed grumbled finally, "I'm not pleased to see blasted Kai and Anna still around. No good thieves, that pair."

Finn snorted. "I believe Anna is entirely different from the woman we first met, and Kai," she smiled, glancing at Àed, "he was always a better man than either of us wanted to admit."

Thinking of Kai, she knew she'd need to speak to him.

There was so much to say. He was her best friend, and she loved him in many ways. Part of her felt that their souls were fated too, just like hers and Iseult's, and Niamh's, even Ealasaid's and Anna's. They were all bound together, through more than just friendship and strife. They were her new world, and she wouldn't have it any other way.

Branwen tossed and turned in her bed, unable to still her thoughts. She'd actually succeeded in her task, and had survived. Soon she would make the journey back to her family's archives. She would record the tale of Finnur, and the stories Druantia had told her. Her brother would have given anything to be the scholar to record those tales. It was the least she could do for him.

A throat cleared.

She startled, then tumbled out of bed, landing hard on the stone floor.

"How graceful," the voice commented.

Her eyes darted around the room until settling on a small round mirror above her washbasin. Niklas' face was framed in the reflective surface.

She staggered to her feet, whipping a blanket off the bed to cover her underpinnings. "What do you want? I did as you asked, didn't I?"

He nodded. "You have done quite well, child, but there is still work to be done."

She shook her head. "No, you no longer hold sway over me. Now with the barrier broken, the power that animates me is all around. You cannot take it away."

He smirked, revealing a few pointed teeth. "I am not threatening you my dear. I am offering you an opportunity. Many changes are soon to come. The Ceàrdaman have been granted great power, as have many other races. New borders must be made, new empires built."

Her heart raced. "What does any of that have to do with me?"

"You are a cartographer, are you not?" he inquired. "Someone will need to map the new kingdom. We will begin with the Realm of the Mages. Perhaps the Realm of An Solas, as they like to call themselves." He tapped his chin in thought.

"You're mad," she breathed. "You can't just create an entire new empire based on your whims."

He tsked at her. "M'dear, the Ceàrdaman have manipulated history for centuries. Now we are more powerful than ever. You cannot expect us to not have any fun with it."

She slumped down onto her bed. She hated the Travelers. They treated humans like dolls, there for their entertainment. Yet, if her brother would have been impressed with the histories she intended to write, how would he feel about her being the historian and cartographer for an entirely new, magical world? Her choices were to go home and continue living her life in the shadows, barely seen by others, or . . .

She raised her gaze to the mirror. "What do I have to do?"

"Good girl," he replied. "Leave the burgh now, and I will join you. Then we will begin to make our plans."

As Niklas faded from the mirror, Branwen stood and began gathering her few belongings. She was utterly mad for even considering this new task . . . or was she? She was still a wraith. Those around her barely noticed her. She'd traveled between realms, spoken to goddesses, gone to the brink of death and back. She was no longer a normal human girl, so why was she trying to fit into such a role to begin with?

No one saw her leave as she departed the estate, and Niklas found her soon after. A new world was coming, and this time, she wouldn't be the one left behind.

CHAPTER SIXTEEN

*A*nna was up with the sun, though she was utterly exhausted. She was simply too grateful to be alive to waste her time in bed. After hastily washing herself and changing, she hurried out into the hall, nearly stumbling over Eywen, who was seated right outside her door, leaning against the wall. She hadn't even sensed his innate magic. While she felt more magic within her, and without, it was no longer jarring. The shine did not sting her eyes. Probably because it now truly belonged in this reality.

"Are you trying to stop my heart!" she growled, quickly recovering from the sudden shock of Eywen's appearance.

He rose fluidly from the floor. His silken black hair appeared clean, as did his white tunic and black breeches. "Forgive me, I've been waiting for a while."

Her heart skipped a beat for another reason. "Whatever for?"

He stepped toward her, taking her hands in his. "Most of my men have dispersed, but a few have remained with the intent of escorting Finnur wherever she should choose to go. We are not sure of our place in this new world. *I'm* not sure of my place . . . " he eyed her intently.

"Well don't expect me to tell you," she answered reflexively. "It's not like I know *my* place either."

He lifted one hand from hers, pushing a strand of her loose hair behind her ear. "Anna," he began patiently. "I would like to remain with Finnur for a time, if only to ensure that this state of freedom for my people is not temporary."

She pulled away and crossed her arms. "I told you I won't be telling you what to do."

He smiled. "Nor I you. What I'm trying to ask, is if you'll come with me."

Her shoulders relaxed. "Follow Finn across the land to make sure she doesn't get herself into any trouble?" she questioned.

He nodded. "At least for a time."

She sighed, dropping her arms to her sides. "Well, it's not like I haven't been doing that already. The woman would be dead ten times over if it weren't for me."

He laughed, then pulled her into his arms.

She slid her arms around his waist, though remained somewhat stiff, uncomfortable with being in the middle of the hallway where anyone might walk up.

"Anna," he muttered against her hair. "Would you be willing to bond yourself to me, not now, but perhaps some day?"

She pulled away, her heart once again racing. "What in the gods does that even mean?"

He continued to smile. "I am immortal. Now that I no

longer need a queen, I am truly immortal. If we were to bond our magics together, it would be similar to what Finn has done. I would take a measure of your mortality, and you a measure of my immortality."

She crossed her arms again. "Which would mean?"

He closed the space between them again. "I would eventually grow old, as would you, but we'd do so on a similar timeline."

She blinked up at him. "You'd be willing to do that for me?"

He nodded.

This man was utterly mad. She debated throwing caution to the wind, but she simply was not that type of girl. "Perhaps, some day in the *far* future, I might *consider* making such a choice."

He grinned. "That was all I needed to hear."

She realized she had an equally sweet grin on her face. She quickly smothered it, but a small smile remained. "Let's go find some breakfast. Surely with all this finery, there must be a hearty meal to be had. We should make the most of it while we can."

He took her hand and walked with her down the hall. Truth be told, she couldn't wait to leave the estate and go back on the road with Eywen, even if Finn and Iseult would be coming along. There were still many adventures to be had, and she didn't want to waste a single moment.

Keiren faced Ealasaid in the meeting room. They'd spent a great deal of time there together, perusing maps and making plans. Now there was more tension than ever before.

Ealasaid crossed her arms. "Well? Say what you have to say. There are preparations to be done for the feast, and I haven't much time to spare."

Keiren's shoulders slumped. Had she not been humiliated enough?

Bedelia cleared her throat behind her. *She* was the only reason Keiren had been granted a meeting in the first place.

Keiren gritted her teeth. "I would like to apologize," she mumbled.

"What was that?" Ealasaid asked smugly. "Do speak up."

Keiren rolled her eyes. "I would like to apologize for using you, though I had very good reason to do so."

Bedelia cleared her throat again. Blasted woman.

"I might have had good reasons," Keiren continued, enunciating each word, "but it is not an excuse for the pain I have caused. I should have been honest with you about why I wanted to break the barrier. Truly, I believed my way the only way."

Ealasaid replied with a curt nod. "Very well." She moved to walk past her toward the door.

Keiren blinked at her. "Very well?"

Ealasaid nodded. "Was there something else?"

Thoroughly defeated, she snapped her mouth shut. There was *no* way she'd be asking to stay to help with the mages now.

Bedelia stepped forward, halting Ealasaid's progress. "Keiren would like to stay here for a time. She would like to help in the training of young mages as penance for her actions."

Ealasaid turned to her, mischief glittering in her eyes. "Is this true? You would like to help others, with nothing to gain in return?"

She clenched her jaw. There was an empty hole in her heart where her mother had been. At some point she'd have to accept that she would never get her back. She had to move on with her life, and there really was nowhere else to go. Plus, an army of mages could prove handy when she finally acted out her vengeance on Niklas.

"Yes," she said finally. "I would like to stay and help others. I do not expect your forgiveness, but I expect you will do what is best for your mages."

Ealasaid rolled her eyes. "Well, no one has moved into your chamber yet. You may as well fill it." With that, she finished her progress toward the door, quietly exiting the room.

Keiren's hands balled into fists. That impertinent little—

A hand alighted on her shoulder. "It's a start at least."

Keiren turned to blink at her.

Bedelia let her hand fall.

Keiren opened her mouth to speak. To say what, she was not sure. She'd treated Bedelia worst of all, even though she was the only person she'd actually come close to loving all these years.

"Why?" she asked finally. "Why do you care what happens to me?"

Bedelia smirked. "I'm not doing it for you. I'm doing it because that's the type of person I want to be. Finn taught me that."

Keiren felt her mouth twisting downward. It always came back to *Finn*. She could see Finn's magic within

Bedelia now, running through her veins. Finn had been able to heal her illness, where she could not.

Bedelia grinned smugly. "You know, she's *your* friend now too."

Keiren scoffed. "Hardly. Finnur cares not what becomes of me."

Bedelia rolled her eyes. "You'll see in time. Now let's go and see if we can help with preparations."

"I'm not a cook," Keiren hissed. "Nor do I intend to sweep floors."

Her back already turned, Bedelia led the way toward the door. "If I can cook and clean, you can cook and clean." She didn't bother to glance at Keiren's reaction to her words. She was her own woman now.

A small smile on her lips, Keiren followed. She still wouldn't be lifting a broom, but she could humor her one-time lover, and perhaps only true friend, at least for now. As soon as things became boring, she'd take off and become someone to be feared once more. At least, that was what she'd keep telling herself.

Kai watched the festivities from a nearby hall, not entirely feeling like celebrating. Though he was glad they'd all survived, he felt a little melancholy that the excitement was over. It meant things were coming to an end. He no longer had a quest, or even a place in the world . . . if he ever really had.

After leaving the Gray City and his family behind, he'd roved about finding adventures with Anna, but he'd never really *fit* anywhere. Now everyone had a place but him.

"Kai," a hesitant voice said from behind him.

He turned to see Finn walking toward him. He hadn't seen her in a dress for quite some time, let alone the violet silks that now clad her body. She was looking healthier now, more human. He supposed it was a result of her sharing her immortality with Iseult and Bedelia.

"What are you doing out here?" she questioned, reaching his side to peek in at the festivities.

"I could ask you the same question," he smiled.

She let out a soft laugh. He couldn't quite remember the last time he heard her laugh.

He didn't mean to ask it, but the words seemed to slip out of their own volition. "Where do we go from here?"

She placed her hand on his shoulder. "Iseult and I are going to return to the fortress for a time. The Pixies have gone ahead to bring news to the remaining Aos Sí, but we would still like to return there, at least for a while to decide where we'll go next. Anna and Eywen will be joining us until they figure out what they want to do. Branwen was going to come too, but she seems to have gone missing again." Finn sighed and shook her head, then looked back up to him. "Regardless, I think you should come with us."

He smirked. "Travel with two couples? How thrilling."

She removed her hand from his shoulder to smack his arm. "I love you too, you know."

"But you love him more," he countered.

She sighed. "Not more, just differently."

He thought about joining them. He had to admit, despite the mild discomfort, the idea appealed to him. They were his only friends in this new world. A world where he fit even less than before. There was no saying what might happen as the new magics settled into the land. If he could still help his friends . . .

"I'm sure Iseult would not appreciate me joining you," he muttered, returning his gaze to those enjoying the feast.

"That is not true," Iseult said, appearing around the corner behind them. Even with his soul returned, he was still annoyingly stealthy.

Kai scowled at him. "Is that so?"

Iseult simply smiled.

Kai balked. Iseult was . . . smiling? How . . . odd.

He heard footsteps coming toward them from the direction of the feast a moment before Anna joined them. Standing near Kai, she placed her hands on her hips. "Why are we all lurking in the hall?"

"We're trying to convince Kai to travel with us to the fortress, and perhaps someplace else beyond that," Finn explained, much to Kai's chagrin.

Anna raised her dark brows at him. "Well of *course* he's coming."

He rolled his eyes at her.

She scowled, jutting her hips to one side. "Are you truly telling me that you would turn down the opportunity to travel with the former Oaken Queen, an Aos Sí, a silent warrior," she gestured to Iseult, "and me, a fully restored Gray Lady of Clan Liath? Really, I thought you had a thirst for adventure. Have you grown cowardly?"

He buried his face in his palm, suddenly overcome with laughter. When he finally was able to speak, he dropped his hand, glancing between each of his companions. His *friends.*

"My apologies," he laughed. "Whatever was I thinking? Surely the path to riches lies solely with companions such as these."

A smug look on her face, Anna nodded. "Well now that your thinking has been un-addled, I believe it's time we *all* celebrate. The evil Snow Queen might not be dead, and the world might not have been set right," she shrugged, "but I'd say it's close enough."

With that, she turned and re-entered the raucous feasting room. Iseult followed her, leaving Finn and Kai alone once more.

Finn took his hand in hers and gave it a squeeze. "So you'll come? You are all so dear to me, I fear I cannot let you go. At least not yet."

He nodded, now smiling despite his reservations. "Why not?" he replied. "Perhaps I'll find another reason to kidnap you along the way."

She scowled, then laughed, tugging him into the celebration. Anna had conveyed the situation perfectly. Evil was not dead, and the world was not *right*, but with friends like the ones he had, it was close enough.

Sitting at the head of the feasting table with Maarav, Ealasaid watched as Slaine attempted to give a very drunken Sage a lesson in swordplay.

She chuckled as the young mage was once again swept from his feet, then turned toward her husband. "Will you be sad to see your brother go?"

Maarav shrugged, then wrapped an arm around her

shoulders. "Fate brought us together after all these years, against all circumstances. I'm sure I will see him again. Are you sad to see Finn and the others leave?"

"Yes," she said honestly, emotion welling up in her at the thought, "but I have all I need here. Wars will continue to brew in this new land, I'm sure, and my mages need me."

"And *I* need you," he added.

She smiled. "And our child needs both of us."

He pulled away and blinked at her for several seconds. When he finally recovered, he asked, "Are you bladdered? What are you talking about?"

Before she could answer, he pulled her close and kissed her, clearly pleased.

She laughed, and her sadness slowly leaked away. She had family all around, and that family would soon become a bit bigger. She would see her friends again, of that she was sure, and in the interim, she had plenty to occupy her time.

Finn picked her way through the forest, searching for one tree in particular. She knew it wouldn't look any different, but she'd know it when she saw it. Loinnir waited not far off, basking in the sun while grazing on dried grass. Finn could feel the new magic all around, slowly soaking into the land.

She stopped walking, sensing a familiar energy. She turned toward a nearby sapling, extending her hand to run across its smooth bark. It was as she'd suspected. By combining her magic with Ealasaid's and Oighear's, they'd managed to seal away *all* Cavari, perhaps even all other Dair as well.

"Hello, mother," she muttered. She hadn't wanted to turn her mother into a tree with all the rest, but it had been impossible to pick and choose.

She summoned her magic, now dampened by mortal blood. Hopefully it would be enough.

The tree's bark began to glow faintly. A tiny spark stung her hand and she recoiled.

A voice whispered in her head, "Finnur, do not do this."

"Mother?" she asked out loud. "I'm going to free you, do not worry."

"No," her mother's voice answered. "It is better this way. I feel . . . at peace."

Finn shook her head. "But mother—"

"No," her mother's voice interrupted again. "I've lived long enough, a phantom for so many years. Now that my daughter is finally free, so too am I. I knew breaking the barrier would free you from us, and you would be able to do what was right."

Finn placed her hand once more against the bark, but this time, did not summon her magic.

"I am a part of the earth now," her mother said into her mind. "I will always be with you."

Iseult walked up behind her, placing a hand on her shoulder. She turned to him, retreating to the curve of his arm. That was, until Naoki trotted over and butted her way between them. The others weren't far off. They'd venture first to the fortress, but beyond that, who knew? There were plenty of adventures to be had in this new land, the fate of which no longer depended on her.

She turned back toward the sapling, a tiny tree ready for a new life, just like her. Saying a silent goodbye to her mother, she felt like she should probably cry, but she could only smile. Everything was finally as it should be, if perhaps a little different than she'd imagined.

The End

GLOSSARY

A

Anna- descendent of clan Liath.

Àed (ay-add)- a conjurer of some renown, also known as "The Mountebank".

Áit I Bhfolach (aht uh wallach)- secret city in the North.

Anders (ahn-durs)- a young, archive scholar.

An Duilleog (ahn Dooh-lug)- the leaf.

An Solas (ahn so-lahs)- the light (organization of mages).

Aonbheannach (aen-vah-nach)- unicorn.

Aos Sí (A-ess she)- ancient humanoid Faie.

Ar Marbhdhraíocht (ur mab-dry-oh)- volume on necromancy

Arthryn (are-thrin)- alleged Alderman of Sormyr. Seen by few.

B

Bannock- unleavened loaf of bread, often sweetened with honey.

Ballybog- large Faie common in swamps.

Bedelia- former lover of Keiren.

Bladdered- drunk

Boobrie- large, colorful, bird-like Faie that lures travelers away from the path.

Branwen (bran-win)- a young, archive scholar.

C

Caorthannach (quar-ah-nach)- Celtic fire-spitting demon.

Cavari (cah-var-ee)- prominent clan of the *Dair Leanbh*.

Ceàrdaman (see-air-duh-maun)- the Craftspeople, often referred to as *Travelers*. Believed to be Faie in origin.

À Choille Fala (ah choi-le-uh fall-ah)- the Blood Forest. Either a refuge or prison for the Faie.

Ceilidh (kay-lee)- a festival, often involving dancing and a great deal of whiskey.

D

Dair Leanbh (dare lan-ub)- Oak Child. Proper term for a race of beings with affinity for the earth. Origins unknown.

Dearg Due (dee-argh doo)- female, blood-drinking Faie.

Dram- a small unit of liquid measure, often referring to whiskey.

Dullahan (doo-la-han)- headless riders of the Faie. Harbingers of death.

E

Ealasaid (eel-ah-sayd)- young mage.
Evrial (ehv-ri-all)- Pixie clan leader.

F

Finnur (fin-uh)- member of Clan Cavari.

G

Garenoch (gare-en-och)- small, southern burgh. A well-used travel stop.
Geancanach (gan-can-och)- small, mischievous Faie with craggy skin and bat-like wings. Travel in Packs.
Glen- narrow, secluded valley.
Gray City- see *Sormyr*
Grogoch (grow-gok)- smelly Faie covered in red hair, roughly the size of a child. Impervious to heat and cold.
Gwrtheryn (gweir-thare-in)- Alderman of Garenoch. Deathly afraid of Faie.

H

Haudin (hah-din)- roughly built homes, often seen in areas of lesser wealth.
Henkies- little purple man fairy that lives in the knolls.

I

Iseult (ee-sult)- allegedly the last living member of Uí Neíd.

K

Kai- escort of the Gray Lady.

Keiren (kigh-rin)- daughter of the Mountebank. Whereabouts unknown.

L

Leon Gheimhridh (leh-oun yeav-jah)- winter lion.

Liaden (lee-ay-din)- the Gray Lady.

Loinnir (lun-yer)- one of the last Unicorns.

M

Maarav (mah-rahv)- brother of Iseult, descendent of Uí Néid.

Meirleach (myar-lukh)- word in the old tongue meaning *thief.*

Merrows- water dwelling Faie capable of taking the shape of sea creatures. Delight in luring humans to watery deaths.

Midden- garbage.

Migris- one of the Great Cities, and also a large trade port.

Móirne (morn-yeh)- member of Clan Cavari. Mother of Finnur.

Muntjac- small deer.

N

Neeps- turnips.
Niamh (nee-ahm-uh)- deceased daughter of Finnur.

O

Óengus (on-gus)- a notorious bounty hunter.
Oighear (Ohg-hear)- ruler of the Aos Sí, also known as Oighear the White, or the Snow Queen.

P

Pooks- also known as Bucca, small Faie with both goat and human features. Nocturnal.
Port Ainfean (ine-feen)- a medium-sized fishing port along the River Cair, a rumored haven for smugglers.

R

Ratchets- Goblin hounds.
Redcaps- Goblins.
Reiver (ree-vur)- borderland raiders.

S

Sand Road- travel road beginning in Felgram and spanning all the way to Migris.
Scunner- an insult referring to someone strongly disliked.
Sgal (skal)- a strong wind.

Sgain Dubh (skee-an-doo)- a small killing knife, carried by roguish characters.

Síoda (she-dee)- Lady of Garenoch.

Slàinte (slawn-cha)- a toast to good health.

Slàine (slahn-yuh)- clan leader of assassins.

Solas Na Réaltaí (so-lahs nah rail-ti)- starlight.

Sormyr (sore-meer)- one of the Great Cities, also known as the Gray City.

T

Travelers- see *Ceàrdaman*.

Trow- large Faie resembling trees. Rumored to steal children.

U

Uí Néid (ooh ned)- previously one of the great cities, now nothing more than a ruin.

NOTE FROM THE AUTHOR

Dear Readers,

I just wanted to make a note to say what a wonderful time I've had sharing this story with you. While this is the end to this series, I do have plans for future stories with these characters (yeah, I'm incapable of letting go!), so this isn't quite goodbye. Please continue on for a sneak peek at my Thief's Apprentice Series!

If you'd like to be notified of news and updates, please consider joining my mailing list by visiting:

www.saracroethle.com

TREE OF AGES READING ORDER

Tree of Ages

The Melted Sea

The Blood Forest

Queen of Wands

The Oaken Throne

ALSO BY SARA C ROETHLE

The Bitter Ashes Series

Death Cursed

Collide and Seek

Rock, Paper, Shivers

Duck, Duck, Noose

Shoots and Tatters

The Thief's Apprentice Series

Clockwork Alchemist

Clocks and Daggers

Under Clock and Key

The Xoe Meyers Series

Xoe

Accidental Ashes

Broken Beasts

Demon Down

Forgotten Fires

Minor Magics

Gone Ghost

SNEAK PEEK AT CLOCKWORK
ALCHEMIST, BOOK ONE OF THE
THIEF'S APPRENTICE SERIES

CLOCKWORK ALCHEMIST: CHAPTER ONE

Arhyen pressed his back against the cracked stone wall. He'd not expected this. He lowered the lantern in his hand as he glanced down at the aged corpse, then kicked it with his toe. It sounded . . . hollow. A pool of long since dried blood had congealed beneath it. It had obviously been lying there for months, but that didn't mean that who or *what* had killed the man wasn't still lurking about in the underground compound. Why couldn't the journal his client needed be somewhere nice? Perhaps an upscale mansion with a lonely, noble lady, just waiting for a dashing thief to sweep her off her feet. Or a cottage where an old man, childless and in his last years, would be waiting to grant a stranger the rights to his fortune. *Nope.* It had to be in a hidden underground compound with a corpse, that required a ten mile hike through the forest to access. He was lucky he hadn't gotten mauled by a badger.

Arhyen wiped the sweat from his brow, pushing back his shaggy, brown hair, then pressed onward down the narrow corridor. His boots, specially made to emit little sound when he moved, touched lightly on the stone floor as he crept further down the hall, holding the lantern in front of him. His client had claimed that the compound's owner had *disappeared*, but Arhyen suspected he'd actually been the dead man in the corridor. Had his client known all along? The journal Arhyen sought was allegedly valuable, containing a new alchemical formula for . . . something, but was it worth killing for?

He shook his head and continued into the next chamber, holding his lantern aloft to light the pitch black space. The stone room he entered was large, yet cozy, with overstuffed sofas, shelves full of books, a roll-top desk, and other expensive wooden furniture, all covered in a fine coating of dust.

Arhyen went straight for the desk, hurrying across the expensive looking dark blue rug that covered most of the floor. He gently pushed back the roll-top with his free hand, then set the lantern down on the desk's surface as he began pawing through neatly stacked papers. He had no idea, really, what he was looking for, so he would simply have to steal anything with alchemical symbols that looked remotely like the ones he'd been given as an example.

"Who are you?" a voice asked from somewhere to his left.

Arhyen nearly jumped out of his skin, skidding backwards away from the sound. He froze and contemplated his options. He'd left his lantern on the desk, but its light didn't push far enough into the room to illuminate the owner of the voice. He should simply run, but he still needed the journal, and the voice's owner didn't seem angry that he was skulking about. Plus, the voice had been female. As far as he knew, the old alchemist had lived in the compound entirely alone.

He cleared his throat. "I could ask you the same question," he stated bluntly, feigning confidence.

The voice didn't answer.

Making up his mind, Arhyen hurried forward and snatched up his lantern, then moved the light to shine in the far corner of the room. Someone was sitting in one of the overstuffed chairs. He hadn't noticed her at first, as she was in the corner, partially obscured by one of the bookcases.

Curiosity getting the better of him, he stepped forward. The girl couldn't have been more than eighteen, and wore a simple dress, with a high-cut neck and tight bodice, a common style. The pale blue sleeves covered dainty arms, ending with delicate, glove-encased hands, placed properly in her lap. Her vibrant red hair, once done in a proper updo, was now covered in dust, with stray tendrils floating about her delicate face. She turned wide, blue eyes up to him to reflect the lantern light.

When the girl didn't speak, Arhyen cleared his throat uncomfortably. "I was told that no one would be here."

The girl seemed confused. "My father is here, but he stopped moving quite some time ago. I'm not sure what I'm supposed to do now."

Arhyen furrowed his brow. Did the girl not understand that her father was dead? More troubling still, was the fact that the compound owner was rumored to have no children. Had he hidden his daughter here her entire life?

He straightened his short, tan coat over his high collared shirt and waistcoat, quietly attempting to devise a kind way of explaining things to her. "Your father," he began, hesitant to break the news. "Your father is dead," he said quickly. "He will not be moving again, *ever*."

The girl's face fell. She turned her gaze down to her lap, straightening the white gloves on her hands needlessly. "What will become of me?" she asked finally.

"I'm not quite sure," he replied, feeling guilty, though he had no reason to. "I'm simply here for a specific set of documents, then I'll be on my way."

The girl's face lit up as she turned her gaze back up to him. "Father has many journals," she explained excitedly. "I keep them all in order."

Arhyen didn't have the heart to correct her on speaking of her father in the present tense. Instead, he lifted a piece of parchment from his breast pocket and unfolded it. He handed it to her. "The document I'm looking for would have some of these same symbols on it. Have you seen them before?"

She looked down at the parchment, then up to Arhyen with a nod. "These are very special symbols," she explained.

Arhyen's eyes widened in surprise. "Are you an alchemist? Most would not recognize anything on that piece of paper." He gestured at the parchment still clutched in her fingertips.

She shook her head sadly. "I only know what father taught me."

He took an excited step forward. He'd been hired to find the journal, and wasn't sure what it detailed, but it was important enough for his employer to hire one of the most prestigious thieves in England. Prestigious in his own mind, at least.

"What is your name?" he asked. He knelt in front of the girl, putting himself at her eye level.

"Liliana Breckenridge," she answered simply, her face void of emotion.

Breckenridge. Perhaps she really was the alchemist's daughter. The great Fairfax Breckenridge had left a legacy after all.

"My name is Arhyen Croft," he said honestly, seeing no reason to give a false name. The girl obviously had no idea what was going on.

She didn't reply, not even with a *pleased to meet you.*

Trying to keep his frustration hidden, Arhyen tried again. "Liliana, do you know what these symbols mean?" he flicked a finger gently against the top of the parchment in her hands.

She nodded. "They're very important."

Arhyen sighed. "Do you know what they're for?"

She nodded again.

"Will you please tell me?"

She nodded, then looked down at the parchment again. "These are the symbols that father used to make my soul."

Arhyen stood abruptly, then looked down at the girl. Suddenly it all made sense. Her emotionless face. Her confusion over her father's death. She was an automaton. An artificial construct. They were all the rage amongst the wealthier classes. Fake humans, entirely willing to do ones bidding, no matter what that bidding might be. As a skilled alchemist, Fairfax Breckinridge had created himself a daughter.

He knew he shouldn't have felt bad, but he was over-whelmed with sympathy for the poor girl. Her creator had perished, leaving her alone in the dark to gather dust. Automatons didn't sleep, nor did they eat, so she'd just sat there in the dark, for who knew how long.

Still, he had a job to do, and Arhyen Croft never failed.

The girl's gaze remained on the parchment. "This is incomplete," she murmured.

Arhyen knelt back down in front of her. "Yes, this is only an example to help me identify the real thing," he explained. "Can you show me the original document?"

The girl nodded. She'd claimed her name was Liliana, but Arhyen was having trouble thinking of her as a human with a name. She was a manmade object . . . yet she claimed her father had made her a soul? It was preposterous. Souls couldn't be made. But then why were these documents so important to his client?

He sighed, realizing he'd gotten himself in way over his head. He should simply procure the documents, leave the automaton in the compound, and be on his merry way, ten times richer for his troubles.

The automaton seemed to be deep in thought, something automatons weren't supposed to do. Finally, she met his eyes. "I'll show you," she agreed, "but you must take me with you when you leave this place. Take me somewhere that's not so dark."

Arhyen inhaled sharply, but couldn't think of anything to say. He couldn't possibly take the girl with him, could he? He had nowhere to bring her, and he wasn't about to emulate the nobility with an automaton in his home. "Of course," he lied. He had to find the documents, after all. Once that was done, he'd find a way to convince the girl to stay behind.

She nodded and stood, brushing the dust from her dress, though she didn't seem to notice all of the dust in her hair. She was small, the top of her head barely reaching Arhyen's shoulder as she breezed past him. He followed without a word as she approached one of the bookcases near where Arhyen had entered the room. He held the lantern aloft to light their way.

The automaton skimmed the spines of the leather-bound books, finally settling on one near the middle of the shelf. She retrieved it, then opened it to reveal pages of handwritten notes. Upon closer observation, Arhyen realized that all of the tomes on the shelf were journals, not books. It must have taken Fairfax Breckenridge his entire life to fill them all.

She flipped through the pages of the journal until she found what she was looking for, then handed it to Arhyen. Taking it with his free hand, he held the lantern close and observed the formulae on the page. Sure enough, the initial symbols matched those on his parchment, though the formulae continued on long after that.

With a smile, he snapped the book shut. Arhyen Croft *never* failed.

His elation was short lived as he turned to find the automaton staring at him, her expression questioning.

"You know," he began hesitantly, "it's very dangerous in the outside world."

She frowned and blinked her big, blue eyes at him. "I'm not afraid," she assured.

Of course you're not afraid, Arhyen thought. *You have no emotions.* "Well have you thought about what you'll do once you're out of here?" he countered. "London is a big

337

place. You might get lost in a sea of people, never to return."

Catching onto his tricks, she crossed her arms. "We had a *deal*," she snapped.

He was utterly taken aback by her anger. Automatons weren't supposed to feel anger. They were *things*. Perhaps she was just emulating emotions she'd seen from her *father*.

Her arms remaining crossed, she tapped her foot, encased in a low-heeled boot, impatiently.

Arhyen sighed. "Fine," he agreed. He would lead her out of the compound, and perhaps she'd even follow him all the way back to London. Then she'd realize that there was nothing there for her, and he might even be kind enough to return her to the compound.

He placed the book under his arm, held the lantern aloft with his free hand, then led the way out of the room. A short way down the hall, he stopped and turned back to the girl following obediently after him. "Do you need to bring anything? Clothes, perhaps?"

She shook her head. "These are all I have," she explained, gesturing down to her dress and dainty boots.

Arhyen sighed and continued down the hall. Fairfax had obviously not been a very good *father*, if he'd only allowed his daughter a single dress. Automaton or no.

Liliana followed after the man down the hall of the compound. She knew they would soon happen upon her father, lying in the hall just like he had been for the past several months. One day she'd found him lying there, unmoving, and she hadn't known what to do. Her entire life had been *him*.

Now this man, Arhyen Croft, had arrived, and was interested in her father's notes. Perhaps he knew what she was supposed to do now that she had no master. Even if he didn't, following him was better than remaining in the dark.

Arhyen stopped ahead of her, and she knew he was looking down at her father. He glanced back at her with a frown. "Don't look down, okay?"

She narrowed her eyes in confusion, unsure of why Arhyen didn't want her to look at her father. She'd seen him before, not long after he stopped moving.

When she didn't continue onward, Arhyen stepped toward her and took her gloved hand. She froze at the alarming touch.

"Just close your eyes and I'll lead you past," he instructed.

She nodded and closed her eyes, used to taking orders, though she was still confused.

He tugged on her hand and she began to walk. Soon they reached the end of the corridor, and her hand was allowed to fall back to her side.

"You can open your eyes now," he instructed.

She did as she was bade, then continued following him down the hall. She felt a pang of sadness at leaving her father behind, but he'd want her to find a new purpose, wouldn't he? She shook her head. Perhaps not, but she couldn't just wait in the dark for all of eternity.

CPSIA information can be obtained
at www.ICGtesting.com
Printed in the USA
LVHW011442080119
603165LV00017B/470/P